A Case Of Peanut Brittle

JACK OCONNOR

DEDICATION

I dedicate this effort at least in part to all the siblings who love each other and learn about the world and themselves at least in part by rubbing their egos against each other. Sometimes it becomes a lifelong style.

ACKNOWLEDGMENTS

I would like to acknowledge the help of the workshops, writer's groups and colleagues, too numerous to enumerate, whose critiques, positive and negative, have helped me along the way. Being told what is negative, being complimented on what is good, and being encouraged to continue is the ultimate support group.

CHAPTER ONE

Audrey's call had left me no choice. "I'm coming to Seattle and I need you to meet the plane." My sister can be a drama queen, so, at first, I didn't let the tension in her voice impress me.

"Who died?"

"Funny you should say that."

"What?"

She gave me the flight information, made sure I had it right, and hung-up. She had passed over an opportunity to talk about something clearly important to her. Now I was impressed—and worried.

Audrey is my one and only sister. I'm not sure I could take two of them. Not that she's a terrible person, she's not. Not that I don't love her, I do. But, God bless America, she can be high maintenance. At an early point in her career she had realized a show business dream. She had been a dancer and even had some success on stage as an actress. Time passed and the realities of a highly competitive business took their toll. She put the stage, where you have to be awfully good and awfully lucky, behind her and went on to other things. But not totally, she performs her life. To this day she assumes personalities to fit situations that she sees as opportunities for role-playing. Audrey is perennially late. Her excuses for habitual lateness are always credible. However, lifelong lateness is not poor time management, it is policy.

My way of coping is to arrange our meetings at places where I can sit and read something or drink something—preferably both.

"Closest bar to baggage claim," I tell her when dealing with airports.

"How about if it's one of those airports where they channel you right from the plane to baggage claim, with no bars in-between," she asks. I see us chasing around the airport looking for each other and, in the end, her being right.

"Then the closest bar to the ticket counter of your airline."

"How about a coffee shop or cafeteria?"

"Only if the bars are closed."

I don't worry about security or how much her flight has been delayed. I don't worry about which baggage carousel her lost luggage should be on. I read and await my one and only favorite sister. I read at a leisurely pace and enjoy a glass of wine or beer. That's how I ended up on a Thursday afternoon at SeaTac International Airport, just south of Seattle, in the Emerald City Bistro, closest bar to the Southwest ticket counter. I eased my bones into a chair from which I could watch the crowd.

Airports are examples of early worldwide culture: airports and Coke. Wherever in the world you land, it seems, the airport signs and gates look the same and you can get a coke. Frankfurt, Narita, De Gaulle, Kennedy. If it weren't for the languages you'd be hard put to tell a big difference. It would take a while to even figure out what country you were in.

"High, handsome, my name's Jeannette. I'll be your cocktail waitress." I looked up to see a stunning young woman with generous thighs and a come-hither smile. Her nametag and cocktail waitress uniform pretty much told the story.

"Well back at ya. I'm Dan and this must be my lucky day."

The uniform, mini-skirt and high collared, white silk blouse with a black felt bow tie, gave her a great two-way quality. I mean, she looked terrific coming and going. She flirted, probably thinking I was safe—sixtyish and looking settled. It's almost insulting and not entirely true. Even after the powers-that-be start short-shotting our hormones, we have instincts; we have memories; we have pride. Inside just about every sixty-ish gentleman prowls at least a shadow of the randy goat he once was. The ones who were never randy goats are lifelong liars.

A few struggling years as a reporter gave me license forever to refer to myself as a journalist. I lucked into co-ownership of a local newspaper, so at places where clean shirts are required, I am a retired publisher. I had a column for several months, and I created the "police blotter" of our little paper, so I'm also a social critic and crime fighter. And now, happily retired from all of it, I have a life that is generally free of surprises.

I ordered a big-beer, draft beer served in a bathtub-sized, reinforced paper cup. In the aviation world of high altitude prices, charging three times what the draft was worth amounted to an airport bargain.

Audrey's plane was due to land at two-thirty. The airlines consider the plane landed when the wheels touch the ground. That it takes another twenty minutes to get to the gate does not affect their "arrived on time" statistics. Perversely, they count departure as when the doors close on the Jet way. That is how they arrive and depart on time so often, yet we, flying in their airplanes, are perennially late in leaving and arriving. We, of the public, count when our loved ones arrive as when our loved ones arrive: when they "de-plane."

So—two-thirty, plus at ten or fifteen minutes for taxi-ing means two-forty-five . . . add more for several foggy passengers to get their carry-ons carried off, a few more to find the bar—I would not stare obsessively at my watch and grumble until then. We would not be ready to de-beer and de-lounge until at least de-three or so.

Meanwhile, I could entertain myself by watching Jeanette glide through her world like it was a video. She put on a nice show. She may not have stooped to conquer, but surely she stooped and bent for tips. Most of the airport bars also serve nuked foods advertised behind Lucite frames standing on the tiny tables. For the price of a fairly good meal, you could get a sandwich or some chicken wings. The muted white noise of thousands of footsteps and voices was almost a white noise like surf. When I look at the frequently intense expressions on people's faces, I realize that they are all doing something immensely important to them. All that importance dashing around was intimidating. Some coming, some going. It would be so much more efficient if we could all swap our importances call it even, and stay home.

I was impressed when, at almost exactly three o'clock, Audrey made her entrance as if cameras were

6

rolling. I don't know how to define charisma, but like good humor and bad art, I know it when I see it. Audrey was the real deal. I won't give her exact age, but we're contemporaries. She's a slender woman with a quick step and an intelligent face. I have heard her called "cute" and even called "sexy." That's pretty great stuff for a grandmother to be called.

She spotted me immediately and performed her perky walk to my little table with the big-beer on top. She wore a comfortable-looking white pantsuit, a broad brimmed hat, and rose-tinted glasses. If the idea was to blend, she ruined it with a huge, multicolored silk scarf she had bought in Russia. Blending was not in her fashion vocabulary. The scarf's Byzantine design was practically an entourage of colors announcing her arrival.

"Audrey." I rose and kissed her on the cheek. "You're looking fine. This is a surprise visit, kiddo. What'll you have? We have time, the guys haven't lost your luggage yet."

Audrey had had some shade of red hair for as long as I can remember. Everything from a sultry auburn to bozo-the-clown red, a shade she had used during her wannabe Maureen O'Hara years. At the airport it was a Debra Messing, red-but-under-control, color. It looked fine, particularly with her green eyes.

Her voice was high-pitched and a little nasal. It still carried a lot more Queens, New York on it than mine did. Several people over the years had suggested that she not sing: not ever. There should be bumper stickers—"Audrey: Don't sing!"

"Some white wine would be nice," she said. "I've been arrested."

"Sure, I'll—you've been what?"

7

One never knew with Audrey. Skinny-dipping in the municipal fountain? Pulling a Za Za with a California Highway Patrolman? Losing her awful temper with a judge at traffic court? She was capable of a lot of bizarre behavior.

She messed with her purse, a chic leather thing that matched her suit. It had a maximum carrying capacity of about a liter. I've seen her jam two liter's worth of essentials into it. She looked at me, repeating it for the slow kid: "Ar-res-ted."

"What for? Who'd want to arrest you?"

She seemed obsessed with finding some whatzit in her purse but finally gave up. "Murder! Those fools think I killed Assemblyman Reilly about a week ago. "

"What . . . how, why didn't you call me then?"

"I thought it would go away. I didn't really want to think about it."

I searched her face for some sign that she might be kidding. She seemed so dismissive. "Oh," I said, a brilliant comment on the problem.

Knowing her, I knew that at least some of this casual, dismissive attitude was play-acting. She simply could not resist it. Once she opted for that kind of behavior, it became her personality for the run of the play. It can be fun, actually, part of her charm, but not when serious things like being arrested are part of her dialog. I knew I had no choice but to react to her as I could, reserving for myself the pleasure of making fun of her, being sarcastic to her, and other brotherly cruelties. Murder, though? Come on.

"Murder is so negative. You know I hate owning the negative." She looked at me and I thought I glimpsed a certain darkness behind those green eyes.

Jeannette arrived. Two giant martini glasses with some pinkish liquid in them were on her tray destined for another table. Two long toothpicks in each glass impaled cherries and stuck in the air. I thought of upside-down ballet dancers. "Jeanette," I emoted, holding my heart. "I've missed you."

"You've already replaced me, you brute," she said, pouting her lips like Baby-Jane. "Another big-beer for you and—"

"—Yes, dear," Audrey said. "Some white wine please. Do you have a nice Pinot Gris?"

Just like her, I thought. Doesn't realize that an airport bar is not going to carry a nice Pinot Gris and lets it distract her from a murder indictment.

"Ma'am," Jeannette said, somehow conveying that "Ma'am" was code for "pretentious bitch." "In whites by the glass we have a nice Washington Chardonnay."

"Oh," Audrey cooed, "Wash-ing-ton," pronouncing it with all the disdain of a Californian. She pretended to think. She knew nearly as much about wines as I did, which is to say dry whites for fish, fowl, and salads, dry reds for meat, sweet whites for before and after dinner, and sweet reds for nausea. "Well," Audrey said, "I suppose I'll try your airport Chardonnay. Thank you dear, you're very sweet."

Jeannette looked about to have a messy accident involving her loaded cocktail tray and the lap of Audrey's white pantsuit. "Thank you, Jeannette," I raised my voice and my eyebrows, apologizing for my sister and implying a decent tip to come. Jeanette acknowledged, teasing me with her best sultry swing as she oscillated away. For a charming moment I thought that marimbas should be playing.

"Arrested? Do you mean really arrested?"

Audrey ignored the question, rose slightly in her seat and looked around the lounge. Apparently some errant thought had evicted attention to the subject from her brain.

"What," I demanded.

"I don't see powder rooms," she said. "You know how awful the airplane facilities are. I need to freshen up. I won't feel clean and civilized until I splash and spritz."

A wise man, Victor Hugo, I think, has said nothing is so powerful as an idea whose time has come. When a woman requires porcelain facilities one must bow to it. "Outside," I said, indicating the entrance. "To your left."

By the time Audrey returned from Euphemism Land where one freshens up in powder rooms, the drinks had arrived. "Just think," she said, "two weeks ago my biggest problem was garden pests. Gopher invaders. So frustrating. I wouldn't mind sharing if they'd put their holes in inconspicuous places. Nature can be rude and inconsiderate, you know."

I pursued the original topic doggedly. Sometimes she dramatized. She had been known to treat the real meaning of words in a cavalier manner. "You were really arrested? By the police?"

"Yes, yes yeeeesss," she said, impatient with my slowness.

"You were processed at the police station?"

She held the wineglass at arm's length by the stem and examined its contents, one imperial eyebrow raised with suspicion. She leaned forward and because of her delicate features, had to put her face right against the glass to sample the aroma. I wanted to say something about rooting for truffles but held my tongue. She sampled the wine, initially swirling it in her mouth, not awkward at all. She swallowed, enologising all the way.

"Yes, police station." She quickly took another sip. "Quite good. Saucy. A blend. Young grapes no doubt."

"Yeah, yeah, yeah, impudent little bastards. Later—you were arraigned?"

"Hmm hmm," she said, having just spotted the snack menu, memorialized in a miniature kiosk of Lucite and sharing the table with the beer and wine.

"You entered a plea?"

She looked up, clearly frustrated by my incompetence. "Dan, honestly, the whole thing. I pled 'not guilty' and, before you ask, posted bail."

I called for another big-beer; somehow mine was empty. I noticed that Audrey had quickly finished her wine. That was unusual. "Audrey," I said, confident I would not like the answer, "You live in San Diego. San Diego, California. That's another whole state." She rewarded me with a dirty look. "Usually, the bail includes things like court orders telling you not to leave the jurisdiction. What the hell are you doing in Seattle?"

"I came to visit."

"You've jumped bail."

"What do they expect me to do?" she said. "I had to get out of there. I wanted to talk to you."

"Jumping bail is a fresh new crime."

"Well, duh." She looked for Jeannette. I think she was beginning to want that second glass pretty badly. "The penalties for murder include the gas chamber, right?" she asked. "So, they're going to execute me then give me six months more for jumping bail?"

I wanted to respond, but—

"I intend to go back. My next appearance is in ten days. I'll be there."

I take it as a fundamental principle of the universe that Audrey can do just about anything—except stop driving me crazy. I've never learned how she maintains patently ridiculous positions, yet makes them sound perfectly reasonable.

"Audrey, they have no way of knowing you'll return. If they find you're gone, you'll be a fugitive. They'll issue fresh warrants and I'm sure that my house is one of the first places they will look."

Her smile was rife with innocence. "Oh, you don't want me to disturb your preciously boring routine."

"Not that again. Yeah, I have a life here and I like it."

"It's Saturday morning, I must be at the farmer's market," she mocked me. "My, goodness, the weekly crime report, I wonder whose dog ran away. Oh, to get to the Kramers you go down the old log road and turn at where the cow was killed last spring, then it's just a jump. If you get to where the well house used to be, you've gone too far." She laughed at her own imitation, then continued, "You've been up here so long moss is growing on you."

She had hinted before that she thought I was just giving up and getting old in my retirement. I disagreed, of course. My life pace is slower and more scheduled, but I like it. I'm happy, "off in the woods somewhere," as she put it. I briefly wondered if this whole arrest thing were not a ploy to butt into my life and light fires in it.

"You're saying that I cannot stay with you tonight?"

"I'm telling you to get the hell back to San Diego. Today. Now!"

"Well that's just plain rude," she said, dismissing me. She flapped her napkin and looked petulant. "Mom didn't bring us up to be rude."

"You're in big trouble. If they catch you jumping bail it will be worse. You'll go to jail."

"You've not asked me if I did it."

"Killed the guy?"

"Assemblyman Reilly."

"Well of course you didn't kill Assemblyman Reilly."

Her disinterested, nearly ditsy expression changed somehow. She looked entirely sane and, for the moment, at peace. "That's why I needed to come here," she said in a voice so low it was almost throaty.

"Not for the airport Chardonnay?"

"No." She looked directly into my eyes, fixing my attention. Got to admit, the gal had something special. I felt speared and gaffed. When she would suddenly drop the role-play and peek out at the real world, like she was doing now, I saw a pretty strong person. She just didn't come out that often. She'd rather play. Sometimes I wondered if she were even aware of this cast of thousands that she surrounded herself with to shield her from the world.

"I needed to surprise someone who loves me unconditionally. I needed . . . not just to be believed, but to be believed without question. I needed to see someone— you—whose faith in me is complete."

I answered with the same depth. "You betcha, Kid."

"Good," she said, back to the pseudo chipper voice. "Because when I tell you the story you'll find it hard to believe. Everyone else thinks it's impossible to believe. Literally incredible. I tell you . . . I wouldn't believe it."

"Well?"

"Not until glass number two," she said.

When Nurse Jeannette's incredible legs carried her to our table with our second helping, Audrey took hers and holding the stem with dainty fingers guided the glass to her lips in one slow motion sip that half emptied the glass. It was a pretty performance.

"It started with peanut brittle, of all things," she said. "Peanut brittle! I swear if worse comes to worst that gas chamber will smell not of cyanide but peanut brittle. It will be in my nostrils when they pass their last."

"Actually, I think they use fatal injection now, Audrey. No smells."

"I'm sure I will smell peanut brittle. I can taste it now. Goes well with the Chardonnay, actually."

"Audrey . . . the murder? What does peanut brittle have to do with the murder?"

"They were trying to get rid of the skateboard park and they got Assemblyman Reilly's support which isn't too difficult if you're part of the moneyed elite which we weren't except for that Miller crowd. You've never met Connie Miller, not a pleasant creature, Dan, not at all. Her whole vocabulary is flash cards and bumper stickers and she thinks she's incredibly profound. She hasn't had a fresh idea in . . . well, I don't think she's ever had a fresh idea."

I was torn between seeing how long it might take for her to get the train back on the track and having to endure the process. It was fascinating, in a way, like seeing how long it takes a buzzing fly to visit the same place twice. That was the part of her games that I liked the least. For whatever reason that popped up in the labyrinthine maelstrom that was her mind, she would fly off in another direction. Like a jazz musician who gets so lost in his

14

sequence of riffs that he forgets the melody he's playing to, she'd play on. I sometimes called it, from the listener's point of view, getting "Audrey'd."

"Murder, Audrey," I said at last. "I don't have many years left."

We got back to the melody in record time.

"So when our committee asked Connie Miller for support she declined. That's all I'm saying. What's the matter with you? Late for something? Are you interested in the murder charge or what?"

"Yes, yes," I said. "Sorry to interrupt. You left me off at the corner of peanut brittle and Connie Miller."

Audrey looked at me as though I had said something inexplicably dense. She finished most of her wine and got Jeannette's attention. My charming, albeit theatrical, sister smiled a politician's smile towards Jeannette and circled her index finger in the air to indicate another round.

Then, she stopped talking. I studied her face and it seemed as though she forgot she had been telling me something. She looked up at me in a thoroughly normal way, showing no signs of stress, then suddenly continued. I wondered if dear Sis had not had a stroke or something, one of those mini-strokes you hear about.

"They were going to shut down the skateboard park the kids had constructed at a good sized plot of ground off the road near the bluffs at the end of our street. Remember, I was going to show it to you once."

I nodded my head, "Yeah. Continue . . ." I plead. I was terrified of shaking the boat into yet another current.

"You remember, it was your first visit since you retired. I was still married to Brad. You never did like him, never appreciated him. We were taking an after dinner walk

. . . I think you just wanted to get away from Brad for a while. I told you about the skateboard park and you seemed interested at first. Then I explained some of the history of it and you went off into one of your long-suffering   I-guess-I-have-to-listen-to-one-of-Audrey's-stories silences."

"Ah, you're kidding. I love your stories. I just wish you'd continue with the one you started with. You know, like the time you got accused of murder and how that came about. Continue that one."

Continue she did, with a passion for detail that left me exhausted, and confused. In her world, the essential elements of a dramatic event include not only the characters and their actions, but to whom they are related, what their current marriage status is and why, with whom they are involved, in what part of town they live, the source from which they subsist . . . and, sometimes, what their history with weight gain (or loss) has been and what they are wearing.

Suddenly, interrupting herself in mid-sidetrack: " . . . Are you serious about this bail jumping business?"

The unexpected leap of topic jarred me back to paying attention and I realized two things. Thing one was that four big-beers are too much big-beer to drive on. Thing two was that after four big-beers my attention skill-set was lacking a few essentials.

"Serious as a heart attack, Audrey," I said. "As far as I know, jumping bail is a felony and here's a news clip, I don't think bail-jumpers get to post bail any more."

"Well that's pretty unforgiving."

"Think of it as the court having trust issues. You're riding a ticket to jail, kiddo. Plain and simple."

"Perhaps you're right. I should be getting back to San Diego."

"Absatively . . . lutely. And, we'd better get some dinner."

"All right. Listen. I'm taking my credit card to the ticket counter right now. You stay here and do whatever is necessary with 'thunder-thighs,'" she said with a dismissive wave in Jeannette's direction.

I resented her cynical picture of the mini-skirted beauty. "But—"

"—Yes, butt—indeed! Work out your fantasy and pay the bill. I'll be back in a sec."

"She's a nice girl," I offered.

"Look at her thighs and ankles. She'll be one of the fat girls on the welfare line before she's thirty." She treated that profound observation like an exit line and left. How like her, after giving no indication that she had been paying attention to anything but her own story, she proved to have been watching so much.

I summoned the fleshy beauty to the table, "I guess we're history," I said. I looked at where her ankles should have been and saw sturdy pylons for support of construction under way. Audrey was completely right, of course. "I need the bill," I explained, "and, she's my sister."

In a voice so dry it could power a litter box, Jeannette drolled, "we'll always have Paris," then added with a perky smile, "it wouldn't work anyway, I'm gay."

And, gay or not, I wished I were forty again. I don't consider my self a stick-in-the-mud. I don't suppose any stick-in-the-mud does. Audrey was wrong about my boring routine. I enjoyed the predictability of it after a dynamic professional life.

17

CHAPTER TWO

Audrey was back to the diminutive table in no time at all. I barely had time to hold a brief memorial service for my vanished youth. It wasn't really that I was feeling so old, more like the vehicle I was driving through life was getting old. I still wanted to be careless and do reckless things but I was too stiff, or tired, or weak. I took one more lingering look at Sappho in satin, then looked up to see Audrey waiting for me to finish the last drops of my beer.

"I'm feeling so refreshed and invigorated," she said, smiling with nearly palpable enthusiasm. "I feel completely optimistic because of you. It was a little pricey, but I've got good tickets and seats for us."

"Tickets? Seats? Us?"

Ever wonder how a mouse feels in that brief interval after it hears the trigger release but before the lethal bar breaks its neck? I stood and she leaned forward and whispered in my ear. "I knew that, after you knew what was going on, you would never let me face it alone. The best I could do is an eleven o'clock flight tomorrow morning. Where's dinner?"

"Sir Loin Haven," I managed, repeating Jeannette's recommendation. "I guess you're staying with me tonight."

"Sure," she said, "And don't claim the negative, okay? This could actually be a challenge. You're starting to rust up here in the great and damp North woods."

"I am not starting to rust."

"What do you do on Sundays?"

"In the morning I watch the pundit parade on TV. In the afternoon I catch up on any writing or reading I had decided on."

"Thursdays," she demanded.

I would prove to her that I had plenty to do. "On Thursdays I meet with a reading group. We bring wine and pu pus and have a great time."

"Friday evenings," she challenged.

"When there's a good play I go to it. Usually our local movie has a good show. And before you throw Saturdays at me, public radio has a nice line-up in the morning and I do the heavier periodic housecleaning that I save for weekends. I belong to a breakfast group that meets on Wednesday mornings and I walk, either in the park or on the beach. Satisfied? I got lots to do."

"Oh, yeah," she said, then commenced mimicking me . . . "Oh, I'm having breakfast with the Geezers, it must be Wednesday morning": "I know it's Sunday, look, there's George Stephanopoulos": "It's Friday, I must be sitting in the theatre."

"So what," I challenged. Her imitation of me was painfully accurate. I did not like it.

"So what is you're so fixed in your ways that you can tell what day it is by what activity is scheduled. You're rusting. My point . . . and you're drinking too much."

"And you are nuts," I countered with incontrovertible logic. "I like my life. What makes you say I'm drinking too much. Do you think I'm intoxicated?"

19

"You're certainly not showing it," she admitted. "That just means you're drinking plenty and building up a tolerance for it."

There was no talking to this woman. She fires an arrow into a wall, paints a bull's-eye around whatever it hits and claims marksmanship.

"And yet, here we are," I said. "How giving of you to get accused of murder just so you can come up here and enliven my life."

"The point is, Danny boy," (a nickname she knew I hated), "I need you now and I need you strong."

"Thought I was an old drunk who's over the hill."

"I know you can be strong."

"Ta da."

"You just have to shake the cobwebs out and re-start that brain we're all so proud of."

I took a good strong breath and affected a good strong posture, thinking good strong positive thoughts. "To dinner then," I commanded with authority.

"I do hope they have something vegetarian," she said, "pasta, salad . . . something."

I felt grouchy. I'd been <u>Audrey'd</u> again. It doesn't matter how many decades you live, some things don't change. Audrey always got the front seat, the first cut, and the nicest parties. Yeah, yeah, yeah, I know it's sibling whining and everybody feels that way. Like everybody else, I insist that in our case, it's all true. She was the favorite and she'd learned how to manipulate people, especially those close to her, like her brother.

"I need to know that something died so I could eat," I said, being mean. "I want bloody flesh."

"I hope that your barbarian instincts will be of some use in solving this murder problem." She made a motherly show of whisking imaginary things off the front of my shirt. "By the way, my luggage still has to be claimed. You'll have time to do it."

During an elaborate but ultimately unsatisfying dinner, Audrey continued her narrative. Her Mediterranean Penna avec Disgusting White Sauce smelled like the stuff they discard after they've cooked the good stuff. My fourteen-ounce steak came from, I think, an animal that used to wear a saddle.

Her voice, albeit nasal and soprano . . . kind of a sopranasal, became a high-pitched droning in my mind. I look back on the dinner as a foggy event. The sound track was her voice informing the rest of the day like the pedal point to a Wagnerian <u>lietmotif</u>. It merged in a new-wave way with the piped-in Stepford Wives Jazz of the restaurant.

Audrey and most of her neighbors had been satisfied with the skateboard park that local kids and their dads had built. It occupied an otherwise unusable lot abutting the great seaward bulge of Bonita Bluffs. Mostly local kids, adolescents and teens, used it. On some afternoons of the week there were several bikes and book bags parked casually. On weekends, the kids held contests of skill and daring.

Connie Miller had complained that the kids skateboarding in the park made noise well into twilight . . . that really annoying sound of young people laughing and challenging each other and having fun. It distracted from the family 'cocktail hour' that Connie and her husband Clyde had from five o'clock till dinner. Rumor was that dinner was often quite late at the Miller house.

There were contra complaints that the Miller's son, now in his late teens, often harassed the skateboarders, hurling insults, rocks, and glass bottles at them.

Connie, nee Consuela DeVargas, Audrey pointed out, had prevailed upon the homeowners association to schedule the issue for discussion and action at their next month's meeting. "It's her damned seductive Latin eyes and the way she rotates her hips when she walks across a room," Audrey explained and I started paying attention again. "She wanted them to authorize some legal action, TROs, that's temporary restraining orders," Audrey explained. "She was getting her way too—there are too many men on that panel. They were just about ready to jump through her hoops."

"How unfair," I said, trying to support her . . . or at least to slow her down now that she was getting excited.

"But our neighborhood committee is a slightly larger volunteer group whose membership includes Bonita Bluffs and several other 'neighborhoods.' Connie is also a member of the neighborhood committee, and so am I. I see no harm in the Skateboard Park and opposed Connie at every turn. They're just kids doing that crazy skateboard stuff off the road that they would otherwise be doing on our streets and sidewalks. This should have been a no-brainer from the beginning."

"I guess her hips didn't so much work on you, eh?"

"I just kept at them and kept at them. I can certainly take some credit that I lead the committee to pretty much back the kids. That didn't exactly cement relations with Connie," Audrey admitted, "We've been on opposite sides of other issues too. Look, it's the kids' neighborhood too. They generally go home after dark.

They make no more mess than occasionally leaving a few empty coke cans on the ground. They've somehow found a picnic table and put it there. They've put trashcans for the fast food wrappers and soda cans. The place always looks pretty decent."

I felt I had to say something. "Good for the kids," I contributed.

"I've seen Connie Miller's place look a lot worse after one of their barbecues," she said, "especially if Clyde's been hitting the Margaritas too much, which is just about every day."

"Oh, those people who cannot control their drinking," I slid in between virtue and outrage.

"Connie Miller had put extra pressure on by appealing to State Assemblyman Reilly, a hang 'em high activist, also a neighbor. I remember him ranting about Wild youths in baggy shorts roaming the community in the dark with no supervision. Well I never saw such a thing. He said that it was no wonder our crime rate is so high. He insisted that if we didn't control them in the neighborhoods today we'd be controlling them in the prisons tomorrow."

"Well," she steamrollered on, "I searched and found the last neighborhood burglary had been thirteen months before. It was committed by an out-of-work, sixty-three year old gardener who had never been known to wear baggy shorts. I was too late. It was now a big law-and-order thingy, escalated to a state assembly issue. A big audience of voters started to pay attention.

"There was a neighborhood town-hall meeting and I ended up in a shouting contest with Assemblyman Reilly. He could be so smug and righteous. He always had an answer for everything and when all else failed, he'd yank out his stupid morality and self-evident Christian values. I got so frustrated that I did some ranting and raving of my own. I complained about him and repeatedly said that something should be done to 'get rid' of him."

Clyde Miller (Mr. Connie Miller) sought a restraining order against any skate park activity pending the passage of an ordinance prohibiting it. The next procedure in the grass roots, American political process had been inevitable.

Fund raisers.

"For what?" I asked with non-activist naïveté.

"It's a scandal," she complained. She rested the fork she had been using to herd some errant peas back and forth on a plate whose dinner had barely been touched. I had asked a question that was not entirely relevant and was about to be punished. I tried to tune her out by imagining myself sitting on my porch, watching the sun set over the Olympic mountains and listening to Beethoven's Pastoral . . . but a screen door persistently invaded the image by sopranasally squeaking in the breeze.

"Everything costs money," she squeaked. "We had legal fees, didn't we? It's our government; what are taxes for? We pay the city, the county, the state and the nation every single year and every single year they all want more. Then, when we want to go sue some damned fool . . . they want more money. Filing fees, copying fees, late fees, stamp fees, courier fees, coffee-break fees . . . I don't know what all. Where did all the taxes go? Not to decent highway signs and clean air, I can tell you that. We had to have a lawyer, didn't we? We had a series of fundraisers, car washes, bake sales. Well, you need fliers and such. Printing is expensive. You have to sell even more. When they say that democracy is the best system that money can buy, they're not whistlin' Dixie, Danny."

She did not call me "Danny" unless she was trying to annoy me or make some rhetorical point. That she could not resist the alliteration at the end of her speech just confirmed in my mind that she had rehearsed and enjoyed delivering a passionately prepared political polemic.

"Well somehow," She continued with a self-effacing shrug, "I ended up being selected as the CP, that's chairperson, Dan, of our own PAC, and that's political action committee. It was an honor and a responsibility that I took very seriously indeed, and I didn't hog everything either. I delegated. Margaret Swenson whose husband plays the banjo and has sound equipment ran the neighborhood hootenanny. Bob Davis let us use a corner of his used-car lot for the car washes on two weekends. We gave each car-wash customer a Bob Davis 'We're ready to deal' flier and a business card. It was a great location and hardly anyone complained—except the kids who had to collect all the wet, crumpled up fliers later. The bake sale, of course, went to Sarah Olsen since you can't keep her away from any baking event. Honestly, her pride in her stupid praline pies approaches hubris. I'll tell you what though, my peanut brittle was the hit of the sale. When I say I make the best peanut brittle you've probably ever tasted, I'm not bragging, just repeating what I've been told."

Her peanut brittle was extraordinary. I remembered it well. In addition to being full of peanuts and pea nutty flavor, there was an indefinable hint of spiciness to it that made it special.

"The holiday lights and your peanut brittle are the only reasons I look forward to Christmas."

"Well, of course," she acknowledged.

"And the music. I like the carols."

"It's the secret ingredient," she went on. "No one, and I mean no one, knows about the secret ingredient. I should probably entrust you with it in a sealed envelope so the secret doesn't die with me."

"I'll deposit it in my safe unopened," I said without smiling.

"So many people wanted more that we had two more bake sales and every one of them sold out all the brittle I could make. Sarah Olsen was furious. She had to donate three un-purchased pies for fellowship at her church."

Audrey paused in her narrative so that I could see that she was neither smug nor vindictive. Her saintly demeanor was belied by a slight smirk that she could not control.

"Lots of brittle, I get it."

Cutting across the grain or with the grain made no difference. That hunk of dinosaur flank was tough. I would get through most of it but I was glad I had ordered a baked potato with everything on it. The salt, butter, chives, and sour cream were so good I dipped some of the meat in them. I did not have to exert myself to contribute to any conversation. The voice, like a grinding wheel in my head, went on and on.

"Well, I thought it would be cute PR, that's public relations, Dan, if I packaged up some of my brittle and presented it to Assemblyman Reilly."

"That was nice."

"Well, it was kind of an apology too," she said with obvious reluctance.

"Apology for what, Audrey? Damn you and your temper."

"At a neighborhood dinner/town meeting he said something stupid and I threw a hard-roll at him."

"Bad behavior, Kiddo."

"The roll was really hard. I caught him on the bridge of his nose. Come to think of it, the corn was cold and they ran out of fish. It doesn't pay to try to save money on catering."

I shook my head. What can you say?

"Then, there was a debate that became a . . . heated discussion—"

"—Shouting contest."

"Well, I cussed at him. I guess I called him a few inappropriate things."

I knew that Audrey had the Kelly gift for cussing and if she was even remembering it, it must have been awful. "Don't even tell me," I said.

"Then, he said something so outrageous that I threw my notes at him."

"Oh. It could have been worse."

"I had no idea my ball-point was in there. It hit him in the cheek. They made a big deal out of it."

"One of these days you're going to get in real trouble."

"Like a murder indictment?"

"Sorry."

"Anyway, so the peanut brittle was kind of an apology and a peace offering. I put it in a neat little gift box, wrapped it in ribbon and presented it to the assemblyman in person and in public."

"In public?"

"That was the last of the community dinners followed by a town hall kind of meeting. Assemblyman Reilly and the Mayor were after dinner speakers."

"The mayor of San Diego?"

"The mayor of Alta Mira, Dan," she scolded. "We are an incorporated city. Everyone just thinks we're part of San Diego."

"City? Fire department, cops . . . the whole Magilla?"

"We contract with the county for law enforcement. Volunteer fire department."

"Sorry."

"Anyway, I made a presentation and gave Assemblyman Reilly the brittle and . . . well, that's about all, I guess."

That "I guess" sounded a bit provisional to me and she looked away quickly. "And?" I prodded. "I'm waiting for the other shoe to drop."

"I included a really unfortunate note, I'm afraid."

"What did it say?"

"I was trying to disarm him with sweets and charm. I wanted the publicity and I wanted people to see that we were not having a personal conflict."

"Not counting that you'd already launched several missiles at him."

"That's harsh."

"The note?"

"Oh, the note was fine. It's just how people interpret things after the fact. That is really annoying. And, it's not fair."

"The note, Audrey."

"It said . . . 'Dear Assemblyman Reilly, I want you to taste some of the kind of love you inspire in your district. I made this brittle just for you. It has a secret ingredient that I can't wait for you to experience. Think of the sweet children as you eat all of it."

28

A CASE OF PEANUT BRITTLE

I had a sinking feeling. "And he ate it?"

"Not then, but, I guess when he got home. He ate about half of it. They found him on the floor of his bedroom the next morning. He died in the hospital without ever regaining consciousness. They tested the peanut brittle and found some stuff that was definitely not my secret ingredient. The same stuff was in his system and . . . well . . . killed him."

I had forgotten about my dinner. I did not notice the tone of her voice. I pictured some anonymous assemblyman dead of a mysterious poison. I felt the power of the state justice system turning its attention on Audrey, then, deciding to accuse and prosecute her.

"Ah, hell, Audrey."

"Well, I guess so," she said, apparently as effected by her own story as I. "Listen. No one at the dinner had gotten sick. The only thing different about the Assemblyman is that he had some peanut brittle after he got home and it killed him. There was no other food and no drink."

"Damn, and you got bail?"

"It wasn't easy. I guess they're waiting for some test results. The district attorney said if they had all the answers there wouldn't have been any bail."

"Well he might get his wish now, dammit," I said. I didn't want her to feel any worse but . . . I knew this guy who was a cop. He told me stuff. On a first-degree murder charge with a case as strong as this one, bail is harder to find than honest oilmen. Now, she had jumped bail putting it in absolute jeopardy.

At my urging she did pick at more of her dinner. She was exhausted. Her legal problems were wearing on her. Audrey being Audrey, of course, she still maintained that public persona of untouchable savoir faire.

We retrieved her single piece of luggage from baggage claim and got the car. Audrey did have a bad temper, usually that just meant that she spoke up when she should not. I could certainly identify with that. She was a phenomenon that the world needed in circulation, an anomaly that helped the rest of us focus. Some birds should never be caged.

My home in the hills of the Olympic Peninsula is a two-hour drive from the airport. It was dark by the time we crossed the Hood Canal bridge that links the Kitsap and Olympic peninsulas. She had drifted into sleep. I looked at her face by the lights of the bridge as we clanked over the steel part of the roadway. She seemed completely at peace in a deep sleep. I realized that was because she was with me. She probably had not slept much since being accused. She had used her energy maintaining the flamboyant persona as a shield against being hurt. For all her gregarious charms, she was a little girl who could not trust strangers. Her trust in me, her opinionated, critical, sarcastic brother, was a pearl of great price.

"Don't worry," I whispered to her, so as not to disturb her sleep, "it will be okay. You're with family."

CHAPTER THREE

The next day, promptly at eleven-fourteen the eleven o'clock flight left the Jet way. Audrey had splurged and gotten us business class seats that were wide enough not to cause internal damage. Those of us so blessed were entitled to board when the omniscient spirit conducting such things called "Zone One loading." Feeling unusually privileged, I thought of the wealthy and the pretty people and how nice it must be to live on their planet: comfortable seats and stretching room in airplanes, first boarding, probably better food, prompt exiting.

We strapped in and, as though the harness was a reality belt, my preoccupation with Audrey's dilemma returned. Thinking that in San Diego I would not have to drive, I ordered what I hoped would be the first of two or three scotches. Audrey frowned at someone being Carthaginian enough to have alcohol before lunch but kept her silence.

"I hope I remembered my cell phone." She rummaged through her travel purse in vain. "I hope it's not still at your place."

"I don't think you ever unpacked it. You said all you unpacked was your night stuff, whatever the hell that is."

31

"Well, it's—."

"—Not that I care at all what your night stuff is. Not that I want to know in any way."

"It's the only cell phone I have."

"And it's still in your luggage. Unpacked."

"You don't really know that."

"Why isn't it in your purse?"

"It doesn't work up here in Seattle. That's silly."

"But you did bring it to Seattle. Yeah, silly me."

"I should get a spare. I depend upon it so much, y'know?"

"If you had a spare you probably would have packed it with the other one."

"What other one?"

"The one that's in your luggage."

"Well that's just what I'm trying to tell you about. I wish you'd pay attention."

These "conversation circles," maddening as they are, are part of what I miss when miles and circumstance separate us. I've never quite decided whether it's a brother-sister game that we're both playing, or there are times when parts of her brain take a break.

The flight was non-stop. Had we been sitting on the left side of the plane, I could have watched the coast slide by slowly. I could have identified the large cities and guessed at the smaller ones. I could have observed, feeling superior like a true Washingtonian, as the world changed from green to brown. However, we sat on the right hand side of the plane and any time I leaned over to peek out the window, I saw the unending blue gray of an ocean from six miles up.

I had no trouble having three drinks. After some almonds and at a very few minutes past twelve, Audrey ordered white wine. We had brief bursts of conversation about family, love interests, travels . . . anything that did not evoke thoughts of trials, imprisonment . . . murder.

She never did apologize for pulling me away from my comfortable life. The only time she did refer to it was to take credit for rejuvenating my retirement. I think she wanted me to thank her.

"Literally incredible," she had said about her story. "No one will believe it," she had warned. "I wouldn't even believe it" I remember her saying. By God, when the woman was right, the woman was right. She makes a special, public presentation of homemade, poison-laced candy to a political enemy that she's thrown stuff at, and includes an ambiguously worded note. No one else touches the candy and the next thing the guy is dead of some poison that they find in the candy.

They talk about witnesses, opportunity, murder weapon and motive. Sis had them all, well, a little short on motive but everyone knows her temper and that she's somewhere between eccentric and whacko.

Daffy Duck could prosecute.

"Jesus, Audrey," I said as we followed the stewardess's instructions to get as uncomfortable as possible for landing.

"You don't have to swear oaths, Dan. Not while the plane is still in the air."

"I wasn't swearing. I was wondering out loud if the good Lord was available for your defense . . . not that he'd be enough."

"Brad will do just fine," she reassured me.

I almost lost last night's "Flank of Mare." Things just got better and better. "Brad? Your ex? Brad? That mammoth sized, sleazy, weasel joke in a three piece suit?"

33

"He's a fine attorney."

"You need a criminal attorney. Now I know all attorneys are criminals but Brad's specialty is contracts. He sues people until they break. He pickpockets the dead."

"You exaggerate."

Her ex was a highly successful corporate attorney who, with two others, had his own firm. They employed a small number of associates and had a complete office staff. They had a particular talent for attracting well moneyed clients, probably, it was that they kept winning things. Their clients got good contracts, the best terms and usually prevailed if they were involved in litigation. All of that meant absolutely nothing to me.

"You should at least try for a defense attorney from your own species."

I do not care for my brother-out-law. It's not that he's an attorney. Hell, I know there are some perfectly fine human beings in that profession—in theory. Brad is one of these people with pinkish faces, that well-scrubbed look that leaves little blood vessel tracks all over the cheeks, like a road map of middle earth. How can you trust anyone who washes and brushes so much that they're pink? Just how much dirt are they trying to hide? His eyes are the pale blue that's sometimes called steely, but I never got the impression that there was a soul driving them. Sooner or later he would hit Audrey. It was in him. I knew it.

"That's not fair, Dan. Brad has been good to me since the divorce."

"You mean his business manager has kept the payments up."

"I'm not rich but I have the house and I don't have to work," she said. It was a mantra I had heard many times.

No, she did not have to work, and she could take one or two modest trips each year. That doesn't make a saint out of Brad (Rhymes with "Vlad," as in "Vlad, The Impaler," Vlad Dracule, historical basis for Count Dracula.) He can easily afford it. In his circle maintaining an ex-wife and a mistress had about the same cache as having season Seahawk tickets did in mine—pricey extra.

"He's meeting us at the airport," Audrey said.

The plane hit the runway particularly hard, momentarily shaking up the passengers. We were thrown forward as the pilot hit the breaks and reversed thrust on the engines, creating an ear-shattering roar. The rapidly decelerating aircraft pitched. In the unpleasant wave of noise that assaulted us, I thought of my sister, accused of murder, depending on good old Brad who was meeting the plane. I couldn't imagine how the day could possibly get any better.

As the pilot and crew, "aware that we have a choice when we travel," gushed over how they had enjoyed carrying us ever so much, the plane came to a rolling stop.

The charming pilot who had had such a nice day flying us down the coast announced that there would be a slight delay at the gate. There was a legal issue that must be dealt with before the doors were opened and everyone must remain in their seats until the doors were open and the "Fasten Seat Belt" light extinguished. At about that time the primary stewardess, walking backward up the aisle toward the cockpit, stopped just past our seats and gestured, indicating us, looking at someone else behind us. She looked frightened.

"Here," she said.

Immediately it seemed my whole field of view was taken up by two hulking figures wearing black leather. The closest one wore a sleeveless jumpsuit that showed off biceps as big as my thighs. He had a craggy face and a great mass of shoulder length blond hair. He leaned close to Audrey and me. "You jumped bail. We're bounty hunters and you're busted. We're taking you in," he said in a gravelly voice right out of central casting.

"Like hell you are," I responded bravely. I tried to push up in the airline seat, difficult enough in normal times. Now Blondie's buddy clamped my shoulders with two ham-hock sized hands.

Blondie shoved some kind of movie-prop looking badge and picture ID at us. "Let's keep this quiet," he said. "Grandma here is busted. It's righteous," he said, an insouciant smirk on his face.

The smirk disappeared in a flash as Audrey's hand hit his cheek like a whiplash. I don't know where she found the space to move, the agility, the speed. I guess those Tai Chi lessons weren't wasted after all.

"Lady Grandma to you," Audrey barked, fire in her eyes.

For an instant I saw the snarling predator that this animal really was, then his civilized mask came back. "You two want to get physical, we can do that too," he threatened sotto voce, "same result excepting that you guys will be hurt more. Law's on our side, suckers." I saw the plastic strips in his hand. "Gimme your wrists Lady Grandma."

I made an effort to protect her. I managed to bring my fist up and hit Blondie in the stomach. I gave it all I could but his belly was made of tree bark. It hurt my hand. I looked even more closely at Blondie and saw that he was in his fifties with windblown skin and the kind of wrinkles that you get from smoking not laughing. His hair, on the other hand, was beautiful, soft, wavy and well cared for. I pictured him cross-dressing and my hand didn't hurt so much.

His partner was an iron-jawed, grim-faced goon in his twenties who had no neck and looked like he might enjoy inflicting pain. When the non-struggle was over, Iron Jaw had pulled me up to stand in the aisle. He had my right hand painfully twisted behind my back, the left arm pinned to my side. Then Blondie pulled Audrey to her feet and to the aisle. We stood there, Audrey handcuffed with the white plastic doohickeys. They maneuvered us to the forward door that finally opened revealing two sheriff's deputies. The deputies took in the scene and looked at me. "Ah," Blondie said, "He was just watchin' out for his sis. There's no fight left in him. You guys ready to sign for her?"

He maneuvered her into the Jet way and gave her to one of the deputies. No-neck stood between us. I tried to read Audrey's face, but could not. She appeared casual. Her lips seemed to flirt with the idea of a smile. There was no smile in her eyes. This was her way of not yielding to them. "Tell, Brad," she said to me in a conversational tone. " . . . And remember to feed the fish for me, would you? The food is in the drawer under the tank. Thanks. Just a shake now; don't overdo it. I don't want the mouth-breeding bounty hunters to get scale rot."

She turned to the handsome young deputy who had just signed for her like a UPS package. "I certainly hope there's a car waiting, Officer," she said. "This is awkward."

There were no fish, of course; that was more show business to let the goons know how important they were in her life.

The other deputy reached past the goons and handed me a card. "She will be here," he said. "It won't be too bad. You won't have any access for several hours. It's a time-consuming process."

Then, the officers escorted Audrey down the long Jet way. I leaned forward to watch her go. It was harsh and confining like an air-conditioning duct. The light was cold and fluorescent like an unyielding tunnel to hell. Her bound and retreating figure looked so helpless. I felt like a powerless old fool. I wanted to cry.

"No hard feelings," Blondie said, "just another job." He offered me his hand.

"I hope your balls rot."

Blondie shrugged, then he and iron jaw sauntered off to look for puppies to kick. I slipped back into the plane long enough to retrieve our carry-on. The crew kept the passengers from offloading quiet yet. Clearly they wanted to be rid of the bounty hunters and me.

The world at the other end of the Jet way did not seem quite real. I know people were coming and going. A human-murmur resounded off the hard surfaces. Information was silently changing on displays and travelers were concerned about time things and place things.

I made it to baggage claim, then, automatically, back to the terminal. As I wandered through the terminal mall, I was aware of food smells from the different concessions, tacos, burgers, stir-fry. Electric carts ferrying the disabled, silent except for the tooting of their little horns, went by. And people, people, people, marching through their fates.

So quickly she had been grabbed and, by now, was in the back seat of a patrol car, driving toward a jail. Maybe her new captors were talking about the weather or their bosses. She was cargo. Secured and ignored.

She had looked so anonymous at the end of that Jet way.

More or less in a preoccupied daze, I nevertheless sought the first cocktail area near the Southwestern ticket counter. People and luggage clustered at small tables. Some young men gathered close to the television, on with the volume very low. There was a game, or a rerun of a game. They watched and commented knowingly. The sign said that this was the Tilted Sombrero. Good enough for me.

The idea of meeting Dan in the bar nearest the ticket counter was a comfortable life pattern that everyone in the family knew. If Brad was around, this is where he'd look. I found a small table and let someone bring me <u>La Especial</u>. I threw the first <u>Margarita</u> down pretty fast. Fortunately <u>La Especial</u> was a two-fer. I contemplated the second, feeling abandoned, but, God love sunshine on this perfect day, help arrived promptly.

"You stupid bastard! Seattle, for Chrissake," I heard my brother-out-law boom in greeting, "are you god dammed crazy or really that god dammed stupid?"

He sat down and I still had to look up at him. He was a big son-of-a bitch, not fat: tall and big-boned. When he raised his arm to signal the waitress, he was immediately seen. "Red wine," commanded the prince, with two fingers in the air, and the handmaiden scurried off like a mouse to do his bidding. "That trip made her a bail jumper," he barked. "Are you god dammed crazy?"

Now where had I heard that argument before?

"I didn't—"

"—She's on bail, goddammit. Bail. Do you know what that is?"

"I—"

"—Washington is a whole other state. A different jurisdiction, goddammit."

"I've heard that."

"You've made her a god dammed bail jumper."

I understood that his vocabulary covered a wider range when he was actually practicing law. I realized I should create an appropriate rejoinder.

"Up yours, Brad," I said. "Bounty hunters got her on the plane. They were on our flight for God's sake. She's on her way to county. She needs a lawyer."

"I'm her lawyer."

"You're not a criminal attorney," I said, uncomfortable with the word order.

"I've hired an associate," he said, "who is. We'll worry about his fee later. This could be an expensive adventure."

"Can Audrey afford it?"

"We'll make an arrangement of some kind," he said. "Audrey's helpless when it comes to business. She wouldn't understand if it were in flashing neon lights."

He had that half-leering smile on his face that needed to be removed. If only he weren't such a big fella I'd volunteer for the removal team. I had to face the unpleasant reality that, like floaters and flies, I could never take this guy down.

His huffing and puffing diminished a bit and I thought I'd wait him out. There were things he knew that I needed to know. We had been related by marriage for God's sake, we might be able to act civilized.

His breathing returned to normal and he looked around the lounge as if confirming, or realizing for the first time, where he was.

"Look, Brad," I said, "Truce, okay? How bad is it?"

Brad looked down at me and I felt he was turning it over in his mind whether to gaf me off or take me in. Whatever faults I had decided he had, I think he had an honest affection for Audrey. This might be unpleasant for him too. Perhaps, at some level, talking to her brother might bring a little relief.

"It's pretty serious," he said, deciding to talk to me. (The steady stare of his eyes seemed to imply that it was a good deal more than that.) "Right now they're charging murder two—but they're just waiting on lab reports and a more solid link to her and it will be murder one."

"She told me it was murder one." It clearly annoyed him to be corrected. "I didn't say murder one, Audrey did."

"And she's the attorney and the accurate reporter, right? We're talking about Audrey here."

"'Nuff said."

"She's got a volatile temper. Hell, I could testify to that myself. She threw stuff at the assemblyman in anger. Some people on that neighborhood committee are remembering radical things that Audrey said about Assemblyman Reilly. Mean, sarcastic, things. She's got a quick and insulting mouth. Makes you wonder where she gets that kind of sarcastic, biting, talk." He hesitated, letting it sink in that it was all my fault.

"That note can be made to sound like a threat and a confession. There's no doubt that the candy was laced with poison and it killed the assemblyman."

I studied this florid giant with the fashionable salt and pepper hairdo and the mild smell of jasmine. I tried to see him as a source of hope. He was a lawyer, doggone it; he had to have something for us. "What the hell is on our side?" I pleaded to know.

"Maybe there's a little wiggle room," he said. He interrupted his own eloquence long enough to sip the wine that had arrived. I made a sign to the waitress for another, but she did not see me, only Brad. His Pomposityness continued, "My associate says that we can always attack the technical evidence, the methodology, the protocol, the accuracy of the tests. Buying our own experts is expensive, but it can be effective. The note can also be read as a peace offering. We'll argue that it was just what Audrey said it was, a gesture hoping to provoke a softening of his position. It can be read that way too."

"That's because it is exactly what Audrey says it is. What's our defense?" I asked.

Brad studied the wineglass, then admired his wonderful gold watch. Clearly his mind was gathering great thoughts. "We're not going to stipulate to a single thing," he said, "understand that. But, the facts seem clear that Audrey did give the tainted candy to the victim. We will plead not guilty, of course. There's justifiable homicide, for example, or self-defense . . . hard to fit either of them with the facts. We may have to go with some mental defect diminishing her capacity to form the proper mens rea, that's literally guilty mind. If she's not capable of a guilty mind, it's not murder one."

"How about 'not guilty' because someone else did it. Isn't it clear to you that someone else put the poison in the brittle?"

"Who?"

"Anyone who could inspire a little of that 'reasonable doubt' I keep hearing about. Anyone else who had access to the candy before or after she gave it to Reilly."

"I would love to," he complained. He started counting points off on his big fingers. "She put the candy in the box, wrapped it, sealed it and gave it to the victim. He put it in his pocket and took it home. Before he went to bed he sampled most of it. They found him the next morning, lying on his bathroom floor in agony. He died the following night. By Audrey's own admission, brittle from the same batch has harmed no one. We're going to have settle for a plea to something lesser."

"There's no way you'll get Audrey to agree to that. She'd lump it all under 'crazy' and start throwing stuff at you."

"Maybe we can argue down to criminal negligence, if we can figure out how the poison got in the candy. Of all the peanut brittle she made that weekend, only the Reilly's candy was poisoned. No, I don't think that will fly. So—"

"—So she's nuts? That's pretty radical, Brad," I argued. "She'll never go for it."

Brad examined the ceiling for a moment then finished the first of his red wine with full lips that were somehow sensuous and cruel. He returned his gaze to me, looking down on me of course.

"We're not talking right and wrong here," he lectured. "We're never going to find the greater truth. We're in a legal battle that we're not likely to win. Our job is to find the best way to escape alive with minimum damages. If that means a negotiated plea bargain—we do it. If it means arguing that Audrey was in an alcoholic stupor and not responsible—we do it. If it means proposing some faultless argument of diminished mental capacity—we do it. If it means pleading to voluntary

43

homicide and taking a few years in prison—we do that too. The idea is to survive for another day. Complete vindication is not the least bit likely."

I didn't like the way he was talking. It was not only defeatist, it seemed he was resigned to it. He was a very smart man and knew about the law. This sucked.

"Are you telling me that the trial is over for Audrey?"

"Of course not," he said. "But, no matter what happens, she's likely to have to accept publicly some form of guilt and punishment?"

"Right," I growled, "that'll happen."

Brad leaned forward, voice low and intense, eyes dead, "The real trial for Audrey will be learning to cope with that reality. Yes," Brad said.

"She just won't do it."

"Well, maybe you can do her some good here after all," he said, looking at the ceiling then back to me. "You may help to save her life by convincing her to take a good deal if we get one for her. I'm not terribly worried about the death penalty but life in prison is a real possibility."

I tried to picture ways in which Audrey might be able to cope with a prison term, even a moderate one. I couldn't do it.

I felt trapped at the table with this bear of a man. I wanted to escape from a world that was increasingly painful and over which I had no control. As long as I had lived and as much as I thought I had learned, I still had the belief that if you're innocent, you're okay. He was telling me in a very convincing way, that it's nearly irrelevant. Innocent in the face of a good prosecution could mean guilty. "That's not right," I pronounced with great indignation.

A CASE OF PEANUT BRITTLE

Brad, elbows on the table, interlocked his fingers in a practiced pose. He looked so pedantic at that moment that I was ready to punch him and take the consequences.

"Stop confusing right and wrong with legal and illegal," he said. "People make that mistake far too often. When society writes laws it tries to make them good and to serve good purposes. It's done with the hope that right will be legal and wrong will be illegal. But, in practice and over time it becomes very imperfect. The state has declared war on Audrey. If it wins completely, it can kill her. A dead Audrey is no one's victory. We need to see to it that the state cannot do that. Two or three years in prison may be the deal of a lifetime."

"I don't see her settling for that," I said. "Ever."

"Then perhaps you should think about trying to convince her. Maybe your being down here can do some good after all."

"I'm committed to doing what's best for Audrey," I said. "I may come to your point of view, but for right now, I say she's innocent, goddamn you, and there's got to be a way to show it."

"You just hang on to that attitude and she may end up doing twenty-five to life for murder one," he said, not even annoyed. "They've got a good case. You've heard of circumstantial? This isn't circumstantial. They've got witnesses that she gave him the brittle. It never left his possession. Extensive testing proves that the same poison found in his system was found on the brittle. The autopsy proves that the poison was the cause of death. They've got a lengthy and hostile history between the two, punctuated with acts of violence that have always been initiated by Audrey. You people had better grow up."

"How about motive? A skateboard park?"

45

"Excellent point," he said and I know it cost him to say it. "Technically, motive is not an element of the crime."

"Ah, bullshit," I pointed out.

"You're right and it may be the strongest part of our defense. Juries still want motive . . . I can't say I blame them. It's almost impossible to get a conviction with no motive at all. However, Your sister, my ex-wife, has got a temper that she expresses with no hesitation. She threw things at Reilly on several occasions, she broke a window at the Millers once, she squirted Jeffry Ballein with a water hose, and she slapped her own minister in the face. Her habit of acting out her rages is enough. The prosecution will argue that over the years she got worse and worse."

"I know about the last one, slapping the minister" I said. "She got to him first or I would've done it. That minister said something incredibly insensitive about a parent we had just buried. Hell, you were there."

"Fact remains, the prosecution can demonstrate a behavior pattern of violent behavior over extremely petty things. In conjunction with the physical evidence, witnesses and an aggressive prosecution, it could be enough for a jury, especially if she takes the stand and starts . . . doing her thing, whatever the hell it is."

"I see your point." I felt defeated. "What are you going to do about Audrey right now?"

For the first time I saw true annoyance on his face. "Arrested her entering the jurisdiction? Dumbest goddamn thing I ever heard of. I'm going to arm twist a judge and try to get her bail re-instated without a hearing. Judas Priest, they arrested her returning to the jurisdiction. They prevented her from entering the jurisdiction. I'll have their asses."

"Good luck. That wouldn't break my heart any."

"I'll get the car and meet you outside baggage claim." He rose, a petty little upturn of his lips suggesting a sly smile. "Thanks for the drinks," he said, tossing down his second.

"Cheap bastard," I mumbled, leaving cash on the table and signaling the waitress.

Brad was going to structure a defense based on the odds. Apparently the professionals on both sides of the law were hardened to using years of peoples' lives as chips in this table game of crime and punishment. "Plead to this and we'll give you seven-to-ten." "Admit to that and we'll drop the death penalty, change the charge to . . ." "Confess this and we'll make that recommendation." The lives of defendants were gambling tokens stretched out on a green felt playing surface, ante'd up, raised, checked and called. The innocent amateurs, like tourists in Las Vegas, were the ones making the sucker bets, bluffing with no hands and not knowing when to quit. When they lost those chips, they lost years of their lives.

Pleading guilty to something she did not do to avoid worse punishment would erode Audrey's soul. She could endure prison as a convicted innocent more than she could as an admitted killer.

Brad and his criminal associate would handle the defense. As far as I knew they didn't need me. Audrey needed me. Audrey needed to know that I believed in her. In that moment I knew my comfortable retirement routine was suspended until this mess was settled.

CHAPTER FOUR

The incorporated municipality of Alta Mira hugged the coastline north of San Diego. In the years before incorporation, US 101 was the commercial and social lifeline on the California coast. Then Interstate 5 was built and the mighty machine of civilization roared north and south a few miles further inland. Many of the coastal communities were able to maintain their charm. Places like La Jolla, Leukadia, Del Mar, Laguna Beach and Alta Mira became irresistible home sites for a growing class of the urban affluent. The University of California, San Diego and an exploding community of hi-tech hard- and soft-ware businesses attracted an educated, ambitious middle class. The arts flourished in a friendly environment on the dramatically beautiful shores of southern California.

The Mediterranean climate, Del Mar Race Track, surfing, sailing, Old Globe Theatre, Mission Bay park, Vacation Village, brought free spending tourists year round. It was the good life. It was the woody smell of new construction. It was prosperity in the sun: a professional football team, a professional baseball team, and professional hockey and basketball teams. Pops in the park in July by a world-class hometown symphony, hosting the Americas cup one year, half a dozen golf courses and miles and miles of sandy beaches . . . and nearly everyone had a California tan.

Much of the labor keeping those gardens so magazine worthy and supporting the wonderful ambiance restaurants was supplied by the labor of people who could neither afford such gardens nor the surf'n'turf special. The Mexican immigrants and other peoples whose color advertised their social status were a great engine supporting the good life. But, hey, that's progress. A good supply of the labor of the oppressed makes for the good life. So, the good people of La Jolla, Del Mar, and Leukadia paid their dues to the ACLU and contented themselves that it would all work out in several generations like it had for their people.

The coastline from the southern tip of Camp Pendleton, the huge Marine base in Oceanside to the Mexican border, was all accounted for in either upscale residences or upscale restaurants and a few beachfront hotels. Camp Pendleton extended for an undeveloped sixteen miles of this magnificently beautiful coast down to Oceanside, the city that supported the El Toro Marine base. If the United States government were to sell off that coastline in residential and commercial lots it could earn several billions of dollars. There was no other coastal land for further development. Add the interior property east of Highway 5 and Uncle Sam could about eliminate the national debt.

Brad, the Impaler, allowed me the front passenger seat of his black Lincoln Town Car. Traffic noises were shamed from interrupting the corporate whoosh as this car, suppressing any bumps and most sense of motion, quietly whisked us northward. We did not speak. Certainly he did not play the radio, which I was sure was an

49

expensive Blaupunkt that would only play discreet string quartets.

As soon as we were on I-5 he pushed a button on his steering wheel and started talking to it. The dashboard answered. He told it to call his office. He hung a black plastic, cockroach-shaped gizmo in his ear, looking like Spock monitoring the landing party. Apparently that muted the dashboard so that passengers, relatives, and other assorted trash could no longer hear both sides of the conversation.

He arranged for several pieces of paper to be taken from one place and to be put into another place: for some to be signed and some to be stamped and some to be recorded. Like a wizard giving arcane instructions to apprentices, he dictated a memo invoking the powers of something called "collateral estoppel." He compelled another minion (grunion, bunion, onion? scallion?) to "wash" a contract. Throughout this display of magic were repeated demands to speak to "Fred."

Maybe, as Audrey has suggested, I have a blind spot when it comes to attorneys in general and good ol' Brad in particular. Certainly his help was welcome right now. He was a big fish in the corporate law pool. Apparently the waters of the corporate law pool and the criminal law pool and the political law pool, all mixed, (which explained a lot). I assumed his contacts, like, I guess, "Fred," were powerful. He was practicing back-door politics, peddling influence, etc. I listened with fascination as a passenger in his luxurious bubble of aloof reality. I didn't comment on his efforts to manipulate the system from inside. I try to be understanding about any kind of corruption that might benefit me or mine. A little politicking in a good cause, helping Audrey, could be seen as a virtue.

I just couldn't get used to thinking good things about Brad. Why was he being so helpful? He was almost disturbing the balance of nature by doing good things. He was a bad guy. It bothered me that he was acting nice. It also bothered me that I was being so small-minded that I almost begrudged Audrey the help.

Finally, his demands were satisfied.

"Fred, Brad here. Right. Listen, I need a favor and I need it now . . . You know the fix Audrey is in, right? . . . Good. Well, in some emotional state, she felt an absolutely irresistible impulse to seek help from her closest loved one— No, not me for Chrissake, her brother, lives in Washington . . . I don't know why, same genes I suppose . . . as soon as she saw him, she came right back to California. It won't happen again because she brought the brother with her. A couple of jackass bounty hunters, lazy as they are stupid, grabbed her. They waited till the plane lands at Lindbergh. Their entire action is within the jurisdiction."

Here, they enjoyed a good laugh. Apparently it is amusing to be so far above the earthlings. While they indulged the thin air of their own upper atmosphere, the hills of home whizzed by in a discrete hush outside, their sere brown turned a tawdry green by the tinted windows.

"Fred, I need this quashed, okay? I don't need poor Audrey back in jail over it. Right . . . . Right . . .. Listen, it's only been an hour. I know that you can jump in and reinstate. What's the edge of being a judge if you can't make a difference once in a while?"

I understood only that "Fred," apparently a judge, was reluctant to make himself vulnerable by doing what was asked. A lot of Latin mumbo-jumbo passed between them. For all *ibuses, erats,* and *vobiscums* running back and forth it sounded like altar boy school. Hell, they could have been saying mass.

"Fred," Brad said, menace in his voice. "I'm calling in a marker. I know you can do it. It's a bullshit bust from the bounty hunters and I want Audrey to sleep in her own bed tonight . . . You're not doing anything wrong, goddammit. It's justice. Bail is meant to suppress flight. She's not a flight risk. She just wanted to see her brother, now that's done and she bought her own tickets back to the jurisdiction . . . Come on, Fred. One for the team. Fourth and inches, I need the down."

Despite the questionable sport metaphor, I wasn't sure what was said. I didn't hear an express agreement, but I'm a stranger to their culture. Maybe they never do expressly agree to do things. They all seem to worship at an altar of credible deniability. The call terminated shortly before we arrived at Audrey's place. "Here's a set of keys," Brad said, holding a small key ring between thumb and forefinger at arms length as though he intended to avoid touching either the keys or me. "House and car. I've got to get back to town. More phone calls to make. I'll let you know when she's getting out."

I got her luggage from the trunk of his car and as the lid closed, he was off.

"Yeah," I said to the curb, "see you later . . . thanks."

Audrey's house, which Brad and she had had built, was one of about a dozen built on a bulge of coastal cliff called Bonita Bluffs. They were upscale manses and most of them blatantly so. Audrey's two-story, stuccoed imitation of a Spanish mission sported an out-of-place portico entrance complete with two columns and a semi-circular terra-cotta driveway. It seemed to shout "We don't need taste; we got money."

The <u>Casa Brad/Audrey</u> shared Bonita Bluff with at least two Georgian mansions that looked like Tara One and Tara Two, a slinking ranch that hid behind dense landscaping, a modern thing that looked like a couple of cantilevered shoe-boxes, and some multi-windowed, main-stream, white clapboard designs that, by comparison, seemed like old-money class. Any of them could be home base for a situation comedy; I could see credits rolling: "Meet The Mundanes." All had long driveways and professional landscaping.

In the center of the arc formed by these houses were yet more houses, also on two-acre lots, the second tier of upper-middle-money homes. They were the latecomers or those who couldn't afford the houses right on the bluff, but who shared the same street and attitude with them. No direct ocean view but beach access and bragging rights to living "on the bluffs."

I knew virtually no one. This was a house and a city that were not my own. I would await news of things far beyond my control. I had a long, boring afternoon ahead of me. I would prowl the rooms of this presumptuous house to get the lay of the land. I would figure out her sound system and look for some light classical or jazz to play. I would definitely raid her bar and probably snoop her kitchen and make a sandwich. It was still bright enough so that I could enjoy that sandwich in Audrey's <u>lanai</u> with its "English, country" (overgrown and a little out of control) garden. But, I had no doubt that I was in for a long, tedious afternoon. In retrospect, if I had listened, I might have heard the gods giggling at my proud assumptions. Just when I had, indeed, located what promised to be a great local jazz station, it was not divine laughter but Audrey's "Ain't we cute" musical door chimes playing an ungodly version of "Ode To Joy," from the album "Welk Plays Bach; Bach Loses."

Some women are born beautiful in a flashy way that suits them through early life. A world that caters to their sex but doesn't give them time to develop personalities spoils them. As long as the dew is still fresh on the bud, so to speak, their lives are idyllic. They are pampered and patronized for what charms they may deign to bestow. When beauty fades, the surprised used-to-be divas wander in a now indifferent world resentfully wondering what the hell just happened. They are usually shallow, angry and confused. Others do not grow into beauty until later in life. They have an opportunity to grow and develop the kind of personal strength that results in great beauty. At the door, an expectant smile on her face, stood one of the beautiful ones.

"I'm Consuela Miller," she said in a voice so rich and full it contributed to global warming. "Connie."

"I'm, uh . . ."

I knew the answer well enough. I was distracted, comparing this woman with the caricature Audrey had drawn of a judgmental housefrau who spoke in bumper stickers. There was a hint of Latin in the depth of her dark eyes, in her olive skin, the near glow of her auburn hair.

"You're Dan Kelly, Audrey's brother," she said, enjoying the moment.

"Of course I am, please come in."

She wore a loose T-shirt and loose fitting sweat pants that hinted at but did not tease. Although she had the body of a playmate, she was not flamboyant. She moved like an athlete, economical and sure.

"I apologize if I'm interfering," she said, heading for the kitchen, I guessed by habit. "I knew Audrey had gone off somewhere up north to visit you. Then I saw Brad drop you off." She looked at me directly and I felt the full force of her smile. "Audrey has told me a lot about you, Dan. It's like we're already friends."

"Me too," I answered, master of dazzling repartee.

Was this the woman whom Audrey had described as never having had an original thought? I had pictured a dowdy, control freak. When friends go to war, truth is the first casualty. " . . . And you're right, Connie," I recovered. "She came to see me. We turned right around and came back to Alta Mira."

She stopped near the coffeepot in Audrey's airy California kitchen. The sun, seen through the sliding glass doors, was low above the Pacific horizon by then. "That begs the question, Dan, where is she now?"

"A couple of no-neck bounty-hunters grabbed her. Brad went down to County to see what he could do. He seemed confident. Would you like some coffee?"

"I'd rather have a glass of wine, or, better yet, something stronger." She raised those dark eyebrows in an inviting manner and resistance or disagreement was rendered impossible. They call them bedroom eyes because when a woman flashes them at you, getting her to the bedroom is all you can think about. Connie was flirting with me, not big-beer-Jeannette flirting, the real deal! I love to flirt, but I do so with the confidence that no one will take me seriously. She was entirely too young for me, but she had me doing age-math in base-iffy. I didn't think of a generation gap, I thought, <u>Gee, I'm on the younger side of</u>

the sixties and she's an appreciative forties . . .if you round up at one end and round down at the other, there's a bare decade or so between us.

"A drink sounds like a good idea" I said. "Just one. I'm hoping that I'll be driving into San Diego to get Audrey."

Yeah, I was thinking of Audrey all right. Decrepit old fart like me sipping cordials with Miss Any-Month-You-Like in a cliff house with an ocean view? Yeah, Audrey.

"Don't worry," she said, returning to the large, pseudo-mission style family room. "If Brad felt confident, it meant he had some power figure by the *cajones* and will get his way. He will either bully the Sheriff's Department to deliver Audrey or he will bring her home himself, simply for the accolades and gratitude it will generate. What's the use of having power if exercising it doesn't put more and more people in your debt?"

Connie delivered this delightfully cynical opinion while she poured a cognac for herself and a scotch neat for me. Bumper stickers? Hell no. My kind of woman.

"That really offends me," I offered. "Brad is one of my favorite people."

"Is that a test?" she laughed. She closed the cover on the portable bar that was made to look like an antique armoire. "You wouldn't piss up his butt if his guts were on fire."

Hearing that kind of language from this beauty was an adolescent turn-on that I'm hard put to describe. I sat on part of a huge, brown leather, sectional that started absorbing me immediately. I held the glass up to save the drink. "Forgive me, Connie, but, I had the impression that you and Audrey did not get along. You're talking like you were best friends."

Her laughter was like a piccolo solo. "We're neighbors and we don't agree on everything. We certainly didn't agree on this whole skateboard park business."

"I heard about that."

"We're both original owners at Bonita Bluffs and we're active in the community. I'd like to think of her as a friend. I'm worried about her. I know she's mad at me right now. That happens."

"I got the impression you were in a state of war."

"We crab at each other. We have spats. We backbite. We invent wonderfully vicious things to say about each other, then we work together to coordinate a crafts fair. Welcome to suburbia."

"Ah, so. When I was married, my wife was my Secretary of State. I didn't concern myself with foreign relations."

Thoughts of my dear Patricia filled my head. Perhaps it was because I felt the pull of Connie's sensuality. Perhaps because I had referred to having been married. The years of Patricia had never entirely left me. They never would. There were still vulnerable times when I would turn my head, nearly having heard her voice. Alone at home, I frequently put flowers on the table when I ate breakfast. Patricia used to do that. She said that starting the day with flowers was a good thing to do. I called it the magic of a loving woman.

Connie had observed my reverie. "How long has it been now?" Her raised eyebrows seemed to imply another meaning to the question.

"Eight years."

"Ever think about re-marrying?"

"Some people cannot be replaced."

"That's too glib, Dan. Shame on you."

"It's true. I can never replace Patricia. But, of course, you're right. There's more."

She nodded her head, waiting me out and for some reason I opened my mouth and some personal parts came out. "I'm not committed to being single for the rest of my life either. I didn't mean that. I'll never love Patricia less, but I could love someone else. At least, I think I could."

"That's better," she said, sipping and smiling. It made me feel good. "I like it when people are candid."

"You touched a button, I guess," I said.

"Sorry."

"Have I met your husband?"

She sighed as though reluctant to change the subject, or, averse to talking about her husband. It was a feeling I had . . . trouble at the Miller house. "You were here two years ago, I think, but we were gone to a convention in Las Vegas at the time."

"Convention?"

"CM, we call him CM because he hates the name 'Clyde,' is an orthodontist. It was a dental convention. I went because Las Vegas is fun and I know a lot of the people. I used to be a dental tech. It's how we met."

I had a quick picture of the younger Connie in a snug little nurse's outfit, flashing her ivories at her boss and just . . . moving. I wanted to ask if he was married at the time but decided that he probably was. I could confirm it later with Audrey.

"And, forgive me for leapfrogging right to the point," I said, being candid which she had said she liked, "but, what do you think about this Reilly business?"

58

"Frankly, I'm shocked and heartbroken about the whole thing," she said. It sounded rehearsed. I looked in vain for signs of shock or a broken heart. She did effect a suppressed sob and wiped at a tear that had never been there.

"You know what I'm asking."

"Yes. Well, Audrey is a passionate woman. Explosive temper. She came to borrow Clyde's shotgun once. She wanted to stick the barrels in the gopher holes and blast away. Clyde said 'no'. She'd probably hurt herself; but she was ready to do it. Some of our disagreements come up because Audrey is too spontaneous with her opinions and criticisms, too quick to anger. You know, some people just don't edit themselves."

"It's genetic," I volunteered.

She suppressed a smile. "I don't know how far Audrey would go . . . or has gone. She was very angry at the assemblyman. She threw things at him more than once. Really angry."

"Did you know him? What was he like?"

She held her knees with her hands and leaned back, smiling as if thinking of something funny. "If anyone were created just to push all your sister's buttons, it was Sean Reilly. He was pompous, authoritarian, dogmatic and, politically, so far to the right that Bluetooth the Vandal would have told him to lighten up. Audrey called him the assemblyman from the Third Reich."

"A bad match," I agreed, keeping in mind that Audrey believed that government existed to do absolutely everything it could do to "keep things nice for everyone."

"And, that was before she met him," Connie said, warming to her subject.

"Oh?"

"The man was fastidious to the point of personality disorder. We, CM and I, and the Reillys, shared a houseboat on Lake Powell for a week. He not only brushed, flossed, and gargled at length after every meal; he almost did it after every drink. I never, during that week, saw him in the same shirt or slacks in the evening that he wore during the day. He brought three bathing suits because he simply would not put a damp suit on. I didn't mind, I thought it amusing. He would dress up for a picnic. His, what do you guys call it . . . shaving kit, was practically a chemical set."

She downed the cognac and smiled over the rim of the glass. "Can I get a little naughty with you?"

"I don't know, can you?"

"CM and Sean did a lot of business together. They were almost partners, but even CM said once that Sean was so uptight he'd step out of the shower to pee."

We had a good laugh about the poor dead guy using the proper drain.

She had started getting silly and she could not stop. "For all that tooth-brushing and gargling, he couldn't bring himself to spit. Biddie, Mrs. Uptight-First-Term-California-Assemblyman-Reilly, whose-stuff-doesn't-stink, told me that when he got coughs they went on forever. He couldn't bring up the phlegm. Of course," Connie had to stop for a moment, she was laughing so hard, "she was so proper that she had to say 'expectorate!'"

I don't know why 'expectorate' was suddenly hilarious. Perhaps it was her comic impression of a pompous, matronly, Biddie Reilly. I was caught up in the mood. This was one funny dead guy.

I got a picture of this fella who would be an absolute nemesis to Audrey. Audrey can be a bit of a poser but she would see all this compulsive fastidiousness as attention getting, 'acting out' behavior. She abhors people who must control, confine, categorize everything and that sounded like Reilly.

Poor Sis. That image from the Jet way returned to somber my mood.

"You're kind of avoiding the big question, Connie."

She would not meet my eyes. "I know." I had cold-watered her little burst of good humor.

"Come on, Connie. My sister drives us both crazy. We've had a drink. We've laughed at bathroom humor. We're pals. Share."

"Dan, I don't know if Audrey did it or not. The evidence sure isn't on her side."

"Fair, but not enough."

"You want to know if I think she could have done it. You want to know if I think she's capable of it, crazy enough for it? Committed enough to do it?"

"That's what I want to know."

"It'll cost Audrey another cognac."

"Help yourself. None for me."

Connie poured another, then let me have it in one blast. "I think Audrey will do whatever she decides to do. I think she makes some terrible decisions."

"Like whether to buy yams or sweet potatoes? Come on. Gimme a break."

"Who knows when and if that hair-trigger temper of hers crossed the line. It's like sometimes she's a completely different person. If she were mad enough at Sean Reilly, could she saturate some of her peanut brittle with poison and feed it to him?"

"Well?"

"Is she capable?" She said, repeating the obvious.

"Consuela?" I tried to sound like an impatient parent.

She was struck dumb, caught in a struggle to say something without using any of the words that would say it. "She . . . You've got to understand . . . Audrey . . ." She sipped at her cognac and fixed me with a steady stare. "If Audrey were angry enough, yes, I think she could do it and not look back."

The telephone rang.

CHAPTER FIVE

"Davis residence," I answered, the way we were brought up to do.

"Right. Come down to county jail. I'm getting her released but I have things to do. You've got the keys; you've got her car. Take Five South till you see signs. She'll be waiting. How long she waits is up to you."

He hung up before I had a chance to say, "Fine, Brad, and you?" or even to thank him for saving Audrey from a night in jail. I related the news to Connie. She tossed off her drink. She even took the two glasses to the kitchen and rinsed them. We walked to the front door together and paused just outside.

"That cognac has put me in the mood," she teased. "I think I'll seduce CM tonight. I'll pick out a romantic restaurant, talk dirty, and try to keep him sober."

"Sounds like a plan," I said, finding out that I was not immune from feeling embarrassed by someone else's lack of inhibitions.

"Do you think that would work?" she said, putting more into the question than words.

"I don't know Clyde but I would think that would work just fine."

"You know, a dark little table in the corner, a casual hand on his thighs . . ."

"Yeah, yes, I, ah, I'm sure that would work just fine. Good plan."

"Of course, he's such an insensitive troll sometimes. I could get all naked and give him a lap dance and he might still reach out for his bourbon instead of my—"

"—Right. Look, Connie, I don't know you all that well and I don't know Clyde at all. You're telling me more than I need to know. Okay?"

"Am I making you uncomfortable? Oh, that's so adorable. It's just that I feel so comfortable, like we've been friends forever."

"I've heard that cognac and felony murder can do that sometimes."

She hesitated and I thought she was going to say something inappropriately personal. "Listen, I don't mean to be paranoid or anything, but that SUV that you can see over my shoulder does not belong in this neighborhood. That's just for your information."

I did look over her shoulder at the maroon SUV. The windows were tinted. I couldn't tell if it was occupied. I wasn't worried; she had planted the thought is all.

"Enjoy your night out," I said as she crossed the manicured green to Tara Two.

Audrey's car was a BMW (yes, she called it "the Beamer"), a recent model in a blue so dark it looked black. It smelled of lavender on the inside and when I fired it off I heard baroque music in the background, some Vivaldi piece. I was disappointed. For public consumption Audrey had her lace-curtain Irish persona, but I would have been delighted at a little window-rattling Gretchen Wilson in the private world of her car. Audrey being a covert bootscooter would've been cool.

64

A CASE OF PEANUT BRITTLE

I remembered how Brad had accessed the neighborhood from I-5 and had no trouble finding my way back to it. A mile or two down the freeway I noticed a maroon SUV in the rear view mirror. I smiled at how silly that was. It was a popular model and probably a popular color. There must be thousands of them. I changed lanes and slowed down. I'd let it pass me so I could scold myself for watching too much TV. The SUV moved to the right and slowed down too. I felt a wave of fear wash over me. It's not paranoia when they're really out to get you.

I slid to the left in the moderate traffic and increased my speed. The SUV matched my movements. When the Beamer and the SUV were exceeding seventy, I took it seriously. I did not have a cell phone. I looked at her steering wheel and her dashboard for any Brad-style buttons I could push to call for help. In a few more minutes we would be close enough to the city for heavier traffic and my options would be even more limited. The Vivaldi concerto was driving me nuts.

Get off the freeway? Then what? Run traffic lights? Get assassinated if I did not run traffic lights? What the hell was I dealing with? This was no damned skateboard park, peanut brittle, neighborhood dust-up. Something was going on. A government official had been murdered. Audrey was caught in the middle, accidentally or by design. Now the SUV. Conspiracy? Christ! I was in the middle of a spy movie. What would Harrison Ford do? Mat Damon?

I slowed down to sixty-five and tried to gather my thoughts. The SUV edged closer. Paranoid, adolescent, panicky . . . I did not care. Nobody gets to shoot me. I sped up. I'd race all the way to Mexico if I had to. I must keep the maroon menace behind me. I changed lanes. I sped up. The traffic got thicker. My heart beat faster. If I knew where the damned "off" button was I would kill the stupid string quartet. I was in a deadly race with a threat I did not understand, terrified that I would lose. Vivaldi was the wrong theme music.

Traffic ahead slowed enough to open a gap between clusters of cars. I nearly lost it cutting someone off, but I made it into the gap. The good old Beamer, designed for the autobahn, acquitted itself magnificently, screaming to ninety miles an hour. My stranglehold on the steering wheel hurt my forearms. As a sour note to the chamber music I heard the wailing of a police siren.

Salvation was at hand.

I slowed down, made it to the shoulder and came to a stop skidding on the ice plant, that gushy, water-packed junk that Southern California grows on the freeway borders. I jumped from the car and waved at the police car bearing down on me. It didn't occur to me until later what a picture I must have made, skinny old guy jumping around and waving his arms like some giant spider monkey, long Einsteinian gray hair blowing in the wind.

The lead Chipmobile had more lights on it than ET's mother ship. The siren died. I pointed to the SUV, waving my arms for them to go after it. The unit stopped and its doors opened. Behind the doors two California Highway Patrol officers stood with their guns drawn and pointed directly at me. You could slice bread with the creases in their starched shirts.

"They're getting away," I shouted. "It's not me, it's the purple ah . . . the maroon SUV that's following me."

"Sir, get down on your knees and put your hands up," invited the driver, his polished chrome aviator's sunglasses making him look like just another CHP clone stamped out of the CHP machine. Another police car pulled up, siren screaming and lights flashing. God, these guys loved flashing lights and big noises.

"Go after the SUV," I shouted, now pointing at the traffic cluster already a quarter mile south. "They're after me."

"On your knees, please," the officer repeated. "Who's after you?"

More reflecting sunglasses and starched shirts showed up.

"I don't know."

By then I was on my knees and the officers in the second car had gotten to me and searched my body. It's called "patting down" by anyone who's never experienced it. Actual "patting" would be more gentle and less invasive of privacy.

"Any weapons?"

"No."

"Any drugs or paraphernalia?"

"Of course not."

"Have you been drinking?"

"No."

"I smell scotch."

"I had a drink."

"One drink?"

"I had a couple on the plane."

"A couple?"

"Three—great police work, by the way. You let the bad guys get away." I knew that was not the most politic thing to say but my mouth has a mind of its own.

They gave me a field sobriety test. In the most polite and politically correct possible manner they accused me of reckless driving, being a deadly scourge on public

67

highways and, oh yeah, crazy. It took some discipline for me to show proper respect to authority. They were so damned young. Authority should be older than you. If I were tending bar I would have carded half of them.

"Is this your vehicle?"

"My sister's. I'm on my way to meet her."

"Where?"

"County jail."

"You got that right," murmured a young officer from behind his glasses. I wondered if he had started shaving yet. At least he was willing to find humor in the situation. A second threatening khaki menace started to giggle but stifled it with a snort.

"Some one was chasing you?"

"Yes. I don't know who. Someone in that SUV that I pointed out to you guys. I pulled over because I saw you as my rescuers, my help."

"Why would someone be chasing you, someone you don't know? Do people chase you often? Do people plot against you?"

Oh, yeah. Now we patronize the crazy old guy. "No, no, no," I explained. "Look, I'm not a paranoid crackpot. People do not plot against me. That SUV was watching my sister's house. When I got on the freeway it followed me. I slowed down and it did. I sped up and it did. I panicked. I'm from Washington State. I just came to help my sister. She was arrested. Now, would you officers please let me go so I can go get her? She needs a ride back home and she's waiting."

I felt surrounded by black leather utility belts with holsters, handcuff pouches, nightsticks. It was like getting mugged at a batman convention.

A CASE OF PEANUT BRITTLE

"What was your sister arrested for?" asked the young one with the engaging sense of humor.

I almost told him the truth out of habit but had calmed down enough to think better of it. "Shoplifting," I said. "Ridiculous. She's had an account at Nieman Marcus for years. It's all settled. She just needs a ride. I don't know who those fools in the van were. They rattled me. Kids maybe. They're probably laughing their asses off right now."

The officers mumbled amongst each other in police talk. I have a friend who's a cop and I assumed that as soon as they had the car's license number and my ID, they called in for "wants and warrants." I assumed further that the answer was negative since I have no record and I seldom get traffic tickets, pay them when I do.

While they were swapping tall tales and pondering my fate, the heavenly forces tired of the game they'd been playing. A high priority call came at exactly the right moment. On their radios a female voice that sounded like she was talking through a kazoo called several numbers that got their attention. The cops decided to let me go with a hastily written ticket and call it a day.

Back in Audrey's car I took several breaths and waited 'till the cops left. Kids in the SUV, my foot! I found the switch to send Vivaldi back to the sixteenth century. For a dizzying second I thought I should have asked one of the cops how to get to the jail. No, I realized, the kid with the sense of humor probably would have volunteered to take me.

At least I knew that there'd be a jail next to the courthouse because the sheriff's department transported prisoners to and from the courtroom. I went downtown and started looking for large, ugly buildings. I found several sandstone monstrosities ugly enough to be built with public dollars and one of them was the jail/courthouse. Then began the quest for parking, circling the courthouse. I was willing to park several blocks away if necessary, but it wasn't.

A minor commotion on the steps of the courthouse caught my attention. It was Audrey, waving her Byzantine scarf. I had missed her on the first pass because I was looking for a lone woman. She was amidst a small cluster of lawyers. In Southern California pretty much anyone around the courthouse wearing a tie is a lawyer. She seemed quite happy with them and as she ran toward the car there were friendly bye-byes exchanged in the twilight air.

"They're really nice," Audrey said, sliding into the passenger seat. "One of them is an assistant district attorney and he's going to look into it."

"The murder? Reilly's murder?"

"No, no, no. Seriously, have you ever been to this jail?"

"Of course not."

"It's deplorable. The bathrooms actually smell. All that money and a new building and the bathrooms smell. They smell Dan."

"It's a jail."

"That's no excuse. They can have bars and locks, clanky things and wear ugly brown shoes, and still use a little Lysol. And the tissue! Talk about cruel and unusual. I'm telling you. I don't think the ADA, that's assistant district attorney, Dan, was aware. He's a nice young man. He said he couldn't talk to me too much because there's a felony case pending. What kind of sense does that make?

Can't talk to me about jail conditions because of some dumb murder charge?"

"I just had a hairy experience too, Audrey. It's why I was late. I was— "

"— I'll say this, those two sheriff's deputies were so much nicer than the bounty hunters. We had a nice chat going to jail."

"There was a car chase. It scared the hell out of me. A hundred miles an hour— "

"— Then there was some mix-up. They were waiting for a judge and some other judge butted in. I sat in limbo for hours."

"I thought they were going to shoot me."

"And they really should do something about the coffee in that horrible place. I'll bet they could raise money for the jail if they'd let a Starbucks in there. As much of that horrid coffee as they all drink, a Starbucks would be a real money-maker."

"Really scared."

"I don't know about biscotti and donuts and muffins. They could do souvenir mugs though. If they had a Starbucks county jail souvenir mug, Dan, I would have bought one. I would have bought one for you too. I should suggest that to someone."

"Honest, really scared."

"And those people who deal with prisoners everyday do not have a very positive attitude. You would think that with the rough tissue and smelly bathrooms and bitter coffee we have to endure, a person would try to put a positive spin on things. Some of those COs, that's corrections officers, Dan, are really surly. I had not eaten since a few almonds on that plane. I just asked for a tuna sandwich, light on the mayonnaise of course, and whole wheat bread. You'd think I was asking for the moon! The matron, or whatever she is, called me something I won't repeat. I'm writing a letter to the editor."

I gave up.

"I'll complain to my assembly— . . . oh, I guess not. I killed him, right?"

"No one cares, Audrey."

"What?"

"What?"

"Were you saying something?"

Back up I-5 we went. I kept the cruise control right at fifty-five. I'd had my fill of uniforms for a while. Audrey had a lot of nervous energy to burn off from her experience. Buried in her frenetic account, that repeated in places, was the reality that she had been badly frightened. She was accustomed to a measure of control that her manipulative charms afforded her. This was a painful experience. I could only hope that it might scare her into taking the whole thing more seriously.

"Was Clyde Miller married when he met Connie?"

"Oh, God! You've been drinking with Connie Miller."

She never failed to amaze me. I just asked a simple question. "What makes you . . . why would . . . How the hell . . .?"

"You just referred to her as 'Connie'" in a familiar way. If she came over to spy things out she probably got you to share at least one cognac with her."

"I had scotch, Smart Ass."

"Yes."

"Yes, what?"

"Yes Clyde was married. He divorced his first wife (I never met her) about a year after he hired Connie. As soon as they were married, Connie insisted on being office manager and hired the rest of his assistants and techs. It was a simple new hiring policy. She saw to it that she was always the youngest, prettiest, and sexiest one in the office."

"You're making that up."

"She told me herself. Four cognacs and she does great girl-talk."

"I underestimate you sometimes, Audrey."

"At your peril, Brother," she said, proud of herself.

I was having fun. This was almost my favorite version of my dynamic sister, the one I believe is under all the others, driving them. She was just a bit too weary for performing at any level and she felt safe enough with me to be honest.

"She says that y'all are friends, just temporarily on the outs right now."

"How many cognacs did she have and how many more scotches did you have?"

"Two and one."

"Did she flirt with you?"

"Is that so surprising?"

"God, men are stupid. Connie Miller can play most men like Liberace plays pianos. She got nearly a million dollars out of her first marriage, a real estate broker. She wiggled her way into Clyde Miller's affections and she's doing pretty well. She and Clyde are playing politics now and I wouldn't be at all surprised if one of them doesn't stand for Mayor of Alta Mira just to step into the assembly. They think they're the Clintons. Why else do you think the Millers were buzzing around the Reillys."?

"I don't know. They liked each other?"

73

"Mutual KMA, that's kiss my agenda, Dan."

"Oh, that's what it is."

"Connie and Clyde (they hate that) helped Sean Reilly get and hold an assembly seat, he helps them in business."

"That's everywhere in the world, Audrey. Nothing new."

"Did she tell you, reluctantly and in the strictest of confidence, how she loves Clyde dearly but sees his life as limiting, how one day she must move on to a fuller, more sophisticated world, how she thinks she is about to meet the man to take her there?"

"No. Damn, I feel cheated."

She laughed the relaxed, real Audrey laugh. It was a very nice laugh. "I don't know whether it's fantasy on her part or Clyde really is just a stepping stone to a better place. Connie and I friends?" She stopped suddenly, "In a way I guess we are. Colleagues, war buddies almost. We're both alone in a jungle where the prey's best bet is to look like the predator."

"Wow."

"Did you ask her if she thinks I did it?"

"Yes. She said she wasn't sure. I asked her if she thought you were capable of it and she hemmed and hawed for a while. At the end, she said 'yes.'"

"Of course she did. She thinks I'm capable of it because she knows she is. Makes you wonder."

"Yes?"

"Either one of us is capable, but I know I didn't. Kinda makes her a suspect, right? Hold that thought the next time she slithers up to you wearing something tight."

CHAPTER SIX

One afternoon two days later, we sat in her lanai enjoying the flower-scented breeze and the brightly colored flowers. She had created a nearly Monet quality in her garden: sprays of color whose effect was more important than their form. Hanging sprays of nearly crimson oleander mixed with violet wisteria, whose conical flower clusters hung like bunches of grapes. In the background splashes of lilac bound the palette together. Closer to the ground was the lantana, almost minty-looking leaves and clusters of tiny flowers, white, lavender, pink. The hues splashed, almost danced, like the garden the great impressionist had immortalized.

I pointed to several rounded mounds of dirt on the lawn near her flowerbeds. "Is that what I think it is?" I asked disregarding grammar for phonics.

"Gopher mounds," she said. "They plague me."

"Gophers?"

"Gophers, moles, goophers, goobers . . . I don't know: creepy little rats that ruin my garden. I can't get rid of them."

From the Lanai we heard the criminally trivialized version of "Ode To Joy," and I volunteered to answer the door. Standing there was a slender youth of, perhaps sixteen or seventeen. He wore jeans and a T-shirt advertising something called the Crud Sluggers that I supposed was a rock group. His insouciant smirk reminded me of Gollum, the sleazy little creature from "Lord Of The

Rings." It had that same creepy part-sycophant, part-sadist quality. A fairly high-pitched, boy soprano voice did not enhance my portrait of him, neither did his habit of aspirating his voice as though he were perpetually on the verge of being out-of-breath.

"Hi," he said, "I'm Eric, I guess you're Dan." He extended his hand toward me just like a human being might. He gathered his breath for the next sentence. "Hi, Dan, I came to see Audrey." Peter Lorre would have loved this guy.

<u>Yeah</u>, I thought, preciousss, preciousss Audrey. I didn't shake his hand, not having a "wipe" nearby. My old guy genes resented all the first name familiarity and I did not mind that it showed. "So, who the hell is Eric and why should Dan care?" I asked, real friendly like.

Eric started to giggle nervously but fought it off. To his credit, he stuck to his guns and maintained his outstretched claw. "Eric Miller," he said, "Connie's son. I came to see if Audrey needed any help. I work around here sometimes."

His extended hand looked like the prow of some bizarre spaceship. In part out of vicarious embarrassment for his position, I took the hand and shook it briefly, risking slime by contact. It was cool and moist: I wiped my hands on the hips of my slacks. "Come in," I said, already tired of this pseudo familiarity. "Mrs. Davis and I are out in the Lanai."

"Yeah," Eric exhaled with a big sarcastic smile that I wanted to stop, "Yeah, Lanai, I like that."

I indicated that he precede me out to the Lanai. I wanted to keep my eye on him.

"Eric," Audrey said, looking up. "I was just thinking about you."

"Audrey, there's stuff to do an' shit."

"Have you come to rid me of the gophers? I'll pay you a bonus for all the little bodies you can deliver. Shoot 'em, blow 'em up . . . I hear poison works well."

"Audrey," I cautioned.

"Yeah, Connie suggested poison."

"Are you referring to your mother?" the old man chided.

"Yeah, Connie, 'Mom' . . . Consuela . . . I heard you met her."

He had added a dirty smirk to the list of masks he presented. I wanted to backhand the creep, but was distracted thinking that it was interesting that "Mom" knew poisons. Perhaps part of her background as a dental technician included some skills at chemistry.

"A charming woman," I acknowledged. Audrey grinned as if she had been witness to my chat with Connie. "Tell me, did she show you how to make poisons too? Do you like knives? Little animals?"

Eric leaned toward me and said sotto voce, eyes flashing with excitement, real or pretended. "I prefer to bait the little fuckers with candy then bite their heads off when I've got them."

"Yeah," I came back, not able to resist a disgusting straight line, "Cool and crunchy on the outside, warm and gushy on the inside. I get it."

He looked disappointed that I knew a punch line.

"You two stop it," Audrey cautioned. "I'm already losing my appetite. Eric, what can I do for you today?"

"There's work needs doing. I need your go-ahead."

"I know, I know. I've been a little distracted, Eric."

"Yeah," the kid said. "I heard. Murder an' shit."

"The Lantana should be cut back before it takes over and I should aerate. We should cut the grass by next week, and feed it."

From his high-water jeans I guessed he was in the midst of a growth spurt. If he were not already taller than his parents, he would be by the following Thursday. He had a fair complexion and, not counting the perpetual impression of leering, he had features so pleasant that it was disturbing in its own right. He was more pretty than handsome—not effeminate, mind you—just pretty features, unusual in a boy that age.

"You do all the gardening here?" I asked.

"Oh, nah," he said. "Since I came home from school, I've been helping people around the Bluffs an'shit. Sometimes I do odd jobs for Clyde at the Association, sometimes odd jobs for my clients, like Audrey."

I knew that all the first-name business was teenage rebellion designed to drive adults crazy but it was driving me crazy.

"Oh, Babe," he said to Audrey, reaching new lows in courtesy, "Got any new ideas for the gophers lately?"

"No," she complained. "Flooding their tunnels didn't seem to do a thing. I don't know what to do next."

"Well, Clyde says you definitely don't get the shotgun. Especially now."

"Why especially now?"

"You know, after Reilly an' stuff. Shotgun . . . shit." He giggled briefly.

"Watch yourself, kid," I said, about fed up. "Audrey . . . Mrs. Davis to you, didn't do a damned thing to Assemblyman Reilly. Got it?"

78

"Sure, sure," he said with no real effort to hide his insincerity. "Got it. Good. Hey, take it easy, I came to see if I could help."

"You've been a big help, Eric," Audrey said. "The garden's never looked so good. You'll be hard to replace."

"Are you firing me?" The sudden change in tone was dramatic.

"You will be going back to prep-school, I would think. Won't you?"

"What have you heard? I don't care. I'm not going back to any goddammed prep-school."

"I haven't heard anything," she answered almost defensively. "I just assumed. You have to go to school somewhere."

"I'll be eighteen soon. I don't have to go anywhere or do anything. I'll be an adult an' shit. That prep-school crap was his idea, not mine. It sucks. Hey, I gotta go. If you need anything, tell Connie or Clyde. I'll be over. If you're not here, just leave the keys in the usual place. Bye. I like gardening an' shit. Bye."

He was gone with a forced, "Later, Cranky-Old-Guy, nice to meet you. You're cool," called over his shoulder as I followed him through the house to the door. I did not care for this kid's action an' shit.

"Connie, Clyde and Eric," I mused, returning to the lanai. "There's a reality show waiting to be made."

"Honestly, Dan. He's been a big help."

"Keys in the usual place?"

"A little key box out of sight. I mean, we're not New York for Pete's sake."

"I don't like the idea of that kid having access to your house. There's something a little weird about him . . . a whole lot weird . . .."

79

"I'll confess that some people have complained about little things missing. But, I don't think anything of it."

"He has this deal with other homes?"

"He came home from boarding school in mid-term and he's been restless. He's a charming boy and he works hard. He has access to a lot of homes. Some of us have already come to depend on him."

"Something not kosher about his wiring. I swear it. There should be a recall out on him. His name goes on the list too."

"Your cranky 'people I don't like' list?"

"No, on the 'people who had access and opportunity to commit murder' list."

"Oh, you don't like anybody," she grouched.

"Sure, I do."

"You are turning into a cranky old man, Dan. It's not very attractive. Not very attractive at all."

"What the hell brought that on? We're enjoying the sun then this weirdo kid makes a visit, now I'm a cranky old man. Who rained on your parade?"

She sat in the wrought iron chair in morose silence. Were it not for a tight, angry set to her face I would swear she was pouting. It couldn't just be Eric's visit or my suspicions of him. "Give a little here," I pleaded. "I'm Brother Dan, remember, one of the good guys."

"I need another lawyer." She suddenly whipped up halfway to full rave.

"Giving up on Brad?"

"I've been had," she practically snapped.

She had been edgy since she got back from a long luncheon with Brad. I had assumed her foul mood was whiplash from a delayed collision with reality.

Her eyes dark with anger, she jumped to her feet and marched to the kitchen. "Tea?" she barked over her shoulder.

I know a direct order when I hear one.

"Sure."

I gave her a few moments to boil the water, presumably by glaring at it. I approached the kitchen with care and stopped out-of-range. Her back was to me. I had a quick vision of her doing mean things to helpless tea bags.

"I am on your side, you know."

She turned to face me. "This morning they told me the price of my defense." She motioned around the kitchen, waving her arms, expanded the gesture to include the whole house. "All this. They want my house, Dan."

I crossed to give her a comforting hug. I thought she'd sob softly into my shoulders: but no. She shouted angrily and it hurt my ear. I didn't know what to do.

"Can't you borrow on the house? Get a second?"

"It's not my house!" she screamed. I tried to look away. I did manage to get her head against my other shoulder. It gave the first ear, the ringing one, a rest. One or two more blasts like that and even aspirin wouldn't help. She was nowhere near to being out of steam yet. "I can live in it but I can't borrow money on it. I certainly can't sell it. It's his house."

"I don't understand," I said.

She pushed me away with amazing strength for a hundred-pound ex-dancer. It threw me back and I grabbed the counter to break a fall. She barraged me, eyes aflame. "All these houses are part of Bonita Bluff Homeowners Association and I was allowed to vote, but not any more.

81

It's his vote. The house is his. The lanai is his. The garden I planted . . . is his. Even the goddamned gophers are his!"

"You mean, like a life-estate?"

"Don't you start using lawyer words," she accused. "Brad said that too, 'life estate.' If I give that up for an alimony settlement I get the defense attorney."

"Well, alimony settlement."

"This is my house, Dan. This is my house . . . I thought it was. This way I have nothing."

The water boiled but it couldn't compare with Audrey. The teapot whistled with increasing insistence. Finally, with her back to the complaining pot, she reached behind and jerked it off the flame. The whistle died, nearly whimpering at the end.

"It's not the money, Dan," she complained. "We built this house. Each room has dreams in it. The view, the placement . . . everything. The last eight years of my life."

"You said alimony . . . "

Her eyes, in anger, were a darker green. "Modest, a smaller house. Leave the cliff. Leave the sunset, the neighbors. Leave the memories. Leave all the associations that make a house a home."

"I'm sorry, Audrey."

"In some new place I'll be the divorcé who got away with murder. I might as well wear a scarlet letter, a big 'A' for Audrey. Life will never be the same." She started pacing. Her high heels stabbed the tile floor with a loud "clack" at each step. It sounded like small arms fire.

I'd never seen her like this. Audrey, even when faking it, always appeared on top of things. I thought, the hell with a fair fight with Brad. At that moment I could have shot the son-of-a-bitch in the back, caved his head in with a shovel . . .

"You won't be next door to Connie and Clyde Miller any more," I reminded, trying to cheer her.

She spun on me and hesitated. "I'll miss her. She's the only one around here with a spine."

"You didn't know about this life-estate business?"

"It was a 'friendly' divorce." She extended the word "divorce" just enough to make a sound like acid eating through metal. "My attorney went to law school with Brad. They showed me papers they knew I wouldn't read and told me I would never have to give up the house and I'd have a monthly payment. I trusted them."

"Audrey, how much money are we talking about for the defense fund? I have some equity in my house. I could—"

"—No way, Dan."

"Really, I could raise fifteen, maybe twenty thousand for you."

She laughed without humor. "God love you, Dan. That's barely a down payment. I won't have you go bust to make a gesture that won't help anyway. Their estimate sounded more like a zip code."

"It's something."

"Don't be hurt, brother. Let's hold your house in reserve, okay? Last resort."

"Yeah, yeah, yeah," I pouted. I knew she was right. In the world of American justice, money makes might and might makes right. We had to face that she'd lost her house.

"If you relocate up North, I promise, for a fee, not to tell people that you're a murderous divorcé. I'll even tell them that the scarlet letter is for adultery, like the original."

She made a very unladylike below-the-wrist gesture at me. "I'm not going to leave the Sun Belt," she argued.

"That god-awful rain forest you live in might be just fine for mushrooms like you who've retired from life and light. I like blue. Blue ocean and blue skies, blue-colored cocktails at seafront resorts."

"On my side of Puget Sound, we have less annual rainfall than LA."

"Yeah, yeah, yeah," she said, mocking me.

"Audrey, I'm sorry and Brad is a real prick, but I don't see what we can do."

"I've just got to cry it off, vent, plot an ingenious revenge then accept what has to be." She stopped attacking the tiles with her heels.

She had vented by yelling: unfortunately at me. My ears were still ringing. The first wave of hurt and temper faded.

She finished making the tea, herb tea, a dark red concoction that almost tasted as though it had some body. She suggested having it in the den, having had enough sunlight for a while. We sat in leather Morris chairs with side tables. She knew better than to put me in a position where I had to balance a cup of tea on my lap.

Next to a roll-top desk was a small lamp table and upon it, on a display frame holding an elaborately hand-painted oriental plate. I admired the bright enamel colors and the intricate floral design. Audrey picked it up, holding it gently at its edges.

"This was a gift to Brad from a grateful Japanese businessman. He's proud of it. It's very old; he had it appraised at several thousand dollars, tells the story all the time. In his words, it's 'found money.' He loves displaying it."

She picked it up and gave it to me to admire. Clearly, it had been hand painted, and I had the impression that it was old.

"He keeps promising to come by for it."

She retrieved it and took several steps toward the archway that separated the den from the family room. She shifted to a Frisbee-like grasp and launched it clear out of the den, across the family room in a gentle arc, and neatly into the fireplace where it shattered to a thousand pieces on the hearth.

I saw sparkle return to her eye.

#

"A potluck? You're kidding. We're going to a potluck?"

Audrey smiled back at me across the white enameled, wrought iron table outside on a rear patio with a small fishpond. A silent pump circulated water to cascade from artificial rocks. The sound of the water was pleasant. We sat on matching chairs with cushions and had been enjoying a light brunch al fresco. She had selected plates with flower patterns. A bowl between us held a fruit salad. She had made finger sandwiches. I felt like the idle rich.

Her smile was sweet and innocent, always a bad sign. "It's a kind of tradition, Dan."

"You mean an honest to God 'who brought the macaroni salad?' potluck? Is this how you tree hugging, California Zen, yuppies deal with your problems?"

"Our neighborhood committee meetings are always pot-lucks."

"And on what planet do I care about that?"

"On the planet that says the odds are that whoever the bad guy is, he'll be at the meeting. He'll be watching us watching him."

I sipped at my iced tea, warming to the idea. "When is this suspect line-up?"

"Friday, and Dan . . ."

"Yup?"

"By 'he', you know I mean 'she' just as quick."

"I know, I know, as in Connie."

Her pink cell phone, lying prostrate on the table, interrupted us with the beginnings of When The Saints Go Marchin' In. It came as a surprise when she answered then held the receiver out to me . . . "It's for you," she said, a question implied in her raised eyebrows. She leaned close as I answered.

"Yes, hello?"

"You drive like a freakin' maniac, Old Man," said the hoarse voice on the other side.

Fears of the maroon SUV and its occupants struck me anew like a slap on the face. "Who the hell are you? What do you want with me? Why'd you chase me?" I blurted out.

"That's all in your head, stupid," the voice said. "We were trying to get your attention."

"It worked."

"We want to talk to you."

There was little he could do to me through the phone. I got brave. "You're talking now."

"We've got information to sell."

"Why do I care?"

"Because someone's maybe framing Lady Grandma. For twenty-five hundred dollars, we have a name."

"Lady Grandma" was the tip-off that it was the bounty hunters. "Everybody's got a name," I snapped. "I call you 'Blondie, the bounty hunter.' No sale."

"Okay, so you know who I am."

"What else do I need to know?"

"Didn't you wonder why we were on to Grandma so quick?"

"Yeah. I did. You don't seem that smart."

"Price just went up another thousand dollars, asshole."

"All right. All right. Who's working against us?"

"Uh uh. It doesn't work that way. You come up with the thirty-five hundred dollars. You meet us tonight with the money and we tell you who we were working for, who tipped us."

"Thirty five hundred dollars! Come on."

"It was twenty five till you opened your big mouth. This ain't a negotiation. Thirty-five hundred dollars, cash, at East Twentieth and Granger, National City, eight o'clock. You can bring Grandma for directions but that's it."

"Eight o'clock tonight."

"I can't have the money that fast, not in cash," I said. "Do you take checks? Plastic?"

"Four thousand dollars, wise ass. Tonight. Eight o'clock. Corner of Granger and East twentieth, National City."

"Damn. Okay. Deal."

I returned the receiver to Audrey. "The bounty hunters. They were in the maroon SUV I told you about. They told me that someone tipped them in the first place. They offered to sell us the name for four thousand dollars.

"It was twenty five hundred before you opened your mouth," she said. The woman had ears like a bat.

#

It's not every day that you prepare for a clandestine meeting with two violent men. We decided not to consult the police. Audrey had jumped bail. Paul Ladish, her new attorney, had assured us that the indictment would be modified to first-degree murder now that the lab results were complete. If we learned anything significant, at this dark rendezvous we could always tell them.

Gun? No gun?

I don't have a gun, neither does Audrey. Even if we could get one, at what point would I use it? Does one parade it openly or wait for the threatening moment? If you draw do you shoot? How sure must you be? Without the weapons experience or combat skills, I was pretty sure that I would delay even showing a weapon until well after they had shot me.

Pretend to have one? I don't think so. Suppose your bluff is called and you're left in a dangerous situation aiming a TV remote at the bad guys.

I decided the best thing I could do was get 911 on Audrey's polka dot cell phone as speed-dial number one. The cell phone would be locked and loaded if we smelled trouble. If I hit that button prematurely, the worst consequence would be appearing a damned old fool. Hell, that no longer embarrasses.

Audrey dealt with her anxiety by considering the evening's dangerous adventure a fashion challenge. I'm convinced she goes through much of her life as if starring in her autobiography. She could not arrange for Spielberg style backlighting through fog, but she could select the costume. Standing in the open door of her bathroom, posing before a full-length mirror, she had called for my opinion.

"Gimme a break, Audrey. A trench coat?"

"There's a distinct marine layer chill that sets in after sunset, Dan."

"And the wide-brimmed black hat, over to one side . . . protection from moon burn?"

"No." She turned away from the mirror, looking back over her shoulder.

"Jesus," I cracked. "Norma Desmond from Sunset Boulevard."

Audrey giggled. "I'm ready for my close-up Mr. DE Mille."

"Will you start taking this seriously?"

"The hat is to protect my hair from the evening mist."

"You wish," I laughed. "Did you call the director for smoke? What's a film noir night scene without some smoke?"

"Sometimes," she said, finished with the self-inspection, "when life call's you to do something that makes you nervous . . . it helps to assume a role."

"Whatever twists your knickers, Sis. Just remember that this is the real deal, okay?"

"I know, but give me room."

"Stay home."

"Not on your life."

"Then take it seriously."

"If I took this too seriously I'd be terrified and useless."

"Not likely," I said. "Are you about ready, Greta Garbo? We shoot the scene at eight o'clock."

"Yes, we should be leaving now. And, please don't say 'shoot.'"

For as long as I can remember, I have enjoyed mocking my sister. Neither truth nor consistencies have ever impeded my progress to a joke at her expense. Never, though, have I made fun of her driving. Now, as she drove through the dark city I could concentrate all my anxiety on the confrontation with Blondie and No-neck. She managed to maintain a constant flow of impassioned opinions and still be alert to conditions and traffic.

From Alta Vista, well north of San Diego, to National City, just south of it, was a forty-minute drive through the night. On the seat between us was the four thousand dollars in cash that we had put together. It had taken three ATM transactions and one savings withdrawal from the credit union. I had lost the argument against stuffing the cash into an old "Piggly Wiggly" shopping bag.

The intersection of Granger and East Twentieth was east of the freeway by a few miles, past the strip malls, the "mile of cars," and the fast food franchises and into the unlit neighborhoods of more modest homes on a series of rolling hills. On one side of E 20th Street, the houses were below street level, opposite atop a gentle hill, was a school building surrounded by chain link. I understood why they wanted to meet here. From several viewpoints they could watch approaching traffic on the quiet street. I assumed there was a handy escape route. I assumed further that we were in their backyard and they knew the layout.

Halfway up the hill, the top of which was lit by a single streetlight, and on the school side of Granger, I saw the SUV. "There it is."

Audrey checked the dashboard clock. "We're right on time. They're early."

"They've probably been checking out the site to make sure we don't have allies watching."

"Right. I wish we did."

We drove up the street at a snail's pace. I could tell nothing through the tinted windows of the SUV. Audrey made a U turn at the intersection at the top of the hill and approached again, parking finally in front of the SUV. We sat there for a few moments with the motor running. A Beamer, an SUV, a polka dot cell phone, and cash in a Piggly-Wiggly bag. No wonder she couldn't take it seriously.

"What'll we do now?" she asked.

"I was hoping they'd come to us. But, it's smarter, I guess, to make us go to them. Look, I'll get out and go alone. We'll leave the money here for now. Have your cell phone cocked and ready."

There really was a slight mist. It had wetted down the streets so that the blacktop sucked up what little light there was. The school building had security lights but they were focused on the immediate perimeter of the building, none of it reached the street. I approached the SUV by first crossing in front of the Beamer so they could see I was carrying nothing, then walked to them on the street side trying to penetrate the tinted windows. Through the windshield I thought I could see the silhouette of the driver. It was Blondie. He didn't move. I got up to the driver's door and tapped on it. I looked through the windshield again. All was quiet. Audrey turned the engine off, damn her. I just knew that something was wrong.

"I have a flashlight."

Audrey's voice so close behind me was like an explosion. I jumped. I was about to ask for the flashlight when she shone it through the windshield. It was Blondie, all right. I looked closer and saw that the dark space between his brows was a bullet hole and some clotted blood.

Against all reason, I jumped back a yard or two when I realized I was examining a dead man. His eyes stared. The safety belt held him. I felt a spasm of fear, an urge to vomit, and a compulsion to run like hell.

Audrey, like a TV cop, moved her light beam around the interior of the vehicle and found Blondie's Neanderthal partner. He looked messy. The first shot had hit his cheek and tore open a good part of his face, creating massive bleeding. We didn't stick around looking for the fatal wound. By comparison, Blondie looked pretty good.

Audrey did better than I, but we were both past complete control of ourselves.

"Let's—"

"—Get the hell out of here—"

"—Now."

CHAPTER SEVEN

We ran back to her car, the flashlight beam making crazy zigzags on the asphalt like kids playing with sparklers. Audrey had the Beamer started by the time I got the passenger door closed. Even on damp pavement the heavy car tore away from the curb with tires squealing. The rear end fishtailed once. We were a block away before she turned on the lights. She noticed the flashlight and extinguished it.

We screamed down the mostly residential street. I suggested to Audrey that she use the cruise control. She nodded and we reclaimed a sensible thirty miles-per.

"What the hell was that?"

"Yeah."

On the freeway, I reminded Audrey once again of the cruise control to keep us literally under the police radar. We sped north on I-5. With each minute or so, another mile separated us from a parked SUV on a dark street in National City. But, the SUV stayed with us too, haunting us in a way that only intimacy with violent death can. Those two men, at the speed of bullets, had had all their aspirations extinguished. These were the men whom I had so casually judged and mocked. How was I so sure that they were not just caught in an unpleasant profession? Perhaps that money, dangerously raised, was meant for food, rent, kid's clothes. Who might be hungry tonight? Who was going to cry tomorrow and wonder why their man was dead or where their daddy was?

"You with me, bro?"

"Yeah, sure. Just thinking."

"You really are the soft one, you know," she said, not unkind. "Don't get sucked down by survivor's guilt. We have things to do."

It was funny to hear her thin voice so businesslike and sure. "I could use one or ten scotches right now."

"No," she said, "not until we're at least twenty miles from . . . that."

"You were great, Audrey. I was ready to mess myself and you probed with that flashlight like a pro."

"Never send a man to do a woman's work." Her voice was clipped. She put on a brave show to lighten the mood.

"Thanks a lot."

"Come back, Dan. I need you."

She was right. The way things were going we didn't have time for moods.

"Okay, okay," I said. "I get it. Still, I'm damned glad you're the one who had my back."

"Tell that to my friends."

"Not likely."

At some point on that dark freeway I realized that my pulse and breathing were back to normal. Audrey seemed calm as well. "We're passing Del Mar," I said. "Let's take a break."

"Bar?"

I thought about it, seriously. People have suggested that I drink a bit too much. I didn't want to admit any of them were right, but, "Not unless you want to. We need to talk."

She found a vinyl and chrome coffee shop near an off-ramp. It had a brightly lit counter and waitresses in beige uniforms. Along an outside wall were several booths with high-back leatherette seats and Formica tops. We chose a corner booth and ordered coffee.

"What the hell are we into?" my obvious question.

"I don't know."

"I believed Blondie when he said someone set you up," I said. "For tonight to have happened, several things had to be in place. First, you were in Seattle not quite twenty-four hours and the bounty hunters were already there ready to get you. They damned near had to have taken the next plane to get up there so quick. Unless they were tipped, there's no way that would happen."

"Connie Miller."

The coffee came and I took an experimental sip. It had been brewed during the Truman administration. "Audrey, you can't lay all the evils of the world at her doorstep."

"We're next door neighbors, Dan. I ran into her right as the cab for the airport showed up. I was standing there with my suitcase . . . you know, the nice peach-colored one with those cute snaps. You remember, you had to get it at baggage claim."

"If I'm really good will you get back to the point?"

"She asked where I was going and I said I needed a hug from my brother. So she knew." Audrey tried to doctor her coffee with non-fat cream and saccharine. I knew it would do no good. This stuff was past redemption.

"All right, Connie Miller."

"And if she knew," she sipped and winced, "you might as well say anyone in that little clique knew."

"We need to find something that distinguishes our suspect list from the neighborhood phone directory."

Audrey nodded, an almost dazed expression on her face. She looked about as though she had forgotten where she was and reached into a deep pocket of her ridiculous trench coat. She withdrew a compact and lipstick. She examined herself in the mirror of the compact. There was a slight tremor in her right hand. It grew worse. She put down the compact and the lipstick and the shaking became visible in her shoulders. Anyone with an IQ greater than his shoe size would know what was coming.

I slid over to be next to her and put my arm around her shoulder. She leaned into me and that broad-brimmed hat hid most of her face from the world as she started crying. There's not much one can do to comfort someone teetering on the verge of a crying jag. Being there, that's about it.

She tried to speak at first but the sobs got in the way.

"Srry . . . hup. Dank oo . . . hup.

"Let it go, Kiddo. You've earned it. I'm proud of you."

"Oo too."

I patted the top of her hat. The waitress glared at me. I was sure a thousand incorrect stories were running through her head. She assumed we were a couple; therefore I was an insensitive brute of a man who had hurt, abused, and otherwise wronged Audrey. The more Audrey cried and I comforted her, the angrier the waitress got. She got so angry she started a fresh pot of coffee.

With, it seemed, every pat on the head that I gave Audrey, the waitress, fussing behind the counter banged something else. Silverware rang out like a sword fight; glasses were replaced with a bang. I couldn't tell whether she was wiping the counter top or trying to rub it out.

Finally, Audrey was spent. She wiped her eyes and smiled, slightly embarrassed. She blew her nose, but not enough. "I'b Sowwy," she said, rising. She pointed to the back, "Powda womb." She patted my slightly dampened shoulder and stood. "Anuder cup, maybe dom pie?"

I got the waitress' attention. "I see you're making fresh coffee," I said. "When it's ready, we'd like two more and some pie. Anything sweet, gushy and fattening."

The waitress returned and served Audrey's place, then slammed down my pie with distinct emphasis. I looked up at her and she smiled.

"Sir," she said.

I decided not to eat the pie.

When Audrey returned she attacked her pie greedily. Sweet things have a different place in the lives of women, I think. Sugars, and particularly chocolate, seem to have therapeutic value, much as Vitamin Beer does for the guys. You hear about broken-hearted women consoling each other with rocky road; guys hit the beer bar.

Having cried on someone's shoulder, rinsed her face, freshened her makeup, and eaten a piece of pie, Audrey was once again ready to take on the world. You'd think she'd had a week off at a health spa.

"Audrey, we've got to take a long look at things."

She nodded her head, wiping a tiny bit of cream from her lip.

"An elected state official has been killed in a way that all the attention turns to you. The minute you leave the jurisdiction, bounty hunters are tracking you. Those same bounty hunters contact you with some information and they are assassinated. We left petty neighborhood skateboard zoning squabbles way behind. I think there's big money and big power involved somewhere. You're in the middle of it. As bad as things seem, something is going on under the surface that we don't know about. We haven't even seen the enemy yet."

"I'm really glad I wore the hat and trench coat, Dan. I never would have made it without them."

"I guess you use what you got."

"Lets make that our strategy," she said.

Sometimes I can't figure out if Audrey is being smart or being stupid. So I asked. "So what have we got?"

"I agree with you. Money or power. Scary money and scary power. It seems like there's an invisible force. If I learned anything from Brad, though, I learned that everything leaves a footprint on paper. We need to find the right paper. Do I have to say 'paper trail'?"

"I'll tell you one thing," I said. "When I hear you guys talking about your neighborhood committees and especially your homeowners association, it sounds like some kind of cabal. If there's an individual or a group working against us, and something's on paper, I'd like some time in the association offices."

"Dan. I might as well be renting for all the rights I have left."

"Do the people at the office know that?"

"Gloria," Audrey said.

"Hallelujah," I responded.

"No, I mean Gloria Pentourno, the association secretary. She likes me and she owes me a favor. An office visit wouldn't do any harm," she said. "What are we looking for?"

"We're looking for some pattern of ownership or financing. I think we're looking for something that binds these people. Hell, I don't know. We're looking for anything that doesn't look right."

"Deeds and stuff?"

"Maybe, hell, I don't know. Notes from board meetings. It all seems to have started with that damned skateboard park. What's so important about that? Maybe there's two board meetings, maybe two sets of books."

"I don't know if I can find it. I'm not much on business."

"At the airport Brad told me that you wouldn't know your business if it were spelled out in flashing neon lights."

"He said that?"

"He most certainly did."

"In those words? You're not embellishing?"

"His words, 'Flashing neon lights.'"

She adjusted her hat, reminding me of Scarlett O'Hara getting ready for the picnic where she'd get all the attention and break all the young men's hearts. Her voice was less impish and virginal. "That son-of-a-bitch," she said, sliding out of her seat. "Oh, he's toast."

She marched to the glass door in that determined way she has, leaving me well behind. I tipped the waitress generously out of a kind of reflected guilt that confused me. What the hell did I do?

#

We left the next morning for the association office. It was located in a mini-mall that fancied itself a turn of the century village green. All the glass storefronts had hand-lettered old-timey signs. The drug store with a lunch counter advertised "Sundries & Soda Shoppe"; the small grocery proclaimed "Bonita Bluffs General Mchdse", the pet store was "All Creatures Great and Reasonable", and the gas station, located at one end of the strip, though a major brand, was made to look like an old stable. At the end closest to the gas station was a mini-mart, "Ye Olde Hitchin' Post," that stayed open late and specialized in beer, soda, magazines, and overpriced snacks. We parked in front of the "Ladies Wear Emporium" at the far end.

"You live in Disneyland," I said.

"I think it's charming and fun."

"Sure, if the prices were eighteen-eighties too. Hell, I'd jerk sodas and make cherry phosphates for all the girls."

At the other end of the mall from the Chevron livery Stable was a modest building containing offices. It had the same "let's pretend we're old" siding, and multipane windows, but the business signs were understated, as though they did not want to be associated with their flamboyant brothers and sisters. "Bonita Bluffs Homeowners Assoc." was at the far end.

Four rented-looking chairs (not trashy but not good either) were placed a distance from the one desk. The desk, flanked by a computer table, had a multi-line phone and was casually cluttered with paperwork. At the desk sat a plump woman in her forties. Her hair was thin, black, and curled in tight little curls. She had black-rimmed glasses that looked pretty thick. She wore a gaudy flowered dress that did nothing to hide her large breasts. She had kicked her shoes off and put the phone receiver down when we entered.

This had to be Gloria, who had yet to say anything. Someone once told me there is something beautiful about every woman. I've never forgotten it and I've found it always to be true. I thought that in this woman, it was the absolute perfection of clear skin, a wonderful hard to define color that so many beautiful Italian women have. It is called olive, but I have never seen an olive that color.

When we walked in, she looked up and smiled, a smile inviting the whole world in, an irresistible smile like that of a child. Her whole face became beautiful and I wanted to be her friend. Her eyes, lit with humor, were as black as her hair.

"Gloria," Audrey said. "You always look so great!"

Gloria answered in a thin, though musical, voice. "It's all the sex," She cast a quick look at me and I felt I was being evaluated.

"Good for you," I said. "It's working."

"And you're the crazy brother who lives in the rain forest or on a mountaintop or something." She extended her hand like a man and we shook.

"It's not that bad," I said.

"It's not that bad," Audrey said.

Behind her desk was a wall and door that, presumably, led to other offices. There was room for, perhaps, three. That door opened and Eric appeared. "Oh, hi, guys," he said casually. "How're you doing?"

"Fine, Eric," Audrey said. "Just visiting with Gloria. I want to introduce her to Dan."

I pointed toward the offices from where he had come. "Got an office here now, kid?"

"Part-time employee," he said. "We're allowed in our offices. Anyway, I just went back there to pee. That all right with you, Cranky Old Guy?"

"As long as you remember to flush and put the seat back down when you're done," I said. "You should be old enough to remember that."

101

Eric did not like being reminded that he was a kid. I liked reminding him. There was an arrogance about his manner, a hostility behind it. I wouldn't trust him out the door.

"Eric," Audrey piped up. "We're going to be out for a while, but, still, if you could just do the grass and do the weed whacking, I'll settle with you for it when I see you next."

"Cool," he said. "Everything's in the shed, right? You got enough gas? Oh, it's all right, if you don't I'll get fresh gas and let you know how much."

"That'd be great, Eric. Sure you don't want me to give you some money now?"

"Uh, uh, I'll get you later. Bye. See ya Gloria," He said, brushing past us and out the door. He waved to Audrey as well.

"You were a little mean to the kid," Gloria said, smiling up at me. "Good. Me? I wouldn't trust him with my trash."

Audrey put her hands on her hips and scolded both of us. "You two are terrible," she said. "Eric has been a good worker for me. The money he earns from homeowners gives him a little independence. How would you like to depend upon asking Connie or Clyde for every penny?"

That was not a pleasant picture. I began to feel a little sympatico for the kid till Gloria spoke up.

"Inventory your valuables lately? Expensive little knickknacks? Jewelry? Camera?"

"Gloria, you're terrible," Audrey said. "No, I'm not missing anything."

"Have you looked? Carefully, even for that little thing you liked a lot but haven't used or seen in a while?"

"You're paranoid."

"You don't get the complaints. There's never a lot missing. It's always something they haven't used in a while. They always think maybe they lost it. But there's a pattern."

"Eric knows that if he asked me for a little money, I'd give it to him. He's a good kid."

"Maybe it's not just money," Gloria suggested. "Maybe he gets off on the doo-dads he swipes."

Audrey was shocked at the outrageous suggestion, but not so much that she and Gloria did not have a good laugh over it. "Sometimes I don't believe you, Gloria. The things you come up with."

"Yeah, Gloria said. I'm something all right." She looked back and forth between us. "Now, why don't you tell me what you want from me, Audrey," she said. "Whatever it is, it's going to cost you. Now that you're a free agent, I want us to go bar-hopping, trolling for men, boot-scootin' for boy-sans. We'd have fun."

"Maybe after the trial," Audrey said. "I'd just like to have a look at some of the records. You know, boring stuff."

"Well you won't get it by patronizing me," Gloria said. She didn't act offended, just wanted to assert her equality. "I was specifically told that you are no longer an owner, so, no longer a member. It's like you're renting or something."

Audrey's lips formed a tight smile and her voice was edgy. "Word travels pretty fast," she said.

"Too fast," Gloria agreed. She allowed us to see some of her anger, her voice raised in pitch and there was an almost teary intensity in her eyes. "Look, I don't know what's going on but I've never had someone say . . . treat so and so like they're renting." She invited us closer to her

103

and whispered hoarsely, "It was a memo from Clyde but I'm sure it came directly from Brad. What the hell did you do to him, Woman? He acts real nice but he's madder 'n hell."

"Pay no attention, Gloria," Audrey said flatly, "He just gets grouchy when I kill people."

Gloria looked shocked but only for a moment. She exploded in a high-pitched cackle of laughter that was infectious and they were off again.

"Yeah," Gloria said between giggles, "lawyers have no sense of humor." She covered her mouth with her hands and giggled again, black eyes shining with mischief.

"Will you two maniacs knock it off," I barked. "This is serious. I know you're nervous but ... damn. We're supposed to be grown-ups, not kids who giggle to hide their fear. We'd really like to take a look at those records."

"What do you want to see, not that I can tell you anything?"

"We really don't know," Audrey said. "But Dan feels, and I agree, that the homeowners association and the neighborhood committee are all over this. I don't want to go to jail, Gloria. I didn't do anything."

Gloria's face showed complete sympathy for Audrey. She nodded her head and sighed, exasperated. "Those guys come in and out of here at all times," she complained. "Especially Clyde. If you got caught past that door and in the files, it'd be my job."

Audrey reached out and momentarily pressed her hand to Gloria's. "We're running out of ideas. Did you hear that the bounty hunters were killed? They called me. They were going to tell us something about this. It's probably why they were killed."

Gloria's eyes became big and her jaw dropped. She even aspirated a tragic "Oh." Her face went pale and she held her hands to her cheeks. "This is terrible," she whispered. "Just awful."

I love Italian opera.

She started thinking so hard it pinched her face.

"I'm sorry I can't help you," she said. Audrey started to speak and Gloria held her hands out to stop her. "These guys take office security very seriously. The number of keys to the offices is tightly controlled and we have a security system that I'm supposed to turn on when I leave. It's that box just to the right of the door. I turn the little key to the right and I have ten seconds to leave the building. When I come back in I have to enter the code and turn the key back to the left. I come in and enter the code and we're back in business. Of course," she giggled, "I'm so absent minded that half the time I forget. I don't get caught though, because I'm always the first one in. Now, if one of them needed to come in after hours, sometimes they do, I'd get busted. I've been lucky. They never know.

"There are only four keys to the office and they all fit the front door and the back door. I got in trouble once because I forgot the key. I had another one made and I never told them about it."

I know this cop and he told me about limited keys. "I thought when the number of keys is limited, they code them so you can't copy them," I said.

Gloria's eyes lit up. "Frank, at the hardware store, is a drinking buddy," she said cupping her own great breasts and lifting them a little, "These guns are loaded and I know how to use them."

I smiled appreciatively. God is good.

105

"Now, where is that damned thing?" she said and made a show of going through her top desk drawer. She took out several keys and matched them to one on her key ring. "Here it is," she smiled. She put the other keys away, accidentally leaving the spare door key on her desk.

We both stared at the key. Gloria said nothing.

"I'm really sorry I can't help you guys," she said, finally. "I just can't let you back in there. I can't tell you anything either. There's a wooden file cabinet in Clyde's office. It has a busted lock. They don't know it, they keep using their keys to open it, then they think they're locking it. Must be something important in there, in that popular second drawer."

"Maybe a flashing neon light," Audrey said with a sidelong glance at me.

Gloria did not understand, just shrugged. "Audrey, I do wish you luck. I'm really on your side. I still think we'll go partying some day. Hey, did either of you guys ever hear of Reinco?"

"Reinco?" I asked.

She spelled it for us. I asked her why she thought of it. "Oh," she said, "I don't know. Name came up somehow. I keep hearing it."

"Never heard of them," Audrey said.

'Well," Gloria said, rising and letting out a great sigh. "I'm sorry I couldn't help but rules are rules, you know. It really was good to meet you, Dan. You can party with us too if you think you can keep up."

"That could be fun."

"Well, listen, I have to use the restroom, guys. You're okay seeing yourselves out, right?"

"Right you are."

She disappeared behind the door. Audrey pocketed the key and we left.

CHAPTER EIGHT

From some mystic source, Audrey divined that appropriate attire for potluck with neighborhood killers was a flamingo pink pantsuit. She wore her rosy locks in a simple upswept hairdo that she did herself. To drill the point home that red was the color of the day, she wore pair of red-plastic framed glasses. Only their cat's eye shape kept her from looking like a caricature of Sally Jesse Raphael. In miniature, she would have made an interesting Christmas tree ornament. She presented herself to me in a Vogue pose after she had dressed.

"Are you sure? For a potluck?" I would go no farther in honestly commenting on a lady's fashion choice.

"The neighborhood meeting is just part of it, Dan," she explained. "It's more cocktail party schmoozing than community service. Connie is hosting and she goes all out to impress everyone with herself and her things."

"I thought you guys were war buddies now."

"Sure, but not always the same side."

Carrying a covered platter of our potluck offering, we walked to Tara Two, the Miller estate. Audrey saw a silver Mercedes Benz and muttered a one-syllable word I hardly ever hear her use.

"What is it?"

"That's Biddy Reilly's car. What terrible taste to come to the meeting tonight. She should be retired at home in mourning."

I agreed with her about at least one thing. In a perfect world, Biddy Reilly would not have attended the neighborhood committee meeting and potluck.

"Careful," I said. "Some people may think it's bad taste for you to be here."

"No, brother. Bad taste would be bringing peanut brittle."

"Audrey . . . you didn't."

"Greek salad, Dan. Jeeze."

In a brief moment of silence, I assumed she was considering her options. "I'll go right up to her. It's not like I'm guilty. I'm not going to act guilty."

"You've got bigger ones than I do, Lady," I said. "I'm in awe."

Eric, the grown up Dennis the Menace, met us at the door. "Audrey, you look so bad!" He said with an enthusiasm that informed me that "bad" was "good" in his demented world. He smiled at me, what I thought was a dangerous little smile. "Hiyah, Gramps. I didn't really expect to see you here, not being an owner or a neighbor or, well, you're nothing really."

"Oh, my favorite Miller kid," I fired back. "You know how it is with those of us who have no real jobs and live with our relatives, free food, y'know?"

"Yeah, well, in this neighborhood you got to be careful what you eat, y'know?"

"Eric!" Audrey almost spat a forceful whisper. "That's in bad taste and I'm offended. Apologize."

"Audrey, ah, hey I wasn't thinking. I'm sorry an' shit. I'm really sorry."

The kid looked so damned miserable that I couldn't resist trying to lighten it, "we probably shouldn't play in front of Audrey," I said. He gave me a crocodile smile and made tracks.

After a uniformed maid-for-a-day accepted the food from Audrey, we made it past the ridiculously large entrance to the absurd dimensions of the salon. This room was furnished with enough cozy little conversation chair circles to seat congress. I could only assume that the dining room would also be formal and somewhat smaller than the one in the Czar's Winter Palace. Along one wall a Champagne and wine table had been established. I was glad to see that even Connie had limitations. There was no ice-sculpture. This farce could be a centerfold in "Better Homes and Pretentions."

Even I could tell who Biddy was. Amongst the score or so people in the immense salon were standing three social clots. One centered on Connie and one on Brad. The expressions painted on the faces in their clots were those of interest and good humor, standard party masks. A third clot attended an attractive woman in her early forties. She wore a classic black cocktail dress, unadorned with any jewelry save a single-strand pearl necklace and earrings. The masks surrounding her showed respect and concern.

There is an air about the very rich who have been born to it and Biddy had that air: essence of "other." They wear quality garments that radiate taste. There's a Teflon aura that separates them from the vulgate. Even arm-in-arm with one of them, laughing at a dirty joke in the midst of alcoholic bonding, their laughter comes from a distant place, a place peopled with uniformed servants and expensive smiles.

As Audrey approached, a wonderfully crafted half-smile on her face, the social clot surrounding Biddy morphed into a semi-circular jury of wannabe peers. Biddy, tall and dark-haired with a creamy complexion, stood with hands folded gracefully in front of her. There was an air of elegance about her, the kind that is nearly impossible to fake.

"Audrey, what a pleasant surprise," Biddy said, betraying an accent that fought not to sound like finishing school. "Almost the last person I expected to see here."

"I thought I should pay my respects to you, Biddy," Audrey said. She extended her hands slightly, anticipating that they would hold hands in greeting. It wasn't to be.

"That's thoughtful," Biddy said. She seemed not the least awkward in withholding her hands in greeting.

"We're in opposition a lot, Biddy, but some things are common to us all."

"And some not so common," Biddy judged neatly.

"One of those is that we share pain at the loss of a loved one."

"Clearly, not remorse," Biddy replied with the hospitality of a cobra.

"Biddy, I feel for your loss, I truly do. Please know that I have nothing to feel remorse for, just shared sadness." I appreciated that Audrey was making a genuine effort. I thought she was pretty good at it.

Biddy responded with a furrowed brow and the briefest glance heavenward, as if an appeal, to indicate that the subject was moot.

I heard the control in Audrey's voice. I hoped for Biddy's sake that she could hear it too. "I know this is awkward," Audrey said, "but you have to know that I did not harm to your husband, and I do offer condolences for your loss."

"You seem to have overcome any anxiety over the awkward, my dear," Biddy said. "I admire that you can overcome anything. That makes you capable of anything."

I saw Audrey's shoulders square and she shifted her weight slightly to assume a martial arts kind of balance. Biddy's regal face showed nothing more than the pseudo affection she had shown from the start. Audrey's rising temper, almost like electricity, was raising little hairs on the back of my neck. I feared for Biddy's long, regal nose. Perhaps, as the hammer was about to fall, Biddy felt it too.

"May I say this, Audrey. I think you've shown a degree of social grace to come and offer me some consolation. It is appreciated."

I could not tell for sure, but it nearly sounded sincere. I have trouble telling with the very rich. They lie so easily. It's another of their gifts.

Audrey's body relaxed. "That's thoughtful, Biddy, and difficult for you, I know."

"And tell us please, what surprise you brought this evening. Wine perhaps? Always appropriate."

"I made a Greek Salad."

"A Greek salad. Wonderful."

I tapped at Audrey's shoulder. She took the hint. She diffused the situation somewhat with the introduction ritual, a great ritual giving everyone something non-committal to say while assessing strangers. It's the PAM spray of social gatherings.

After the widow and the jury expressed their joy at meeting someone new (me), it was comfortable for Audrey and me to turn our backs and seek another clot of people. That's when Biddy released her missile.

"Hear that ladies? Greek Salad. Beware of Greeks bearing gifts and God-knows-what."

Biddy got a satisfying round of giggles from her audience. Fortunately I had Audrey's arm and was strong enough to keep her from turning. "I can't take you anywhere," I scolded in sotto voce. "We're here to watch suspects not draw blood."

Audrey remembered. "Why, honestly, Captain Rhett Butler, whatever do you mean? I was simply expressin' heartfelt condolences to the widow. Miss Biddy and I are quite close, you know."

"And you can eat with a mouth that lies like that?"

"I think I'll avoid the Greek Salad," she said with a grin. "Everyone will notice." She saw Connie approaching and removed herself to tend to some imagined business elsewhere.

Connie walked up to me with a drink that did not come from the Champagne and wine table. "Scotch neat, right?" the siren sang.

I nodded my head appreciatively. While nodding, I could admire the cleavage her green satin cocktail dress was designed to exploit. What had been modestly hinted at before was now a storefront window display. I felt no shame. I have been on shopping duty often enough with ladies and have seen them check their boobs and bums in the full-length mirrors. There are no fashion accidents. Any gal who wants to put her all or a few component parts on display could not ask for a more unabashedly appreciative audience.

"I see you like my dress."

"Enough to thank you for wearing it."

I sipped at my drink. I don't know much about wine but I know a properly aged malt scotch when I taste one. "To the good stuff," I said, raising the glass in salute to its contents and hers.

Her smile was innocent but the devil danced in her eyes. This lady could not help but seduce. I appreciated it. I even allowed myself to feel honored.

"It's time for you to meet Clyde," she said.

"Absolutely." I agreed with genuine enthusiasm. His name was prominent on the suspect list. "I look forward to it."

I followed her derriere to the baby grand piano nearly lost in the corner of what I had heard someone refer to as the sitting room. Yeah, sitting room for the Mormon Tabernacle Choir.

I would never have pictured these two together. His male pattern baldness was in progress above an intelligent, hawk-nosed face. He wore black-rimmed bifocals. I had a few inches on him and I'm barely five-eight. I pictured him in his tooth workshop and wondered if he used a little footstool to reach his work or had his victims nearly upside-down in the double-jointed torture chairs the dentists use. He was about the same age as his wife but had the dry, wrinkled skin of a smoker. As we shook hands, Connie went to his side and I could see that his face came to a place between her lips and her breasts. He was a highly successful dentist and a very lucky man.

"Sorry about this whole Audrey-in-trouble business," he said, dismissing it. "We're all on her side, you know."

"That's good to hear," I said, thinking that it would be even better to believe. "We need the support of her friends and neighbors right now."

"Uhm, yes." He agreed. It seemed his mind was elsewhere, a malignant molar perhaps, appointment to a commission, a passing itch.

114

"Suspicion fell on her very quickly," I offered. I had to learn from these people. I needed their versions of the truth and their opinions.

"Unfortunate, but surely a byproduct of some of the things she said about the deceased," he said. "And, of course, there's the business of the peanut brittle."

"It was part of a fund-raiser to save the skateboard park, right?"

"Yes," he said. "So unnecessary. Surely those young people could find some other place to skate."

"Pesky young people." I tried for a patrician sigh but I don't think I pulled it off.

"It's an inappropriate location. It's really sad that Audrey knows so little about business."

"Apparently." I didn't know how else to respond.

"Right," came the booming baritone of Brad the Impaler, stalking us from behind. "I still have to do her taxes. Well, I used to. Now I have my business manager do it."

"Just as long as Audrey doesn't know what's happening, right?" I accused, hating to have to look up to meet his eyes.

"You misapprehend the situation again, Dan." Brad put his arm around my shoulder in the nicest neighborhood way. "Audrey does not have a head for business."

"I'll bet deeds and property rights elude her understanding too."

"Right." He was un-offended. "I tried to make the divorce easy on her. She would never have to move from her beloved bluffs. She gets expense money. She's even still on my health plan. But, there are limits. I cannot toss out six figures for an adequate defense without consequence. I need the asset back."

"Basic business," the dentist agreed as his wife nodded her head. I was overcome by a feeling that approached absolute knowledge that these three shared something hidden from me. If necessary, I would go ahead with that damned equity loan and hire a private detective. What the hell did a skateboard park have to do with business? What was important enough to kill a man for? What secret was so heinous that keeping it justified killing two more people.

After much stimulating banter about gold futures, bubbles in the housing market, and the importance of massacres to the spread of evangelical religions, Clyde eyed my drink and brought my attention to his own. "Looks like scotch," he said. "Me too. Come, let's refresh them."

He led me to a room off the grand salon. It was a mini gentlemen's club with two bookcase walls and an ego wall decorated with degrees, signed photographs, and testimonials. Several modest red leather chairs attended an antique mahogany desk. Opposite, two high-back armchairs book-ended about a small fireplace. The fourth wall was completely draped with a heavy, wine colored fabric that looked like it was never opened. Compared to the other rooms, this one was so small one could barely raise a decent echo.

"Inner sanctum," I said.

"It really is," he answered. The drapes did their job to mute our voices, providing an air of seclusion. I could live in a room like this. The draped wall could mask a giant video screen. Add a beer tap, microwave, and a bathroom . . . I'd never have to leave.

"Connie loves the showplace stuff and to be perfectly honest, so do I. But, here, in a room she seldom visits, I have my little nest." His voice was a sharp-edged baritone.

"I'm jealous of your little nest," I said, wondering if we were talking aerie-of-eagle or pit-of-snake.

I emptied my glass at his urging and gave it to him. While he accessed a portable bar, I examined his library. It looked like a library that was used. The books were not display sets with virgin bindings and unread pages. There was an eclectic mix of classics and several titles from the Times Best Seller list. Two shelves contained trade magazines that were just messy enough to indicate they were used.

I spotted The "Prince," "American Caesar" several books by and about the Kennedys and "Ambition: The American Virtue." "Where's 'Mein Kampf' and 'The Gallic Wars?'" I asked trying to be obnoxious.

Clyde guffawed from his belly. "You caught me," he said. "I have a copy of 'Mein Kampf' upstairs and I have studied the strategies of Julius Caesar."

"Should America be afraid?"

"Probably so, but not of me," he said easily, handing me a fresh drink. His moist and slightly reddened eyes testified to, perhaps, an afternoon of scotch. He was approaching the 'sincere' stage of his buzz. I could barely wait to here him say "No kidding, I love you guys."

"I believe in the dark side of ambition," he boasted. "I believe in knowing the rules of whatever game I'm playing. So, I read Machiavelli and Hitler and, while you're asking, I read Chairman Mao, Stalin, Churchill and Malcolm X as well. It would amaze you to know how informative these thinkers can be in understanding American politics."

"Just how ambitious are you, Clyde?" His last name was okay, but I just couldn't imagine Governor Clyde or President Clyde. Clyde was the name of Clint Eastwood's chimpanzee, as in, "Right turn, Clyde."

"I want political power," he bragged. "I'll go as far as circumstances allow. That may not be beyond this state, but as far as I can."

"Gee, thanks for the scotch and all, but aren't you afraid that someone like me might drop a dime on your naked lust for power over our lives?"

"Not at all," he said, friendly as pie. "You're a nobody and always will be a nobody . . . politically speaking that is. You're probably a splendid human being; you certainly seem nice enough in a sarcastic, curmudgeon kind of way. But, in my world, you're a nobody, a retired old fella living in the woods and full of opinions that no one really cares about."

I was hooked and having almost as much fun as he was. "You don't even know what my opinions are."

"You still don't get it. You have no power so I don't care what your opinions are. You have no power so no one cares what your opinions are. You have no power so you can drop all the dimes on me you want. No one's taking your calls."

I should have been angry but the scotch was so good; the room was so cozy; he sounded so right. What a performance artist. "You're having a good time, aren't you?"

"Absolutely," he raised his glass. "To you, and I mean that," he said. "I see the intelligence and character behind your sister's ways and I see it in you too. I'm having fun talking to someone with whom I can relax."

". . . Because you don't see me as a threat?"

"Oh, don't dismiss yourself so quickly. That's part of it, but you're also intelligent enough to understand me. We could be friends, actually. I don't think you care about my world any more than I care about yours. You're making my evening. Thank you."

"Do you think my sister killed Reilly?"

I had asked the question as unexpectedly as I could. I wanted to read his face. I shouldn't have bothered. This guy had an impenetrable avuncular mask. He answered with no more change of affect than if I had asked him what time it was.

"I seriously doubt she killed him. I think she's in terrible trouble over it and may be convicted. But that's another matter entirely."

"If she didn't kill him, then who did?"

His face lit up with sudden delight. "I've got it now," he said. "I'm a suspect! I guess several of the people in my house tonight are your suspects."

"As far as I know, all the likely suspects are here."

"Grand . . . let's see, there's me, Connie, of course, Biddy—"

"—Help me there, Clyde. Why Biddy?"

"Why should I tell you?" His eyes shone with fun.

"Helping me widens the number of suspects, maybe takes my attention off you."

"Wonderful! Okay, then. It's no secret that Biddy is ambitious too. Sean Reilly was a pretty face and had a little youthful charm but was mostly an empty obsessive-compulsive shell. She realized that she'd hitched her star to a guy who wasn't smart enough, sly enough or ambitious

119

enough. Divorce is ugly and a political negative. If someone hadn't helped him out the door, he'd be an assemblyman till he retired and she'd be stuck with him."

"How do you know all that?"

"Pillow talk, spying, observation. Biddy has her eyes on Sacramento . . . Washington. She needs to trade up."

"You had a lot of business dealings with him though, didn't you. And you were friends, friends enough to take vacations together. The Millers and the Reillys on Lake Powell?"

He shrugged. "Business and politics. We're all whores. We use each other. Friendship has nothing to do with it."

For a minute I felt like Jimmy Stewart finding out how congress works—but that was the scotch. I had learned a generation earlier that Frank Capra's America was a myth. There are always wheelers and dealers out there playing pickup games of "Who can we screw." I couldn't quite figure out if these guys were wannabe big frogs in a small pond or the dangerous psychopaths they pretended to be.

"Break's over."

I looked up from my scotch to see Connie at the door, glaring at Clyde with a lot less than conjugal affection. Clyde, as though caught at something, was looking about for the poise her presence had just destroyed. "Oh," he said. "We were just . . ."

"You were just a couple of kids smoking in the locker room," she scolded. "We have guests, CM. Get your ass out there. Sound competent. It's good practice."

Clyde looked chastised for a brief moment. The expression changed quickly as the politician in him took control, but I had seen it. My initial impression about trouble in the Miller house was confirmed.

"And you," Connie turned to me. "I enjoy your company and your ridiculous flirting, but you're coming into our house as Audrey's brother and you have your own not-so-friendly agenda. At least the police were honest."

"I like my ridiculous flirting too, Connie." I rose, confident in the presence of her embarrassment at her moderately drunk husband. I momentarily contemplated Clyde, the imperially ambitious dentist cowed by his woman. "I'll tell you what my agenda is. I know that my sister is innocent and I will do whatever it takes to prove it."

"Understood," Connie said.

Clyde had refreshed his scotch, then looked at Connie and drank it off in defiance. He seemed afraid that she would not permit him back in the salon with it. "We were just talking about that, Connie," he said but stopped at a quick gesture from her. How the mighty had fallen.

"I ask you, her friends, for help," I said directly to Connie. "But almost surely the guilty one is one of her friends too, probably that person is here at the party. Before this is over, I'll find out who it is."

Connie laughed. "How gallant of you not to use a personal pronoun that would betray gender," she said. "Well enough, then. I'll give you all the help I can. I would like to see Audrey out of this mess. Who else would I joust with if she were gone off to some horrible prison?"

"Two or three layers down, Connie, you and Audrey are the same strong woman."

Clyde, hurrying past us to get back to the party grumbled. "Christ, there's two of them?"

CHAPTER NINE

The hired help set up the potluck offerings on what had been the Champagne and wine table. No honest macaroni/tuna casseroles in this crowd. The ambrosia salad was in a cut crystal leaf-dish; smoked salmon filets with capers were cut in a floral design. They must have hired a Las Vegas dealer to fan out the prime rib slices, each one with a dollop of sour cream in a precisely cut hole . . . etc. I could not believe that some of these entrees were not catered. No one seemed to care. This was potluck Cordon Bleu and they were all used to it.

We took our glorified pupu platters to the dining room where several large tables had been set. There were four small crystal chandeliers surrounding a large one. I hadn't seen so many dancing points of light in one place since disco died. A pleasant murmur of conversation rode on a background of piped-in chamber music. It was all very uptown and civilized. I looked about for Audrey Hepburn.

A business meeting followed, presided over by Mrs. Prescott, a lady, Victorian in demeanor, who spoke a lengthy homage to the departed assemblyman and his courageous widow. The following applause was a public show of support. It set the mood; henceforth nary a speaker would pass the salt without sharing the loss again and honoring the widow anew.

A CASE OF PEANUT BRITTLE

Clyde rose and read from a piece of paper whose bold letterhead I recognized as Brad's. He announced that since the as-hoc skateboard park property abutted the Bluffs, there should be a meeting of the Bluff's Homeowners Association to take action as appropriate. Apparently they were treating the homeowners association as a kind of executive board of the neighborhood committee. It was hard to be present and not be cynical.

Audrey controlled herself wonderfully throughout the meeting. Toward the end, she sought recognition from the chair. "A tiny bit of new business, Madam Chairwoman," she said.

"New business is on the agenda at the beginning of meetings," Madam Prescott replied coldly. "It was called and there was none. You are out of order."

"Then I rise for a point of order," Audrey said.

Mrs. Prescott tapped her little gavel and hit a saucer by accident, shattering it. There was muted laughter in the background. "Not recognized. Audrey, you are not going to personalize this meeting for your own ends."

"Then I rise now for a point of personal privilege and if you don't recognize me I'm going ahead anyway and maybe some more of Connie's beautiful table service will broken. I will speak my piece."

"The chair will yield to your bullying, Audrey. The secretary need not take notes, however, the speaker is out of order."

"Thank you." Audrey stretched to her full five-foot six-inch stature and forged ahead. "You all know that I've been accused of things," she said. "I just needed this opportunity to assure my friends and neighbors that I haven't done anyone any harm. I feel strongly about issues and I speak my mind, sometimes harshly. I ask you not to hold that against me. Some are far more courteous than I and much more dangerous. I am innocent of any wrongdoing. I . . . I guess I just wanted to reassure my friends and neighbors of that."

The silence that followed lasted longer than her statement had. I hoped she was not expecting applause in support. She got none.

"That was a bit short," I whispered to her.

"It might have been too short," she replied with a brave smile.

"This is all new," I said. "They don't know what to do."

While I was speaking, Mrs. Prescott wound up the meeting and declared it adjourned. People broke up immediately and one or two did come near Audrey to offer subdued support in passing. It would have been touching had they not acted guilty about it, kept moving, and tried not to be seen.

We exited quickly with our cut glass platter of barely touched Greek Salad. "This is the place you don't want to leave?"

"I didn't expect much more. I just had to say it. It's the same everywhere, Dan."

"Not where I live, dammit," I said. "You haven't been back to the home planet in a long time. California suburbia is an asteroid that orbits too close to the sun."

"We have plenty of Greek Salad for tomorrow's lunch," she said bright and cheerful. "We'll have it with a little pita bread and some bisque."

#

A CASE OF PEANUT BRITTLE

Richard Ladish, Audrey's Attorney, was a wiry guy no taller than I. He seemed always ready to zip off somewhere else like a humming bird. He had an energy that, though he was approaching fifty, showed no signs of waning. He had a straight, sharp nose that nearly looked like a beak. It gave support to his sudden, birdlike movements. The day after the potluck we met in the conference room of his office downtown San Diego. He greeted us himself and asked an intercom named "Beth" to get us all coffee.

"I don't like you being here for this," he said to me.

I looked this little guy over and didn't think too much of him. "Why, do you intend to abuse Audrey?"

"Yes, I do," he said. "And you are too much of a comfort to her."

"I don't know what to say," I said, not knowing what to say.

"We don't need to waste time with this," Audrey said. "It's my decision and Dan stays. He's my support."

"That's why I don't want him here, Mrs. Davis."

"Brad's behind this," I mumbled.

"In a way you're right, Dan," Ladish said. "Brad has impressed on me that Audrey has a tendency to speak before thinking it all out. That can be fatal in the midst of a trial."

"Yeah, blurting out the truth can be messy," I cracked.

Ladish turned on me in a second and I saw the energy of a bantam cock in him. "The jury has a few days at most to see truth," he said, stepping toward me. "Any truth they get will be incomplete. That's the nature of things. You can't sum up a complicated reality with chunks

125

of testimony. Anything the jury hears is partial: an almost this and maybe that. We don't want incomplete truths that hurt us. Audrey has insisted on testifying and I agree. But, she's a dangerous witness. I want to start practicing right now with mock interrogations and I don't want you here comforting her."

"I'm in the room," Audrey said.

Now it was her turn to get his energy. I quickly revised my initial impression. I wouldn't want to match wits with this fella. "I want to stress you," he declared, turning and practically stalking her. "I want to get in your face, twist your words, piss you off, jump on the slightest error and bully you to tears. Why should I have someone in the room with whom you're comfortable?"

I got up to leave but Audrey did not skip a beat. "Because we are preparing me for a trial that Dan will attend. If you're convinced I have all these deficits, then we better start right now with me learning to be aware of Dan before I open my mouth. Besides, I rely upon his memory and his advice. He stays."

Ladish was used to getting his way. He muttered something about "goddammed amateurs." I didn't get all of it.

"She surprised you didn't she?" I said. "Don't rely on the opinions of Brad the Impaler when it comes to Audrey."

A tense moment seemed frozen in time: Richard Ladish trying to intimidate me into leaving: Audrey forbidding it. Finally, the Bantam rooster turned away from us both and walked to his desk. "Brad the Impaler," he said softly, then chuckled. "I'm going to use that," he confided. "You've initiated a courthouse nickname."

It made my day.

A CASE OF PEANUT BRITTLE

Over the next hour-and-a-half I learned why he did not want third parties present. He machine gunned her with questions, turning this way and that in distracting ways, making quick approaches till he was close, shouting from across the room. He seemed not to believe a word she said, not the hint of an emotion she expressed.

"Tell me about this peanut brittle of yours."

"It's just peanut brittle."

"You have a secret ingredient?"

"Yes."

"What is it?"

" . . . a secret."

"Then I appeal to the judge," Richard snapped, turning to an imaginary judge. 'Unresponsive, your Honor,' I say. 'The witness will answer the question,' he says. Now, you've already lost points with the jury by holding the truth back and you have to answer the question anyway. If you don't, the judge can put you in jail for contempt. If you even resist, you look bad. Either way, the jury is watching the whole thing. You know what they'll remember? Not the damned peanut brittle. They'll remember your arrogance. They'll remember that you tried to avoid a question and had to be threatened to give up the truth. You're on trial for your life. Stop playing Nancy Neat the suburban housewife. Now, what is the secret ingredient to your peanut brittle?"

"Allspice and a smidgin of allspice."

"Jesus, really?" I muttered, I thought I was muttering.

"Shut up, Dan," Ladish snapped.

"Really," Audrey said.

"And as soon as you made the brittle, you put some of it in this blue box we'll talk about later?"

"No. I didn't put it—"

"—If you're answer's 'no' then leave it at 'no.' Don't expand or explain anything. The fewest words possible. Less is better."

"When did you put it in the box?"

"I had some left over. Not a—"

"Less is better."

"I had some left over the night before the meeting."

"A lot or just bits?"

"Several bits, not enough for potluck . . .."

"Where had the candy been since you made it?"

"In my kitchen. On the counter."

"Covered in an airtight container?"

"No."

"Are you fully aware of all the health codes involved in food handling?"

"Not all."

"Are you, in fact, certified for food handling?"

"Yes."

That took him aback. "You are?" he said in his real voice, not the sneering prosecutor that he had been for the last hour. "That's good. I should have asked you. How'd that come about?"

"We do a lot of fund raisers involving food and I volunteer at the soup kitchen. I took food handlers school from the county and got certified."

"Great, I'll work that in. Back to it."

Audrey took a breath.

"So," he ranted again, "even knowing about the proper handling of foods, you left a sticky, sweet confection lying about your kitchen where it could be contaminated by anyone or anything."

128

"My brittle is not sticky, sir," she said.

"No. It's deadly."

She held her tongue.

"Was there anything special about these particular pieces of brittle that you put into the box?"

"Yes."

"What was special?"

"Ordinarily, you break up the brittle and serve the pieces at random. When I selected the pieces for the gift box, I made sure there were no really small pieces and that every piece had at least one peanut."

"When did you box the brittle?"

"Right before I took my shower."

"So the brittle was unattended for some time."

"Yes."

"All right. You boxed the brittle, took your shower, then . . .?"

"I dressed for the meeting, wrote the little note, picked up the box and left for the community center. The box was with me until I gave it to the assemblyman."

"Did he open it right away?"

"No."

"When did he open it?"

"I have no idea."

"You have an herb garden?"

"What? Oh, why yes. I do."

"You pick your own herbs?"

"Yes."

"And dry them and grind them or whatever."

"Yes."

"So, you're familiar with processing plants and plant products."

"Yes."

"You have, in your garden, what you call a lanai?"

"Yes."

"Describe it, please."

"Well, it's a veranda off the side of the house, decorated in a Hawaiian style. I can't get plumeria to grow but I do have crimson oleander, multicolored little lantana, and pale violet wisteria growing in and around a nice lattice structure. It's very colorful. There's lilac close by that blends with the wisteria."

"And you do your own gardening, trimming, pruning."

"Yes. Well . . ."

"Go ahead."

"There is a boy who comes around and cuts the grass, the lawn areas for all the bluff homes. He also does any whacking I need."

"In this climate, I'd avoid that wording."

She nearly giggled. "Weed whacking, of course."

Ladish scowled.

"Weed removal," Audrey said, then smiled.

I smiled too at the image of the suburban housewife suggesting to the neighborhood kid that, for an extra ten, he whack this person or that. Of course, given that the kid was Eric, there might be some truth to it. I was half-tempted to mention it, then remembered that half the other people in the room did not want me to be here.

"Okay, well, the boy who cuts the grass also keeps the weeds under control. Yes?"

"Weeds under control. Yes."

"You have the expertise to cut and harvest various herbaceous plants."

"Yes. Yes. Yes" she said, tiring.

"Don't be so dismissive," Ladish barked.

"Why all these gardening questions?" Audrey demanded.

"Because we got the forensic lab results on the poisons that killed Assemblyman Reilly," Ladish said. "It was a combination of Lantana and Oleander extract. You have both and you have the knowledge to extract a concentrated potion to lace your brittle with."

"That's ridiculous, Ladish," I said. "You're supposed to be on our side."

Ladish ignored me and offered Audrey a tissue. "I want you people to see how serious this case is. If the peanut brittle link weren't strong enough, now we have you growing the poison in your backyard."

"Richard," Audrey said. "They'll have to do better. Oleander grows in half the houses in southern California. Lantana is considered an invasive weed. I like the little flower clusters. This isn't the common lantana."

"No," Ladish said. "I'll bet it's the lantana camera, most commonly grown in Texas."

"That's right. I got cuttings from Connie. She brought hers from Corpus Christi. She likes the tight little flower clusters too. How did you know?"

"It is the most toxic variety."

"Oh . . . I had no idea."

"Back to work."

"No, let's take a—"

"—Back to work!"

"My, you're bossy."

"The court awarded you bail."

"Yes."

"You were told not to leave the jurisdiction."

"Probably."

"No equivocating. It makes you look dishonest. You know what the answer is. Don't let them see you trying not to answer correctly. Again. You were told not to leave the jurisdiction."

"Yes."

"But you did."

"Yes."

"Why?"

"I needed to talk to my brother."

"No phone?"

"I needed to see my brother."

"Why?"

"I needed to look in his eyes and see that he believed in me. No one else did."

"You are active in the community?"

"Yes."

"Committees, fundraisers, causes, charities?"

"Yes, yes."

"Know a lot of people?"

"Yes."

"Your ex-husband is an attorney?"

"Yes."

"When you were married, you entertained?"

"Yes."

"Met a lot more people."

"Yes."

"And they know you?"

"Yes."

"And of all these people who have known you now for years, who have worked with you, seen you under stress, seen you socially . . . not one of these people believed in your innocence? You were so desperate to find one person to believe you that you violated court orders to do so. No one within a thousand miles believes in you, you're ex-husband does not believe in you. These people know you. Why should this jury believe in you?"

His attack had wounded her. I saw the three quick swallows and the stealthy tear-wipe as she pretended to straighten a strand of hair. "The business associates of my ex-husband, the friends and neighbors who do community and charity work with me, all have their own interests in our common activities. My brother is not involved in any of these things and he trusts me completely. The jury is not involved with me in any of these things and I trust them to be objective. That's why."

Ladish approached and kissed her on the forehead. "Excellent," he said, "except, edit out the 'that's why' at the end. It's too confrontational, makes it sound like you're trying to get the best of me."

"I was."

"Of course, but never show it."

"I'll work on it. Are you getting all this, Dan?"

I treated them to my favorite hillbilly impression. "Yep, missus ma'am, 'ceptin' for the real big words I got it mostly recollected in my remembery."

"We'll work on this at home, now that we know how to do it," she told him. I heard the respect in her voice.

Ladish tried to measure my character with his eyes. I winked at him. "If you guys decide to practice," he ordered, "I want you, Dan, to be rough on her. Make sure her answers are absolutely responsive, direct, on point and brief. Don't rehearse words; just rehearse her getting battered and handling it gracefully. Got it?"

"Got it," I said.

"Don't worry about Dan," Audrey said, "when it comes to being abusive and sarcastic, he can make you look like Barney the friendly dinosaur."

"Good," he said and out of lawyer character, he was back to this birdlike guy. "You did well for the first session. Be spontaneous on the stand, not rehearsed. It's a thin line. Even with a strong case, and they've got one, we can throw enough doubt to make it about character."

CHAPTER TEN

Before we left his office I wanted to satisfy my curiosity about a few details. "Richard," I said, "Can you fill-in some things for me?"

"I'll try."

"I want to follow the box. Do we know that it was not opened or left around at the meeting?"

"As far as we know, he put the box in his side jacket pocket unopened. As far as we know, he and his wife went straight home after the meeting. He was found the next morning, after nine o'clock, on the bathroom floor barely conscious and in agony. He was taken to the hospital where he lost consciousness and several hours later, passed away. While we're at it, I'll tell you that they got very little stomach content, but there were several peanuts. The autopsy revealed, as we found out this morning, a combination of poisons found in oleander and lantana. The brittle remaining in the box tested positive for the same toxins.

"Where was Biddy Reilly when all this was happening?" Audrey asked.

"Biddy was at home. They have separate bed and bathrooms in different parts of the house. She claims she heard nothing."

"Could anyone have gotten to the candy?"

"I suppose Biddy could," he said, but there was no conviction in his voice. "There could have been a third

135

person, it would explain things, but it's a stretch. It really looks like he got home and decided to try some brittle."

"Could the brittle have been poisoned with a syringe through the box and everything?"

"The police are not stupid. They specifically asked their forensic people to examine the ribbon and the box for evidence of tampering."

"God they're thorough," Audrey said. She sounded disappointed.

"Could the box have been opened, the candy doused and then the box re-tied?" I asked.

"Again, he said, "it's possible."

Audrey surprised us. "No it's not," she said.

"Why not?" Ladish and I said in unison.

"After I've tied the bow, and left long tails leading to it, I run the ribbon tails against the back of a scissors blade; it separates the silk into individual strands and they curl up. I do it all the way to the knot, it makes a gay nest of curled satin. But, it would be almost impossible to untie the bow and get it back the same way. I'd notice it immediately."

I nodded wisely as though contemplating profound things. I had no clear idea of what to do. I felt increasing fear for Audrey's future.

We scheduled another meeting and left the building, one of those redwood and sandstone things that are supposed to evoke comfortable rustic feelings, like the information centers at state parks.

The witness preparation session had taken a toll from Audrey. "Richard told me that in future sessions he's going to let other people pick on me."

"It's all in a good cause, Audrey."

"Let's find a good donut shop," she said. "If I don't indulge myself with some sweet pastries, I'm going to get in a sour mood."

"Then to the hardware store."

"That's right. Last night we had dinner with the killer crowd. Tonight we're committing our own felony. We need burglar stuff. But first, something gushy."

"A couple of flashlights maybe."

"Something cream-filled with soft, rich chocolate icing."

"I'm almost ready for a sandwich," I said.

"How can you be thinking of food when I'm going to be on trial for my life?"

"Hello? Gushy donuts?"

"That's not food; it's therapy. I didn't say, 'gee I'm upset and frightened let's get prime rib did I?"

"No, but—"

"—But what? This is serious, Dan. Do you know what's at risk here? Everything's at risk, that's what."

"Sorry." I changed the subject to things more relevant. "I think we're lucky with Ladish. He seems like a competent guy."

"Remember those multi-layered pastries they have in Europe? France, I guess. I don't know the French name but on the East Coast they call them 'Napoleons.' I wonder if there's any place around here where you can get one."

"In France they call them mille fouilles, a thousand layers, a thousand leaves.

Audrey knew of an upscale patisserie in La Jolla, a good distance from Ladish's office. Nevertheless, we went to La Jolla where she indulged in some creamy, puffy things that I cannot even describe. Apparently they were good enough to inspire many "mmmms" and "oohhhhs" and she was kept busy wiping excess cream from her lips. From the effect these things had on her, the detour to La Jolla was worthwhile. When her taste buds were sated and my coffee was finished we headed back into the downtown area to the Impaler's offices. I had been there just once before, at a champagne thing for a partner while I was visiting Audrey.

A blond Debbie or Buffy or Bambi or whatever greeted us at the reception desk to the suite of offices . . . "Davis, Cummings and Crabbe." She flaunted an expensive row of impossibly white teeth and blue eyes that would never wear out from too much reading.

"Good Morning, Mrs. Davis," she said. "We've been expecting you. Mrs. Greene will meet you in the conference room. It's right around the corner. Would you like some tea or latté? Spring water?"

We decided 'no' and did not ask for menus.

"Have a nice day," she ordered.

I had a big grin on my face by that time. I knew we were there to sign some papers that, essentially, would separate Audrey from her home irrevocably, but still, I love theatre of the absurd.

Mrs. Greene, an attractive woman in her forties, joined us almost immediately. Her face and manner transmitted an air of competence and intelligence. Brad the Impaler was entirely too smart to become Brad the secretary chaser. He and his partners paid for competent associates and staff. I'm not counting the window dressing up front.

"Good morning, Mrs. Davis," Mrs. Greene said and turned her welcome to me " . . . and you must be Mr. Kelly. How are you? Angela Greene." She extended her hand and I shook it. How was I going to have any fun if I couldn't mock the office help?

"Audrey," Mrs. Greene said after we sat at the end of a long conference table. She placed a thin folder of legal papers on the desk and started arranging them for signature. "I would like to say that I admire you, Audrey," she said. "I know that these papers, and several others I've seen you execute, aren't without emotional consequence. One woman to another, you're a graceful lady."

Audrey nodded. I think she was grateful. "Hear that, Dan? I've got grace. Tell all my friends."

"Not likely."

Mrs. Greene smiled. It looked like she wasn't sure what else to do. "We've been through this before," she said, moving the first paper forward on the table for Audrey's signature. "Quitclaim for consideration, agreement to amended alimony agreement, preservation of rights and privileges not mentioned. It's all there. I really have checked."

Audrey informed the ceiling. "Brad can do a lot of things, but I don't think he'd cheat me in this," she said.

"Yeah, there's no icebergs tonight; full speed ahead. We're unsinkable." I couldn't resist.

The double doors of the conference room opened and His Magnificence loomed there, dominating the frame, live and in full color.

"Right," he said. "Just a few signatures and we're back in business. Tiffany told me you were here. I only have a moment to say 'hi.'"

He used part of his moment to lean his tall frame down to kiss Audrey on the head and she did not bite him. He nodded his head to me and aimed a reptile smile down to my level.

"I'm sure it's all in order," Audrey said. Maybe she just liked looking up at him and smiling. "I'm signing it all. The settlement is generous."

It was a sorry sight to see. She knew he was a jerk but in his presence she melted like ice cream on a hot sidewalk. He had cheated on her. He had lied to her and about her. He had forged her name to some loans and he was verbally abusive with a real cruel streak. She was still hoping he'd ask her to the prom.

He stood up, drawing pleasure, I think, from being above the rest of us in so many ways. "I'm waiting for an important phone call. Stick your head in my office before you go, okay? Don't bother to knock."

"Sure. Right. Yes, we will," Audrey crooned. It was embarrassing.

"Jesus, Audrey. Re-read your divorce papers. He's not Johnny Depp."

"Dan, there's no reason why I shouldn't at least be civil to the man. Isn't that right, Mrs. Greene?"

Mrs. Greene seemed to be fighting her conscience. "He's my boss," she said. "Now, I'm a notary and, Dan, you can be a witness. We'll be finished here in a few moments."

She was true to her word and a few minutes later we padded down to the partners section on carpet so plush it felt like new sneakers.

Brad the Impaler was at his most imposing and intimidating when he was in his own lair. Being a large man and probably frustrated by normal sized furniture, he had been sure that his desk was the size of a pool table. The leather chairs of his office, the paneling, the faint echo of cigar smoke from days done by . . . he had it all. This was my favorite setting for him. He strode the halls heavily like a bear. It was well worth the trip. I would not have been surprised to see trophy head mounts on the walls, vanquished litigants and their attorneys, perhaps a careless judge or two.

He was seated at the desk and waved us in when Audrey tentatively opened the door and knocked softly like a supplicant. He finished his call as he stood. "Right. Right . . . but not too much. Don't over do it, we're conciliatory not weakened, right? . . . Right. Look, got to go. Important visitors. Right." He hung up.

"Right. Well then, everything go smoothly?"

He wasn't asking me.

"The settlement is generous, Brad," she said. "But, I'm going to miss my home."

"Ah," he said, dismissing it with a wave of his hand and sitting back on his throne. "I'm not exactly evicting you, Audrey. I need the equity value to make up for the defense expenses. I'm sorry. It's the real world. It's necessary. You should be glad we can do this and, I don't mind saying so, you should be glad that I'm willing to do it. I'm not under obligation, you know. I just want to support you. I believe in you."

"Brad, you're a brick," I said, then, to Audrey, "Did I pronounce that right?"

"Thank you, Brad," she said with a lump in her throat, trying to sound brave like Meg Ryan. "I'll make it through this. I will."

"I posted bail for you in the first place because I believed in you."

"Yes, Brad. I know you did."

"Did you hear that those two idiot bounty hunters who arrested you were found murdered in National City?"

"No, oh my goodness!" She looked so convincing.

141

"The bonding agent they worked for called me wondering if there were some kind of connection. Isn't that interesting?"

"Gee, Brad," I piped up, "I know you were furious with them the other day. Did the guy think you did it, or what?"

Brad looked at me with a degree of menace that I had not seen before. Maybe that's how he won a lot of cases, intimidating the opposition into bowel discomfort. "Dan, I'm going to really miss you around the Thanksgiving table. I do enjoy your humor. Apparently the cops think it might have been a professional."

"Why?"

"Because, this was done up close and with no warning. A good con man, an expert. These two were too street smart to let just anyone get so close to them." That reminded me of something, something important, from a movie, but I let it slip away.

CHAPTER ELEVEN

Time stood still in the pitch-dark alley. The back of the building was a darker than dark mass. I was anxiously aware of the unseen neighborhood close by. Our whispering, amplified by nerves and fear, sounded harsh and loud. Audrey rattled a ring of keys loudly seeking the one we got from Gloria.

"What's taking so long, sis? Someone will see us."

"I can't find the right key. It's dark, you know."

"There's only one key."

"I put it on my key ring so I wouldn't lose it."

"So?"

"Well, keys are keys, Dan."

"How many can there be?"

"There's the house keys, there are two of them: and two for the car, my car, I probably still have two keys for Brad's car, garage key, the shed, my locker at the women's fitness center, the post office box, our home safe, honestly, there's a few here I don't remember about."

"Yeah, yeah, yeah. Keep trying."

"Why don't you give me some light?"

"Because there are half-a-dozen houses fifty yards from here, that's why. They see a flashlight in this alley and they call the police."

"Whisper lower. You want someone to hear us?"

"This is my whisper. Live with it."

"God, you're a cranky criminal."

"Give me the key ring. I'll try."

"You'd have to start at the beginning. One at a time is good fishing."

"Just hurry. We're vulnerable out here."

"Ah, got it."

"Glory, hallelujah."

"I'll thank Gloria later."

We had planned our burglary with all the enthusiasm of movie-going amateurs. I was proud of the final plan. I didn't want to be in a strange neighborhood with no good story. Audrey had created our costumes as a couple of elderly joggers, old sweat pants for me, they stopped awkwardly at mid-calf. The important thing is that they were a dark color. I had brought a dark T-shirt with me, also a pair of sneakers. I talked Audrey out of looking like a Ninja warrior. We settled on sweats, headband and running shoes for her . . . all dark colors.

The plan was to go to the Hitchin' Post in our jog-togs and buy two small bottles of water for our fanny packs. We would play out a little theatre within the cashier's hearing, make a show of deciding to leave the car at the Hitchin' Post and jog around the neighborhood. Then we would jog into the alley and voila we're on the scene of the crime with a cover story. We would execute the plan at about eight thirty, early enough to be credible, late enough to be dark.

It worked exactly like that and I started feeling cocky until Ditzo had trouble finding Gloria's key in a morass of her own junk. I don't know how long we were in the alley while she tried key after key but it seemed a lifetime. Finally, the lock turned. Once inside, I took he key ring from her and put it in my pocket. I lit the small mag light. We had rigged the lens with red cellophane and even that I partially covered with my fingers. I wanted a dim light for the inside in case the outer doors and windows were not lightproof.

We were in a small hall, with doors to our right. The first one was the one used by the association president, currently Clyde Miller. It even smelled like an office; I guess that much paper has a smell, almost musty, almost woody. In Clyde's office was the wooden file cabinet with the no-lock. I went directly to the second drawer and pulled. No good. Gloria had been wrong. It was locked.

"Goddammit," I observed.

Audrey chided, "Dan, honestly, I would think with all your time in business you would know just a little about offices." She jiggled the top drawer and it opened, then she went to the second and it slid open easily.

"When you do it right you don't have to grunt and cuss." I felt her smug expression in the dark.

"We didn't lock stuff in my offices," I lied.

I rifled through the files while she held the small flashlight. There were not many files. Most of it was detailed property descriptions, old county and city property records, some old plat and zoning maps and a list of names. It was not hard for Audrey to verify that the names were Bonita Bluff homeowners. Beside most of the names was a check mark. Brad and Audrey's names were there, with no check mark. At the bottom of this list was a scribbled note with a recent date. It read, "Confirmed to Reinco."

"Wow!" Audrey whispered.

"Wow? What wow? Wow what?" I demanded.

A thin slash of red light illuminated her awed face. "Reinco," Audrey whispered, as though it were a powerful

145

sacred word, and in her best Nancy Drew voice, "Just like Gloria said."

We were in a 'B' movie.

"We already knew there was a Reinco link," I said. "Gloria as much as told us that. We still don't know what the hell it is."

"Oh, yeah." She sounded deflated.

We found a few more vague references to Reinco in the second drawer but could learn nothing from them. Most of the records were the same real estate junk and I could understand little or nothing of it. Descriptions, legal descriptions, etc. I was hoping for names, actions, plans, money. I wish there had been a "Detective Work For Dummies" book that I could have read. I had no idea what we were looking for.

The first drawer was far more interesting. I immediately grabbed a file called "Miller, personal." In it I found a letter from the Ridgecrest Academy For Boys. It was addressed to Clyde in apparent response to a letter he had written. It was a refusal to refund all or any part of the year's fees:

> "Eric occupied a position which otherwise would have been occupied by a full term student. The fact that Eric's behavior and demeanor became unacceptable was not a breach of obligation on the part of Ridgecrest Academy for Boys. On the contrary, it was a breach of implied commitment to honor academy regulations and respect the other students on the part of your son." And, "We regret we were unable to help this young man. We do not have the

146

facilities we feel it would require. We recommend ongoing therapy."

I pointed the salient parts out to Audrey. "Told you the kid had a screw loose. You're a bad judge of character."

"No I'm not."

"Come on, you marry lawyers."

The rest of the drawer contained a lot of confidential association correspondence. There was correspondence between the association and homeowners, contractors, the city. Some of it was fairly personal, internal memos–not really incriminating—just embarrassing reminders of who's a jerk and who's bitching about this and that, what contractor's not to be trusted . . . stuff you wouldn't want everyone to read, but hardly incriminating.

"If I didn't know better, I'd say this place was a Condo," I said. "I thought you were all homeowners."

"We are," then, with regret in her voice, "they are."

"Yeah, well . . . " I couldn't complete the thought.

"But still, it's subject to the CC&Rs of the association, that's conditions, covenants and restrictions, Dan. It keeps the standards high. There are things we can't do . . . work on cars in the driveways, have metallic roofs or television antennas, paint our houses garish colors, neglect the landscaping, store boats or RVs, that's recrea—"

"—Yeah, yeah, yeah, a Condo. You live in a damned condo only the units aren't attached."

"What's that got to do with anything?"

"Nothing, I guess. Let's try the desk and the other office."

147

The desks were locked, except for Gloria's and there was nothing in hers but telephone directories, tell-all magazines, candy, some make-up and a book about meeting men in bars. While we were up front looking at her desk, a police cruiser showed up in the parking lot. We fell to the floor behind the desk, Audrey balled up like a crazy Yoga thing deep under the desk and I, hugging my knees, pressed right next to her. The police unit stopped close, headlights pointing through the plate glass. We heard an occasional radio squawk but not clearly enough to understand it. Red and blue lights flashed on the walls of the darkened office.

We heard a single set of footsteps approach the front. We saw a bright flashlight beam scan across the office space and we desperately prayed to the God of all burglars and sneak thieves that we wouldn't be detected.

"Come out," came the demand. "We know you're in there."

The light scanned again.

"I think I peed a little," Audrey whispered.

I heard a second voice, a little further away. "No joy here either," it said. "False alarm. Probably animal noise from the pet shop."

"Our" cop answered. "Let's go to the Hitchin' Post for coffee and donuts."

"Yeah, I know the RP. She's an idiot. Nothin' here."

"RP, that's reporting party, Dan." Audrey just couldn't shut up.

"Yeah, I guess," the first voice said. "Who the hell would burglarize an office? What are they going to steal, stamps?"

"That was close, Dan."

"Shhh, I didn't hear any footsteps going away. It's a trick."

After a few minutes we did hear footsteps fade away, but I didn't trust them. We stayed there until muscle cramps began. I snuck a peek from the desk and there was no longer a police cruiser in the parking lot. We groaned and grunted to our feet. Bent like a couple of question marks, we sought the back door. Our taste for crime had disappeared. We let ourselves out.

No red and blue flashing lights nightmared the alley. No blinding spotlights bathed us. No mechanical voices demanded that we lay face down in the dirty asphalt. In silent agreement, we jogged back to the car and went home, not sure whether or not we'd been on a fool's errand.

#

"That was exciting," I grouched on the short drive back to Audrey's house. "We risked a felony arrest, came pretty close to it, and got out of there with absolutely nothing."

"We know that Reinco is somehow connected with the association, don't we?"

"Only a few cryptic notes. We knew that going in from Gloria's hints."

"Dan, you've got to be positive," she said. "You can't go around celebrating the negative. You'll never discover what's right."

"That's right, by gosh," I said. "We should gather everyone together, drink green tea, and sing John Jacob Jingleheimer Schmidt, that should work."

Audrey laughed. "Maybe it wouldn't, but it beats sitting around grouching."

"Yeah, yeah, yeah."

"Oh, that settles everything."

"Okay, but no more burglaries, okay?"

"Absolutely. I've had enough of that," she said. "Unless we have a better idea of what to look for."

"Have you got any ideas about what to do?"

"You mean besides meditating?"

"Yeah."

"I don't know. Maybe some centering the two of us together, clear our spirits. I feel a gathering cloud of the negative trying to steal my chi."

"Can't have that now can we? Once the chi is gone the whole neighborhood goes."

"I wasn't kidding, Dan."

"Yeah, for Pete's sake, let's keep your chi safe."

"You shouldn't make fun of it."

"Sure, burn incense, some of that meditation music of yours, the stuff that has no melody or rhythm, ring a few chimes. Hell, we'll be home free. Chi's back in its cage."

"Age old philosophies, Dan. Don't knock it."

I did admire that she was able to keep her spirits up. I could only ascribe so much of that to being airheaded. If nothing else, her "airy fairy" stuff did keep her cheered and energetic.

Then, she did the unexpected, bursting into enthusiastic song, doing the actions with gusto:

"If you're happy and you know it

Clap your hands (clap, clap)

If you're happy and you know it

Clap your hands (clap clap)

If you're happy and you know it
Just clap you're hands and show it
If you're happy and you know it
Clap you're hands. (clap clap)"

Audrey threw herself entirely into it, smiling like there was no problem in the world, bobbing her head from side to side with the rhythm of it. Her voice was the grating sopranasal that could induce metal fatigue, but her energy would not be denied. When the song called for the clapping, she took both hands off the wheel and clapped.

I tried complaining and grouching but she would not be denied. Finally, out of desperation, I joined her. We went through "clap your hands" to "hit the dash, tap your head, say 'ha ha', jerk the wheel, stamp your foot" and my personal non-favorite, "love the world."

Without any break, she led us into Michael Row The Boat Ashore, On Top Of Old Smokey, Sloop John B, and Row, Row, Row Your Boat, which she insisted upon doing as a round.

That took us home, and, although I'm loath to admit it, my spirits had lifted. Just laughing had some effect. I did not know what we would do the next day. I knew we would do something. I knew we would keep trying. And I knew with my sometimes-nutty sister's indomitable cheer and energy, we'd find something.

#

The next morning came too early. I missed the comparatively regulated life that I had created back in Washington State. There, it averaged out that I had something to do most days of the week. My excitements were funny things that happened, parties, hearing things going bump in the night at my isolated house. There were no car chases, no "pat downs," no urges to commit burglary. I did not find murder victims in the streets. There, I generally woke up thinking about what I had planned for the day, looking forward to it. Here, I woke up tired and a little depressed. My sister was in danger and I seemed powerless to help her.

Audrey was already up and about. I went to the kitchen and she had not made the pot of coffee she had been in the habit of making since I got there.

"Fire the cook," I said, standing there with an empty cup.

"Good morning, Grinch," she said, a superior smile on her face.

"Then I'll make some coffee, I guess. I know where everything is."

"There's no coffee because we're going out. I know a place where the coffee is fresh and the giant blueberry muffins are homemade."

"Bingo," I said. "My shoes are upstairs. Gimme twenty seconds."

Before we left the house Audrey's cell phone interrupted us with an infuriating version of "Alexander's Ragtime Band" only in four-four time instead of swinging five-eight. I gave Audrey a dirty look for choosing it as she answered with her cheeriest "hello" making it a three-syllable singsong thing. "Good morning . . . calm down Brad . . . don't talk to me like that . . . I will not even discuss this with you until you are rational." She covered the mouthpiece with her hand. "He's angry. He's very angry and we're divorced. I don't have to endure this. You take the phone. See what he wants."

" . . . goddamned stupid stunts I've ever——"

"——Brad, it's me, Dan. What's going on? What's wrong?"

"You two idiots are incorrigible. I should get her bail revoked. I should get you kicked out of the state. Right. The two of you deserve it. You're dangerous."

"Tell me what's got your knickers in a twist or I'm hanging up. You're not my favorite guy to talk to and I don't need your shit for breakfast. *Capice*?"

The line was silent for several seconds. I pictured him muting the phone and shouting cusses in his office, making women scream and grown-men flee in panic. Finally, he came back on line. "Clyde Miller went to his office this morning and found a fanny pack lying on the floor by the back door, in fact, its strap was caught in the door jam. He looked around the office, checked the files and, clearly, someone had been messing around in there. He called the police and he called me. I recognized the goddammed fanny pack you friggin' idiot!"

"An office break-in? I thought Alta Mira was a nice place." That was my way of letting an anxious Audrey know what Brad was all pissy about.

"Not break-in. They, you, had a key and there's only one place you could've gotten it. Clyde fired her this morning. Nice work, you two."

"Oh, come on, don't take this out on Gloria, for God's sake."

"Think about that the next time you recruit accomplices to your felonies. Gloria's goddammed lucky we've decided not to prosecute her right now."

"I don't know what the hell you're talking about," I said.

"It was Audrey's fanny pack and if she was there you were there. You two are joined at the hip, a partnership, 'Crazy and Goddammed Crazy, Ltd.'"

I asked Audrey, assuring that Brad could hear, "Audrey, did you burglarize any offices last night . . . rob any banks, anything like that . . . steal any cars? Brad seems upset."

"I was with you all night, Dan. We played cribbage and I wiped the floor with you. You owe me seventeen dollars."

"There you go, Brad," I said to him. "I guess we can't help you. Did you tell the police this crazy story?"

"No. I wish I had. I want you to grow up. We have a trial coming up. We don't need you idiots playing junior G-man. Suppose you'd been caught last night. Nice preparation for a trial, don't you think? Caught in a burglary? Right. We really need that."

He was scaring me a little, but it was a delight to hear him so angry that his control was loosened. "Oh, Brad," I said as lightly as I could, "while I've got you on the line, I have a question for you. You can help me out, here."

"What now?"

"Ever hear of an outfit called Reinco? R-E-I-N-C-O-. Do you know who they are or what they do?"

"What the hell is it to you?"

"Just came up, is all. You're a corporate lawyer, thought I'd ask you a business question."

"You have enough trouble with your own business. No, I've never heard of Reinco. I don't know who they are or what they do. How important is it to you?"

154

That sounded to me like negotiation. "Gee, Brad, I'd really like to know. It's gnawing at me, y'know? One of those little things that's hard to put down."

"Right. Right. Okay, you two promise to stop playing Columbo and I'll find out about Reinco for you. Deal?"

"More than fair, Brad," I said. "Thanks for calling," and I disconnected without waiting for a response: served the rude son-of-a-bitch right.

CHAPTER TWELVE

"Fanny pack?" I shouted at Audrey. "Fanny pack?"

She returned my angry stare with a face that was a study in innocence, eyes wide and clear, lips pursed as though hurt, eyebrows raised in confusion.

"You lost it!" I scolded. "It got stuck in the back door. Brad recognized it. Clyde called the police. Audrey, for God's sake."

She blushed, something that does not happen often. Last time I saw her busted so bad that she blushed was when Mom found the birth control pills in her book bag.

"What about 'take it out on Gloria,'" she asked. "What did that mean?"

"Clyde fired her this morning. They know a key was used. There's only one it could have been. Anyway, they're smart enough to figure the security system was off."

"Oh, God. We've got to talk to Clyde and get him to take it back. That's not fair. Gloria needs that job."

"Okay, but I don't know what we can tell him unless we confess. Do you want to do that?"

"It's not plan A, that's for sure. Come on, Dan. You're supposed to be the smart one, the one who went to college. Come up with something."

"I'll try, Sis. Honest, I'll give it the best. Damn. Fanny pack!"

"I knew I lost it and all. I was hoping it dropped in the alley or the car or something. Sorry Dan."

I was too hard on her. In all the fear and excitement, either one of us could have screwed something up. "Don't worry about it. It's not like we're pros."

"Did Brad tell the police it was mine?"

"No."

"See? He does have a sweet side. You've never appreciated that."

Sweet-Ass Brad the Impaler? Hard concept. Milk of human kindness running through his veins and dripping from his fangs? Nope. Doesn't work. "So, he said he'd find out about Reinco. Do you think he will?"

"Oh, sure," she said without hesitation. "Brad wouldn't lie."

"He lies for a living."

"He wouldn't lie to me."

"He wasn't talking to you."

"Dan, if Brad told you he would find out, he will find out."

"And, in return, we're supposed to stop playing Columbo, whatever the hell that means."

Audrey had an unusual expression on her face that I believed was meant to convey that she was thinking. She smiled and said, "Lunch, then," and we went out to the car.

"I don't know about 'Columbo,'" she purred as she started the car, "but my big brother is visiting from up North and I can certainly take him around to chat with my friends and neighbors. I'm sure we'll chat about this and that and such, whatever comes up."

She had been right in recommending the little café. The coffee was fresh and the blueberry muffins were extraordinary. They were the size of a super-carrier. Each one could feed a whole first grade class. Mine was still felt warm from the oven and the blueberries were large and tasty. The world started looking better. Audrey insisted, and I agreed with her, that the first thing we had to do was speak to Clyde and try to get Gloria's job back. We located him at the association office. Biddy's car was just leaving as we drove up. Audrey beeped and waved at her and she must have seen us but she kept driving, eyes front and never acknowledged us.

"Upper crust," Audrey practically snorted.

"Just a bunch of crumbs stuck together at the top," I said, resurrecting the old saw. Sometimes I can't stop myself in time.

Gloria's desk, cleaned out, was a reminder of the consequences of what we had done. There was a death quality about it. Yesterday she was there and this space was filled with her personality. Now, it was just a reception area with an empty metal desk. I've been told not to play poker because my thoughts and feelings are all over my face. If Clyde was at all perceptive, he'd have no trouble reading guilt and regret there.

"Come on back to the office," Clyde said. "Someone you should meet." As we walked the brief distance to his office, Clyde continued. "Your timing is perfect, this fella wants to meet you too."

Sitting across from Clyde's desk was a middle-aged man in a slate gray off-the-rack suit, white socks, and brown shoes. I have several friends who are cops and some of them you can just spot at a distance. This guy noticed me staring at the wooden file cabinet. My ears burned and I knew I looked guilty. He rose, smiled, and extended his hand, first to Audrey, then to me. "I'm detective

Morrison," he said, "San Diego County Sheriff's Department."

Audrey and I expressed how doggoned happy we were to meet Detective Morrison of the San Diego County Sheriff's Department, and we all took chairs. Clyde perched behind the desk, his symbol of power. I realized that his chair was on a platform that elevated his position.

"Detective Morrison is here because we had a burglary last night," Clyde began. He was really enjoying the catbird seat. "He's looking into it. Maybe you can help us."

Clyde, and the cop. It was almost too much. I wished I could rewind the last twenty-four hours and give it another shot.

"Did they get much? Do you keep money here?" Audrey asked, an innocent third party.

"Detective?" I said, surprised.

"My Captain was a friend of the assemblyman," Detective Morrison explained. "There are no small crimes. We're interested in anything involving friends, family and parties of interest."

"So, you've indicted my sister but your not real sure, or, you know your case is weak. I'm curious which it is. Can you tell me?"

Detective Morrison ignored my question. "Mrs. Davis," he began with a toothy smile that seemed somehow menacing, "Do you have a fanny pack?"

"Almost everyone I know has a fanny pack."

I thought she was doing very well. She had quickly identified a role and was playing it with conviction. She was the nothing-to-hide neighbor.

When you do go out jogging or whatever, you're supposed to carry a little money and some identification

159

with you. It would be just like Audrey not to carry any ID. I could almost hear her saying, "Why should I, Dan. Everyone knows who I am." That attitude might save our bacon.

"If we were to go to your home right now, you could produce this fanny pack? You wouldn't have to buy a new one to replace one you lost?"

"No trouble at all, Detective," she said. "We can take your car if you like. Why would you want to see my fanny pack?"

I wondered, why weren't they asking me about fanny packs and such. If they were stuck on the idea of one fanny pack, Audrey was right to be so relaxed. She could readily show them the one I was wearing. They were identical. Smart kid. Good liar.

Morrison relaxed even more in his chair. He was being so casual, so friendly. The most horrifying thing about a cat playing with its doomed prey is that the cat is not angry or passionate, just casual, almost friendly, with its victim. He continued with a friendly, almost apologetic manner. "There is some conjecture that you two might be involved in this," he said. "Can you help me with that?"

Stinking goddammed Brad the friggin' impaler. Sweet my ass! He'd dropped a dime on us. "I don't know," I said. "Who thinks we're involved? How would you get an idea like that?" Audrey was a better liar, but I think I'm smarter. I wanted to see what cards Morrison was holding.

"Tell you what," Morrison said. "I'd like your opinion on something." From his briefcase he withdrew a portable DVD player. "We dubbed this off the Hitchin' Post security tape. It's a bit fuzzy. The original's better."

He held the six-by eight-inch screen toward us and hit a button. There we were, Audrey and I, paying for the water. The bottom of the screen was time and date flagged. The fanny pack on Audrey's hips was clear. However, the big T-shirt I was wearing occluded mine and the camera never got a good shot of it. One fanny pack! They had nothing.

"Oh," I said, "that was here?" I shook my head and smiled. "I'm a visitor. I didn't realize that the 7-11, or whatever it is, was right here. Wow. Burglary, huh?"

Morrison rewarded me with a brief flash of a smile that carried no humor. "Are you a visitor too, Mrs. Davis?" he asked.

"Of course not," Audrey, the good liar, said. "I knew where we were last night. I heard about the break-in from my ex-husband this morning. I've had a little trouble in the community and I didn't want to have anything to do with the association any more, not their rules, not their burglaries, not their airs. I came down here because I heard that Mr. Miller had fired the receptionist, thinking she had something to do with all this. That is ridiculous and we'd like him to recall her."

That's my sister!

"What were you doing at the Hitchin' Post?"

"That's kind of obvious, ain't it?" I piped up. "When I jog I like some water. I didn't bring my water jug with me all the way from Washington State. Couldn't carry it on the airplane if I wanted to. So, we went to get a couple of mineral waters."

"Is this where you usually jog, Mrs. Davis? There's no track or park here. It's some distance from your house. Why here?"

Again, I answered for her. "Look, we were running off a little too much dinner. What difference where you run when it's dark? We were here. We were parked. We had the water."

Detective Morrison made a play of returning the tech-toy to his briefcase. He and Clyde exchanged helpless looks.

"As long as I've got you here, so to speak," Morrison said. "There is one more thing I'd like to bring up. Mrs. Davis, do you remember the bounty hunters who captured you?"

"Of course," Audrey said, a little color in her cheek. "They were brutes and those plastic handcuffs or whatever were too tight. If I'd had to wear them for much longer I would have had abrasions. Then you'd hear about me, and you'd hear from me too. Some of those people are outrageous. Absolutely outrageous."

I almost couldn't wait. I saw it in the enthusiasm of her expression. She was about to "Audrey" him.

"Do you know that they were killed," the Detective asked.

"And I'll tell you something else for all the good it might do. You're a detective which is an officer, right? Well that's got to mean something. Have you been to that jail downtown? It's disgraceful. I pay taxes and from what I pay in taxes I just know you could go to COSTCO and get lots of halfway decent toilet paper that doesn't scratch. While you're at it"

"Mrs. Davis, I——"

"——Did I say I was finished, young man? While you're at it you can tell those people to use some Lysol for God's sake. The place smells like a bus terminal. And that matron, or whatever, who wears the ugly brown shoes is very rude. Someone should speak to her. Not only does she have a poor attitude and shows no respect, but her language is deplorable. Not professional. Not professional at all."

"None of this is my department," Detective Morrison said when he could.

"Well, you people are always bragging about how you protect and serve. You paint it all over your cars for everyone to see. Can't some effort be made to serve innocent people who are put in that smelly, dirty place with tight handcuffs and abused by crude, bitter women with bad hairdos and filthy mouths? I mean, honestly, we're all innocent until we're proven guilty, right? Isn't that right? Isn't that what our constitution says. It's what mine says. So you're treating hundreds of thoroughly innocent people like criminals. It's not fair. It is just not fair."

"The bounty hunters, Ma'am. They were killed."

"I was thinking, just to show you that I'm fair. If it's a matter of money, why don't you suggest to your superiors that they put a Starbucks in the jail? A decent cup of coffee would be a world away from what they're drinking now. It would make money. It would make enough to clean the place up. You could even have San Diego County Jail souvenir mugs for sale. I would have bought one. That's what I told you, Dan, right?"

"You sure did, Sis," I said, trying not to laugh.

"Mrs. Davis," He raised his voice a bit. "Those bounty hunters were shot at very close range. Murdered. Did you hear about that?"

Something about being shot at close range. I had a déjà vu moment, reminded again about something from a movie. Once again it slipped away before I could identify it.

"Of course I did," she said. "Are you accusing me of not being a good citizen either and not reading the

163

newspaper or seeing the news on TV? Even if I hadn't known about it. Is not keeping up with current events a misdemeanor now? That's just awful."

"Do you, by any chance, remember what you were doing the night they were killed?"

"No, Detective Morrison, not by chance do I remember such things," she said. "Since people have started accusing me of killing other people, I've taken to noting events and their sequence. Not by chance at all."

"And . . . ?"

"And what? Oh. That was the night that I took Dan downtown and even over the bridge to Coronado to see the lights. San Diego is so pretty at night. It's such a pretty city, don't you think?"

"And, of course, Mr. Kelly will verify that statement as well, will he not," he said, sounding a bit tired. He looked in my direction.

"That's the way I remember it," I said with a straight face.

"And, no one saw you."

Audrey smiled as though he had said something well beneath him. "We were inside the car, Detective Morrison, I mean, really."

Detective Morrison nodded his head in agreement. I don't think he really suspected us of having anything to do with the bounty hunters. The detective rose to his feet and said 'goodbye' to us. He had a strange half-smile on his face. He knew damned well we were lying about the break-in. I knew from lots of chats with my cop buddies over beer and pool that this no-forced-entry, nothing taken, everybody-knows-everybody, all-in-the-family burglary would be considered chicken-shit and nothing much more would happen. Friends of the assemblyman or not, case not exactly closed, but not active either. Morrison's best hope would be that the experience had scared hell out of us, which it had.

After he left, Clyde changed his posture. "Actually," he said to me as if continuing our conversation from his den. "This burglary thing raises my respect for you. Didn't know you had it in you."

"Hell, Clyde, I'm just a crazy old guy living in the woods. No one even takes my calls."

"Touché."

"Clyde," Audrey said. "You've made your point with Gloria. She really needs this job. How about giving her a break, okay?"

"I'd like to, Audrey. I really would. But, I've got to maintain respect and credibility for my position."

I wondered if he got that from one of his military-style strategy books, clear chain of command and all.

Audrey's voice was friendly as she pressed the point. "Oh, I know Gloria respects you, Clyde. Why, I heard one of the temporary employees call you an obstinate martinet last summer and Gloria was all over him. She wouldn't allow it. 'That's my boss,' she said, and 'get out of here.' I honestly thought she was going to hit him."

Clyde puffed up a little at that. God, the man was easy.

"And, yesterday, I came in here, we both did, and asked if we could see some stuff and she said a flat 'no.' Didn't she, Dan? She even said, and it hurt my feelings a little, that I had no more rights than a tenant." She turned to me, passing the ball and we double-teamed the poor bastard.

"Swear on my mother's grave." I passed back. I was not lying, she had said 'no.'

"You think some new-hire is going to give you that kind of loyalty?" Again, she passed.

"Yeah. You're missing a valuable asset to your system, your machine. You've probably invested a certain amount of leadership in training her. That's an asset."

" . . . And, remember, Clyde, Gloria and I are sort of friends. It wasn't easy for her to say 'no' to me but she did. That's integrity. I was disappointed but I respected her for it. And you fired her this morning. Dammit, Clyde, you should be ashamed."

I had a golden stroke of inspiration and played it for a three-pointer. "Clyde, this wasn't Brad's idea, was it? You shouldn't let that guy intimidate you into doing things you don't want to. That won't get you any extra respect from the help and I bet you'll catch hell from Connie."

We got to him. I know we did. He changed his whole demeanor and tried to pretend that he was important and things mattered. "So, what was it you wanted, Audrey? Why didn't you just ask me?"

"I probably should have," she apologized. She shifted position in her chair and I realized that she was flirting with him. I had never seen her flirt. "Clyde, with all this murder nonsense, I didn't want to bother you with little things. I know you've got important things to do."

It was fascinating, from the remote perspective of a brother, watching a woman flirt: the crossing of her legs, the leaning forward in an intimate way, the inflection of her voice. I thought she must be doing it wrong because it seemed a little obvious and silly, but then I realized it was working on Clyde. He softened in his attitude, his spine less rigid, his forearms no longer crossed. He concentrated on her with a degree of real pleasure.

"Sometimes, I ask Brad or I go to Connie," she cooed on, "but lately we've been spatting. I don't know if you've noticed."

"Oh, yes."

"So, I just wanted to know about this Reinco thing. Are they contractors to the association, some kind of software or accounting service? What?"

"Audrey," he pontificated, "As association manager, my job is mostly supervisory. I deal with the owners and, yes, arrange contracts for this and that. I don't know everything but I don't remember having this outfit of yours do any work for us. You didn't have to get Gloria's key or break-in to the offices."

"I didn't say we did, Clyde. Why fire Gloria? Is it because she's not on the board of directors? She's just a 'little guy' and doesn't count? I'd like to think better of you." He started to say something but she cut him off. "I already know that someone has set me up with a murder charge. Why are you so sure that none of your colleagues, who also have keys, hasn't run this masquerade just to distract you? Maybe convince you to get rid of your best, most loyal, employee?"

Audrey stopped. She allowed a long and very uncomfortable silence to follow. Clyde kept changing position in his chair and looking on his desktop for something to say.

"We've got to go, honestly," Audrey said, rising.

I got up too and extended my hand to Clyde. It felt a little clammy. I wondered if he weren't thinking forward to the start of happy hour.

At the door, Audrey paused, "So, I can tell Gloria to come back tomorrow, or do you want to do that yourself?"

Audrey and Clyde stared at each other for some time. I could almost see Clyde thinking of Machiavellian plots, and counter plots, schemes, ambitions, and betrayals. Knowing him, it would all be predicated on the fear that someone had manipulated him into doing something . . . therefore, perhaps he should not have done it.

"I'll tell her," he said in a small voice.

CHAPTER THIRTEEN

Gloria dancing was a sight to see. She shuffled, swayed, and shimmied her rotund body with a refreshing lack of self-consciousness. She wore a dress the color of lima beans on which were printed huge, red, orange and yellow tropical flowers. It was loud, garish, out of style, and (according to Audrey) clashed with Gloria's skin tones. Perfect. It reflected Gloria's thoroughly blind joi de vivre. No one ever would have recommended the hideous dress but she wore it well and proved them wrong.

There was no dance floor in the Home'n'Hearth, a neighborhood beer bar; and without a cabaret license, dancing was probably against some municipal statute. The jukebox and the festive mood, however, repealed all ordinances. A few tables were moved apart to make room for two or three happy couples to flounder about.

Gloria made it her business to flirt with every man in the bar and with some of them seriously. Built something like a five-and-a-half foot high cherubim whom only Rubens could get exited about, she nevertheless seemed to attract men, God bless her.

After she had been reinstated, she had assumed correctly that Audrey had been behind it. A celebration had become mandatory. Gloria would not be denied. We agreed to it, thinking of dinner and a few drinks. Gloria was determined to have a party at the Home'n'Hearth. It was worth real money watching Audrey get out-maneuvered and suckered in by a master.

169

The name of the game was beer and wine served by the owners, Wanda and Ralph, two retired postal workers. Wanda had been the postmistress of a town in the county. The jukebox was mostly country and classic-rock, so loud that it was sometimes hard to tell which. The crowd was regulars, working class neighborhood people bent on shooting pool, drinking too much beer and enjoying their Saturday night. The only negative, and I am drawn to discover the negative in anything, was that it was so loud you had to lean into whomever you were talking to in order to be heard. That's fine for a while, about twenty minutes maybe. We were starting our second hour.

One of the best things about the beer-bar party was that Audrey, sipping at a snail's pace, was nevertheless on her fourth wine. I love it when Audrey gets a bit snockered. The personas she loves so much fall away. The controlled delivery fades. What is left is a really nice, warm gal whose laughter is no longer the tight "heh heh heh," but a hearty "Hah hah hah," open, relaxed, and genuine.

"This place is really fun," shouted the real Audrey in my ear.

I nodded my head and refilled my mug from the pitcher. Another Somebody Done Somebody Wrong Song was blaring its way into my brain. Gloria was slow-dancing with Chuck, a tall, muscular truck driver who was apparently a Rubens fan. He was a head-and-a-half taller than she but still managed to get his hands on her butt as they danced. Not only did she not mind, I believe she moaned once or twice.

"I wonder why no one has asked me to dance," Audrey said, assessing the men overtly.

"You're looking at them like they're produce on display," I shouted in her ear.

"I'd like to squeeze a few to see if they're ripe," she said, laughing.

"They think we're together," I said.

Gloria, after doing a little butt squeezing of her own returned to the table and reached for her glass. "Hey, Gloria," I shouted in her ear knowing that Audrey would not hear. "No one has asked Audrey to dance. They must think we're together or something. Could you quietly spread the word, talk to a guy or two . . . she'd like to dance too. Be discrete, you know."

Gloria nodded her head in agreement and stood up. She put her pinkie and index finger in her mouth and produced a shrieking whistle that should have broken glass; people in graveyards started moving. Even the jukebox was silent. "Hey," she shouted to the suddenly attentive audience, "when I introduced Dan and Audrey Kelly, I forgot to say they were brother and sister. Isn't there a man in this bar who isn't afraid to ask my friend Audrey to dance?"

Audrey tried to slide under the table.

Willie Nelson started singing "Blue Skies." Gloria returned to the dance floor with a skinny little man who kept trying to nuzzle his face between her breasts. Four guys came over to the table like shy kids on prom night. Audrey, over the embarrassment enough to window-shop, said yes to the youngest and tallest of them, promising the others to dance with them later.

"How 'bout you, Dan? Dance?"

I looked up to see Gloria. I felt I knew her well enough to be honest.

"Nope."

"Good." She sounded relieved. "I need to sit down and finish my beer. Hey, we need another pitcher." She got Wanda's attention and signaled for more.

"What happened to the little guy?"

"He kept sticking his head between my tits."

"Oh."

"I didn't mind that, but every time he did it, he started crying."

"Crying?"

"Him and his wife broke up. He misses her . . . he misses her tits."

"I guess I see."

"Too much beer. He's nice enough; I just don't want to stain this dress. I got it on sale."

"On sale, you say," I commented without laughing. "Good crowd," I said. "You got nice friends."

She smiled, almost automatically, then, she looked around the bar more slowly, appraising her friends and neighbors. "Yes," she said, dark Italian eyes moist with emotion, "Yes, I do. These are nice people. We work. We play. We make love, have families, fight with each other . . ." She finished her mug. "We get faced, regret it, say we're sorry, and do it next weekend."

"Only in America."

"How's Audrey? Sometimes I can't tell. She's got walls."

"Yeah, she's got walls all right. Sometimes I can't tell either and I've known her all my life."

"One of my ex-boyfriends would have called her a hard read."

"I think she's okay. For all her bullshit, she's pretty strong."

"Right," Gloria said. She too was more perceptive than she let on.

I could not resist asking, *"How did that book help you?"*

"What book?"

"The one about how to meet men in bars."

"How do you know about that?" A shy, almost embarrassed smile flashed across her face. It was charming.

"While I was burglarizing your office I took the opportunity to invade your privacy too. The book was in your desk."

"Oh," she said. The pitcher came and she refilled our mugs and took a generous pull on hers. "That's a great book. It really works."

"What does it say?"

She laughed, blowing beer foam from her upper lip. "I haven't got the damndest idea," she said. "I never read the goddammed thing. I just go into a place and I slap it on the bar, face up. Guys come to talk to me about it. So the book works. I'm meeting guys in bars."

It's a minor miracle how beer makes things funnier and funnier.

"Hey," I said. "You know all the homeowners. When we went to the office yesterday morning, we saw Biddie Reilly leaving. She didn't see us, or maybe she pretended not to. Is she really that big a snob?"

"Oh, yeah, but it's more than that. You caught her."

"Caught her what?"

"Caught her going to see her luh-vah." Gloria giggled with pleasure.

"Her lover? Clyde? Jesus! Clyde Miller and Biddie Reilly?" It was a potentially valuable bit of news but I

173

couldn't help picturing the two of them clumsily working their way through the Kama Sutra. Sometimes I really wish I could draw. Caricatures would be enough: Clyde, face all contorted and serious, violently asserting his passionate manhood atop socially confident

"Just tuning-up the old snoring machine were you?"

"I don't snore."

"Right," she said. "Then what were you doing running a noisy power tool for an hour? It sure sounded like snoring from the other side of your door." Biddie yawning at both ends. It'd be great.

"Biddie and Clyde sounds almost as bad as Connie and Clyde," I offered.

"Anybody and Clyde is a bad combination," she proposed. We both laughed at the truth of that. This was a really nice bar.

Once rested, Gloria did not wait to be asked to dance. She walked to the bar and grabbed the trucker for round two. Audrey's dance card was full now. She had been a dancer and was good at it. Her age didn't make a bit of difference. All the guys, it seemed, wanted to dance with her. Then, a guy, who had been the center of attention in his little group at the far end of the bar, asked her. It was soon clear that he was a dancer too. In no time, the other couples gave up and Audrey and this fella had the dance floor to themselves. It was great to see. What they danced during LeAnn Rimes' Blue was worth paying for, a romantic and dramatic near-ballet of two bodies expressing themselves. It was followed by a fast "boot-scooter," Gretchen Wilson's "All Jacked Up," and they did a part lindy/part polka thing that was exciting.

A CASE OF PEANUT BRITTLE

All this I watched from the best seat in the house, up front and a nearly full pitcher within grasp. It's not that I do not dance. I do. I just have to be in the mood, really in the mood. The only exception is that I'll force myself in order to impress a woman. I'd dance in a fire-pit to get hooked-up. But, my dancing was like everyone else in the bar except for this fella and Audrey. It's like they had rehearsed, like an improv Jazz quartet jamming in the zone. How do people do that?

Tired at the end of their exhibition, while the bar's applause and cheering rewarded their efforts, they spoke briefly, then Audrey returned to the table. "I didn't even know how much I needed that, Dan," she said. "Ken is wonderful?"

"Really and truly?"

She smiled a spontaneous smile and buddy-punched me in the shoulder. "He's a married guy," she said. "He told me his wife is not really a dancer. In fact, it was her that suggested he ask me. She knew he wanted to."

"This is a nice place," I said. No sarcasm. "Hey, I found out that Clyde and Biddie . . ." I made a crude gesture with my hands.

"You're kidding," she said.

"As Gloria would say, they're luh-vahs."

"That's really interesting," she said. "I didn't have a clue."

"That makes the assemblyman one leg of a cheating triangle. Murders have been committed over less."

Audrey took my hand in hers and pressed gently. "Tomorrow, Dan," she said. She stared directly at me. Her eyes were a bit watery and her lids were tending toward half-mast. Tired and tippled. "Tonight I'm having fun and

I want to have some more fun. I need it. No murder tonight. You need a rest from all this too."

I didn't bother arguing. When Audrey is truly Audrey, she's seldom wrong. Assuming that we'd call a taxi at the end of the evening, I let myself get into a honky tonkin' mood. I left the table for the restroom and on the way back fell into conversation with two sports fans. We talked about the Chargers, the good old days of Fouts and Air Coryell . . . the bad luck of the red zone and several other things that I recall being passionate about at the time, making half of it up. I don't know much of anything about football and could care less. But, it was fun.

I ran into a cranky old so-and-so at the end of the bar who wanted to "nuke" all the foreigners and Arabs and most of the Democrats. "Goddam right," I remember saying. "People don't care anymore."

The next morning I appreciated how right Audrey had been. Other than getting up a few more times than usual during the night, I felt more relaxed than I had been in a while. My head was more clear. My stomach had not voted yet, but I was pretty sure my only discomfort was a case of birdcage mouth. Since I was first up, I made the coffee. I tried to make enough noise to wake her but nothing worked until I banged the frying pan on the stove several times——hard. She rushed into the kitchen.

"What the hell are you doing down here . . . building a ship?"

"Oh, I'm sorry. Just making coffee. Did I wake you?"

"People in Long Beach fell out of their beds, Dan. What has the frying pan got to do with coffee?"

"I was thinking of making some scrambled eggs like we used to get at home."

176

"Yeah, well, you scramble the eggs, Mister, not the pan."

She wore an oversized bathrobe that had once belonged to The Impaler. It was terry cloth, deep brown, and as unpleasant as its original owner. Her hair looked like it was afire and the wind was blowing the flames around.

"How do you feel?" I asked, extending a full coffee cup to her.

"Okay, I guess. I'm not used to that much drinking. My mouth tastes funny."

"It'll go away after you eat and brush your teeth. We didn't have that much; you're just not a steamer."

"Yeah, I feel okay, but I'll pass on the scrambled eggs I don't want to tempt fate."

"Okay. I recommend dry toast or dry cereal. Good for the tummy. Then we can get dressed and call a cab. We need the car back."

She started laughing at me so hard she had to put the coffee on the table and sit down. "I'm not a steamer, eh, experienced and worldly brother-of-mine? You haven't the foggiest notion how we got home last night. You don't remember."

"We didn't take a cab? That was plan one."

"Gloria wouldn't hear of it. She drove and got the trucker dude to follow us, then he drove her home."

"I'll bet he did, too!" I said. "Good for Gloria."

"So, our 'taxi' is waiting in the garage like every other morning."

"Yeah, yeah."

"Where are you in a hurry to get off to?"

"I thought that sometime today we should see Biddie and try to embarrass her. We can also ask your last big mistake if he found anything out about Reinco. I'm

177

calling my own lawyer to do the same thing. At least my lawyer's not a suspect."

Audrey was about to sip from the cup but put it back on the table and stared at me. "Do you really think Brad had anything to do with this?"

I tried to be diplomatic. "Listen, Babe, if you weren't who you are, you'd be on my suspect list too. Someone laced that brittle with poisonous goop. It damned sure wasn't me. How the hell do I really know it wasn't you?"

"That's so reassuring."

"We're looking for someone who knows the people involved, someone who knew about the brittle, someone who knew how to make the poison or get hold of it, someone who'd have easy access to your house or Reilly's house to plant it."

"It could have been random and an accident, I suppose," she said. It was weak.

"If it were, we'd have nothing at all to work with. I'm assuming that someone in your circle is responsible."

Audrey sipped at the coffee, holding the cup with both hands. She seemed lost in thought. She held the cup up for more. "You were more fun last night," she complained.

After a moment or two of silence, her mood completely changed. "Do you really wonder, once in a while, if it was me after all?"

She was serious, even a little worried, but she was overdue for a reality check. "It ain't rocket science, Audrey. You guys were confronting each other all the time. You have a history of losing your temper at him. You made the peanut brittle. You gave him the peanut brittle in front of a hundred people. It was laced with poison. You even gave him an ambiguous note. He ate some of the peanut brittle and it killed him. None of this is even contested. For you to be innocent we have to come from the outside all that with a whole new theory. So far, any outside theory looks too fantastic."

"Isn't there some Sherlock Holmes thing about when you've tried all the common sense things and they don't work, the crazy thing that's left has to be the answer?"

"You've got that so screwed up I can't remember the right quote. Anyway, it's fiction."

"Well, then," she said, "I guess I should just confess and let everyone go home."

CHAPTER FOURTEEN

We decided to split our efforts. Audrey felt that Biddy would freeze up or become too hostile in her company. On the other hand, she was concerned that my quick-draw-McGraw mouth would launch Brad into some erratic orbit. She gave me the car and instructions to Biddy's house, and to the "Rumpled Rhineskeller," a yuppie dump in La Jolla where we could compare notes later.

I called Biddy. She was not at all enthusiastic about talking to me.

"Believe me, I understand," I said, trying to sound like a sympathetic counselor.

"Then you will not mind that I decline to see you."

"I will be alone, Mrs. Reilly, I promise."

"Audrey?"

"No, good Lord, I am sensitive to your position. Please understand mine. Audrey is my sister and I'm down here trying to help her."

"By doing what, exactly?"

"I don't want to see her convicted of this without at least knowing that I spoke to everyone I could . . . that I tried my best."

"I can understand that."

"It would haunt me."

"What happened, and what will happen, are not your fault."

180

A CASE OF PEANUT BRITTLE

"Mrs. Reilly, may I call you Biddy? You seemed a generous and gracious woman when I met you at the Miller home the other night." I was a bit ashamed of myself for being so unctuous, but, in for a dime, in for a dollar. "I ask a few moments of your time and attention. Then, my conscience will be clear that I tried my best."

"Well . . . If you are so determined . . ."

The fish were starting to nibble. I tugged gently on the line. "I'm afraid I am. At the same time I want to be fair to everyone. I certainly don't want my only information about you to be based on what other people tell me."

"I would hope not."

"This is a terrible thing. I'd like to understand it better. Wouldn't you?"

"I believe that I already do . . . Dan."

I knew I had her. Now, set the hook and bring it in. "And if you do, you can really help me. I know I'm asking a lot. Can we meet for coffee or tea or something? I promise it will not be for long——a few moments is all."

"Then I suppose we'd best be done with it. Do you need directions to my house? I will have Sarah make fresh tea. I have a bit of time right now."

"I can be over in a few minutes."

"You get very limited time, Dan. This is, after all, an imposition."

"I'll respect your needs," I said, and we "rang off" as the Brits say.

Within ten minutes I had parked Audrey's car outside the Reilly house. It was a two-story frame house, white with shuttered windows, a classic Cape Cod form, its proportions swollen by affluence. The builders had eschewed a columned front, though there was a circular drive with access to a multiple car garage. Its understatement oozed class. Even the white of the clapboard was an off white, the shutters were more baker's chocolate than black. Only up close did the visitor realize how large the house really was.

A middle-aged woman answered the door. She wore a simple gray dress that, though not quite the classic servant's uniform, gave the same effect. She led me to a sitting room off the entry where Biddy awaited me. This sitting room, unlike the palatial excesses of Connie's salon, was a normal size room with one sofa, a love seat, and several upholstered chairs. The curtains and upholstery were in small, delicate floral patterns, as was a large rug covering a wood floor. Several colored glass vases held freshly cut flowers. This room was definitely for the lady of the house. I imagined that the deceased probably had had an office that served a similar function for him.

Biddy, wearing a skirt and blouse of subdued earth colors, sat on a delicately adorned but comfortable looking chair. Her poise made it seem throne like, perhaps it was her height . . . apparent dignity is frequently attributed to the quite tall, as long as they have been graceful enough to stay out of their own way. With an arm extended like one who has studied ballet, she indicated the end of the couch closest to her, inviting me to sit. On a walnut coffee table was a china tea set. She had already poured for herself and, dismissing Sarah, poured tea for me without asking.

"Sugar, cream?" she asked. She was being gracious with no signs of her reluctance to have me in her home. The elite reflect their good breeding—much the same as do properly certified horses and dogs.

"No thank you," I said to the sugar and cream. I took the seat and reached for the proffered teacup.

A CASE OF PEANUT BRITTLE

The cup was sitting on its stupid little saucer and I wasn't sure what to do. Do you put the saucer on the coffee table and deal with the cup like ordinary people? Do you hold the saucer with one hand and remove and replace the cup with the other? Pinky up or pinky down? I looked to her but she sat, hands gracefully in her lap, idly toying with a lace hanky-looking thing. Her tea and saucer sat smugly on the coffee table. That's where I put mine: didn't want the damned thing in the first place.

"Audrey's offer of condolences was genuine, you know," I said to her.

She moved her lips slightly in the direction of a smile. Clearly, I had not chosen the right opening. Once more into the breach, dear friends, "Among the reasons this will be a short visit is that it is extremely awkward . . . for both of us, I'm sure."

"Then, in the privacy of this parlor let us drop the ordinary civilities and get to the sharpest points we can," she said in a clipped voice. "Is that agreeable?"

"Absolutely. Some of my questions will be personal, Biddy, but they are relevant."

"I have heard that you are an opinionated, obnoxious, unpleasant boor," she said in the sweetest conversational way, gently winding the doily dingus around one forefinger. "Yet, you are acting like a considerate gentleman. I wonder, does that hurt?"

Good shot. I could like this broad.

"Perhaps not everything that you've heard or think you know about me, or my sister for that matter, is the complete truth. No, it doesn't hurt. I'm impatient with fools and posers and I'm at the age where I'm not afraid to say so. That does not mean that I don't know how to act in the presence of a lady, much less a widow."

"Touché," and this time, she smiled, even her amber eyes were smiling. By god, she was enjoying this.

"I . . . uh . . ." I actually stammered. Dammit, she intimidated me, sitting there so pristine and somehow remote. I wanted to know some intimate, sweaty things about her and her husband and she was playing with a lacy thing too delicate and too pretty to have any use whatever. No way would you blow your nose or wipe up a spaghetti stain with it. Maybe, she being a widow and all, it was meant to dab discreetly at teeny tiny tasteful tears.

"Do you know what Reinco is?" I asked out of desperation. "That's an acronym for some kind of company."

"Yes, actually," she said.

I hoped my jaw didn't make too much of a racket when it hit the coffee table. Two lawyers working on it with no success and I only asked her because I was looking for sensitive questions to open with. "Yes, actually," indeed! It echoed in my brain.

"Well, 'yes' and 'no,' I guess I don't," she continued, letting all the air out of my new balloon. "I've heard the name and it's something that was bothering Sean. He was angry about it. I don't know, really."

"Something about it made him angry? Do you know what?"

"No, just that he was angry about it. He kept promising to 'get them all.'"

"'Get them all?' Who?"

"Who knows? With Sean, everything was a conspiracy. Who? Audrey and her neighborhood crowd, her skateboarding hooligans. I don't know."

"But Reinco?"

184

A CASE OF PEANUT BRITTLE

"I'm sure Reinco was all part of 'them.' 'They' were always out to ruin the world and Sean was always uncovering their conspiracies and fighting them. We didn't share too much on issues. The skate park annoyed me. We agreed on that. Sean even advocated the injunction against its use to county board members."

"I've heard some unkind things about Sean's objection to the skate park." "Unkind things" included Audrey railing against him for being pro-business and anti-kids. "He could stomp on orphans on his way to church," Audrey had said.

"My husband was, perhaps, the last Boy Scout in politics. People made fun of his righteousness. They thought it was a pose. It wasn't."

"Are you saying he was an honest politician?" I couldn't resist.

Biddy looked at me and smiled in a kind of confidential way. I got the impression that, since I was a nobody just passing through her world, she could afford to be frank with me. "Dan, Sean was obsessively fastidious, a bit of a hypochondriac, and fanatically devoted to the principles of law and order. He was forced to make some compromises in the assembly in order to be effective at all. Each point he had to yield, each line that had to be struck, bothered him. Some would say he had extreme control issues, perhaps so. Some called him a zealot. But he was honest and dedicated. He was against the skate board park because it was not authorized, supervised and controlled."

"Just kids having fun, huh?"

"That's an inane simplification," she corrected, like Sister Agnes with a three cornered ruler. She circled the lacey surrogate for my neck with her fingers. "It was kids without knee pads or helmets, without proper lighting or design, throwing themselves around with abandon as they out-dared each other in growing darkness. It was fractured skulls, broken bones and bitter lawsuits waiting to happen. Sean was working to prevent all that. He had no objection to having a legitimate skate park built."

"I'm sorry," I said. "I guess I've never heard the other side of the argument."

"And we agreed on that little creep who thinks he's a gardener."

"The Miller kid, Eric?" I guessed . . . I mean, after all, she did say "creep."

"Not only am I missing an amber brooch in a silver setting, but also, and I couldn't testify to this, I think some of my delicates are missing." Since Eric's name had come up, Biddy started wringing the lacy thingy with considerable force.

"You suspect the Miller kid."

"Strongly enough so that Sean was going to try to get him banned from working in the Alta Mira community. He makes my skin crawl."

"I met the kid only recently. I had forgotten that I even had hackles till I met Eric."

"He needs help, but not from us. He should be in an institution somewhere. He needs ongoing therapy."

That was the same phrase used in the letter to Clyde from the Ridgecrest School. "What might be your connection with the Ridgecrest Academy? Do you know why Eric interrupted his term at Ridgecrest and came home?"

"I'm sure that such things are confidential."

"Come on, Biddy, dropping the civilities and all, how much do you know?"

She conducted a very brief argument with herself, presumably about ethics and confidentiality, then committed to gossip. "Sean had connections to the managing board at Ridgecrest. He wrote a letter of recommendation as a favor to Clyde and Connie. When things went sour at the prep school, some people there thought Sean should know about it."

"What happened?"

"I don't know exactly. There were some things missing and a boy was somehow abused, attacked . . . I don't want to use the word 'molested' because I'm not sure that they did . . . I don't know." She glanced at her watch.

"Were you and Sean close to Connie and Clyde? I understand you vacationed together."

"We had similar interests, of course. It was convenient."

"And you are still close to Clyde?" I said, evenly.

She looked away from the intricate lace design. I saw color rise at the base of her neck where there was no make-up to disguise it. "He's been a great help to me," she said.

"Yes, I saw you leaving the association offices the other morning. We waved 'hello' to you, even tooted the horn, but you looked away. Didn't see us, I suppose."

"I'm sure I don't know. I don't recall."

Her eyes avoided mine again and the alarm at the top of my lie-o-meter started going "ding-ding."

"How about Sean and Connie, were they close too?"

"That's an offensive question, the way you're asking it, and it just ran out the clock, Mr. Kelly."

"If we leave it at that, I'll have to assume that I hit a hot spot," I said.

187

"Think what you're bred to. We are a neighborhood of families. Like all neighborhoods we form friendships, interlocking friendships . . . it's part of what makes a community. The Millers are an interesting couple and we have spent time with them, as couples and as singles. They face challenges with their son. We all face challenges of one sort or another. It's life, not 'school for scandal.'"

"The night of the awards, you and Sean came home together?"

"Yes, of course."

"Did he comment on Audrey's little gift in any way? Open it?"

"No. We were both tired. Sean spoke of having some work to do. I went straight to bed and remember nothing till the next morning."

"You have separate bedrooms."

"Yes. Many couples do. He sometimes kept irregular hours. Also, he had sleep apnea and slept with one of those noisy breathing machines. I'm a light sleeper. His bedroom is downstairs at the other end of the house, near the kitchen. It was intended for a live-in housekeeper, but we never had one who met Sean's impossibly high standards. It even has its own door to the outside. When he's working in the office, raiding the refrigerator or watching television in his bedroom, I do not hear him."

"So you found him and . . . "

Biddy rose to her feet. "You may now have a clear conscience that you've spoken for your sister," she said. "I told you I only had a few moments."

I stood too. This was one of the nicest houses I'd ever been thrown out of. "We never defined a few moments," I plead.

"We just did," she said and extended her hand toward the door.

With what I thought was a sufficient amount of dignity and a somber tone, I thanked her for speaking to me, acknowledging that it was surely difficult. I said the obvious things about finding my way out and wishing her well.

Outside the house I allowed the smile to spread. She and old Clyde were definitely boffing each other. The Miller kid was confirmed as a perv-creep, and there was a hint that Connie and Sean made the eight-legged monster once in a while. Why, that private entrance of his might have had a sign: "Hi, Connie, welcome aboard." A productive few minutes.

I drove down I-5 far enough to get to some working people's neighborhoods for some straightforward leisure facilities. I killed the time before my meeting with Audrey by swilling a few brews at a beer bar that had the good grace to be called "Joe's" and the good sense to be open at ten thirty in the morning. I spent some of the time trying to get hold of my own lawyer. That is always a lengthy procedure involving "not in the office just now," or "in conference," or "in court" and always followed with, "can he call you back?" Well, I was "in conference" at Joe's until time to leave for the "Ruined Rhinoceros" or whatever the oak'n'brass yuppie dump was called.

At eleven thirty I went back north to La Jolla. La Jolla is (contrary to what its residents frequently pretend) a neighborhood of San Diego. It is named after and built around the beautiful cove on the Pacific. Scripps Institute is ensconced happily on the coast as is UCSD. There's a rich cultural life of painting, classical music, gardening . . .

189

very much of the best of what California has to offer. It is scenic and charming past postcards.

Like many beautiful things and people, it takes itself entirely too seriously. All those college professors and scientists and artists thin out the air. What with the plethora of Town Cars, Beamers, Jags, Prius's, and Ferraris, it's almost impossible for a hard-working Chevy to find a parking place.

The "Rumpled Rheinskeller" clung precariously to the till cliffside, and had a cantilevered outdoor dining area that was almost literally over the ocean. Audrey, having just gotten there, was sitting comfortably in the waiting area. A post-doc maitre d' escorted us to a table near the safety railing. The view was a spectacular panorama of thousands of miles of blue Pacific. It was the sort of place, I just knew, where at the moment of sunset, all the gentry would applaud politely, one or two wags calling "Author, author."

"Isn't the ocean beautiful?" Audrey coo'ed.

"I understand it's the largest ocean on this coast," I said, trying to help.

"How did things go with you and Biddy?" she asked, accepting, then perusing a menu board big enough to be a lamp table.

"We're engaged," I said. "After all, she's free now and Clyde can't get it up any more. Why not?"

Audrey leaned forward speaking barely above the drone of the surf below, "You wouldn't think it, but they have the very best fish stew in here. They call it the Neptune something or other and it's the best bargain on the menu."

"Works for me," I said. "So, we're going to honeymoon in Barbados. She's paying of course."

190

"That's good, I . . . what? Are you making fun of me again?"

"If you'd actually listen to me once in a while you can always tell; I'm very funny."

"Tell what?"

"Whether or not I'm making fun of you."

"So what's that got to do with someone getting engaged in Barbados? Who?"

"I have no idea. Listen, the interview with Biddy was awkward but interesting."

"Yes? And?"

The waiter returned and we ordered a half-liter of their house Chablis. He poured a bit for my approval that I signaled. He actually had a neatly folded hand towel draped over his forearm, " . . . And are we ready to order?"

I wondered what his major was. "Two Neptune Something Or Others," I said, getting Audrey's assent.

The waiter smarmed at us with his perfect teeth and withdrew. I decided his major was Far Eastern Mysticism or Italian Renaissance Literature.

"All right, you've had your revenge, Dan. What did Biddy say?"

"I'm sure that she and Clyde are boinking each other. No big surprise, that. There's a possibility that Connie and Sean were going at it too."

"Is everybody but me and Brad at each other?"

Doing my best D. C. Reilly impression, I sang, "This is just another Peyton Place and they're all Harper Valley hypocrites."

Audrey giggled. "Anything else?"

"Yeah. Sean wrote a letter of recommendation for Eric at the snooty prep school. When the little perv got bad enough to get kicked out, the school let Sean know the

191

whole story. He was out to get Eric banned or ostracized or burned at the stake or something. He didn't want him in the neighborhood. Apparently, Lady Chatterley, your gardener is a sneak thief who pilfers panties, and attacks little boys."

"Wow."

"Eloquent. How did you do with Brad?"

"Wow."

"Brad? Reinco? New lawyer for your civil needs? Earth calling?"

We interrupted matters of life and death long enough to sample the house white, after all, we were on the Côte d'Azur de La Jolla The wine was outstanding.

"I'm very angry at Brad and I told him so," she announced.

"That'll fix'im."

"Mr. Ladish is fine for my defense, but for everything else I'm going to get another lawyer. Brad gave me a list of very nice ones."

I rolled my eyes heavenward seeking solace and mercy for all creatures great and stupid. "Yeah, and the one you're going to fire for screwing you used to be on the top of that same list. God. You need a baby-sitter."

"Well how am I supposed to know?" Raised eyebrows, injured innocence.

"In the first place, my own lawyer is supposed to call me today, I'll ask him if he can find a lawyer down here. In the second place, ask your favorite bully, Ladish, if he can recommend anyone. But not Brad, for Chrissake. Never Brad."

The "Neptune Whatever" was served and further conversation was limited to one- or two-word comments. The seafood chowder was magnificent, wonderful fresh fish, crab, clam, etc. in a spicy tomato/cilantro base that was a creative masterpiece. With it were served small loaves of freshly baked bread, crusty on the outside and warm and soft on the inside with a slight basil aroma. For whole moments at a time I forgot where I was and why.

Finally, sopping up the last bit of chowder with the last crisp end of bread, Starship Dan landed back on Planet Earth. "So, did you remember to ask about Reinco again?"

"Yes, I did and he doesn't know anything about it. He seemed annoyed that we keep pestering him about it."

"I am of the opinion that anything that annoys Brad is good for us."

"You never did like him."

"Good for me."

"Is there more wine?"

"I only ordered a half-liter."

"Well?"

She was right. That lunch did deserve a bit more wine.

#

A lot of older men get accused of being cranky. There's a good reason for that. A lot of older men are cranky. There's a good reason for that too. We're not getting enough sleep. Half of us are sleep-deprived because we have to get up every ninety minutes to pee. It's a rare night when I can get four or five hours uninterrupted sleep. We begin our lives as babies hoping to sleep through the night, and end them as cranky old men, hoping to sleep through the night.

193

I enjoyed staying with Audrey, even had fun with her ersatz California missions interior decorating. However, getting chased down the freeway, hob-nobbing with dead guys on dark streets, nearly getting caught committing burglary and being daunted by an escalating sense of doom, had an effect. It was doing bad things to an already lousy sleep pattern. I was having disturbing dreams.

One night I had a couple of shots before bed. Some time later, I escaped from a dream about being chased and shot at by gargoyles. For a second or two of disorientation, my mind transitioned from the dream world to the bed. I still felt the fear. Then, I felt the urge to urinate.

I was used to her guestroom and could navigate to the hall bathroom in the dark. (Neither one of us liked lights on after bedtime.) I was a bit surprised to open the guest bedroom door and find some light in the hall. It was filtering up from the first floor, dim, but light. I figured that since this was my third or fourth trek, it must be at least three o'clock in the morning. The need to urinate subsided. I heard a creaking from below, as if someone were opening and closing cabinet doors.

I knew that Audrey slept like a rock and little sounds from downstairs would not wake her. If I tried to rouse her I'd have to shake her, then she'd likely make a loud noise that could be heard from downstairs. It might scare off whoever our visitor was and I'd never know who it had been. Curiosity overcame kidneys and common sense. I crept toward the stairway, damning myself for not sleeping with a shotgun at hand. I recalled there was an Indian walking stick displayed in the archway near the foot of the stairs. Not a shotgun——but . . .

A CASE OF PEANUT BRITTLE

By the time I was down the stairs it was clear that the noises and the light were coming from the kitchen. I eased the five-foot, ironwood, walking stick from its display constraints and crept toward the kitchen light.

At the center island, back to me and nearly silhouetted by the light from the hood over the range, was a caped and hooded figure. The cape was a thick, dark material that touched the floor. The hood was also a dark color, but different. I heard low rhythmic chanting, but could not make out the words. On the counter I saw starkly outlined by the low angle light, oleander branches with a few leaves and flowers. There was another kind of plant that I would bet money was lantana. I raised the stick to what I thought was a threatening position and pitched my voice to a deep, threatening tone.

"Who the hell are you, and what are you doing here!" I demanded.

My quarry turned and I jumped back. The disfigured face was mottled and dark green, the eye-sockets black with the whites of the eyes seeming to glow from their depths. The sight froze me to the floor. I felt a dream-like paralysis. I took a psychological inventory to see if I were awake.

The specter took a half step towards me and from it came a cackling laughter. It approached steadily and I prepared to swing that ironwood stick. Finally the cackling stopped, replaced by the sopranasal "heh heh heh" that was all Audrey.

"Do you know how ridiculous you look? Standing there in your skivvies, holding that stick in the air like a light saber?"

I gathered my wits, still feeling vulnerable to illusions. "You scared the hell out of me," I complained, breathing again. "What did you do to your face?"

"Oh, . . . night cream," said the hideous specter. "Wrinkles."

"You look like the wicked witch of the west," I said, taking a desperate gasp of air after having not breathed for a while.

"How gallant you are." She made a show of examining my bare legs. "Jesus, Dan, get some sun: ride a bike."

"I thought you were some kind of evil monk. What's with the hood?"

"I'm embarrassed, but I have to admit, Brad's old robe comforts me, you know, his smell, his presence. No hood, a towel. It's comforting too."

I didn't want to know where the towel had been. "What the hell are you doing down here?"

As I approached, native walking stick, boxer shorts, pale legs and all, I saw that she had been grinding up leaves and flowers with a porcelain mortar and pestle. Her hideous face was lit from the side and she had a manic look in her eyes. I reasoned that it must be the lighting and the night cream and . . . it was still scary looking. I hoped she was not sliding into a dark role from which she wouldn't be able to escape.

She looked at the workspace and at me and said in a chilling monotone. "Silly man. Assemblyman Reilly was only the first one. I'm just getting started. I'm going to take out the whole goddamned homeowners association."

She sounded serious.

"Don't play too hard, Audrey," I said. "You didn't kill anyone."

A CASE OF PEANUT BRITTLE

"Well, everyone seems to think I did, so, why not? I don't like most of them anyway. Don't get in my way, Dan, or I'll invite you to tea, Oleander au Lait, Lantana Latté."

I found the switch to the track lighting. We needed fewer shadows. I didn't like the way she looked. I didn't like the way she was acting. "Christ, Audrey," I complained. "You look like the 'Portrait Of Dorian Gray.' Can't you wipe that stuff away and save it for Halloween?"

"It disappears when the sun rises," she cackled.

I took little comfort that she was having fun scaring me. I knew that she could run with an all-consuming enthusiasm over a role and leave our world behind her. "So, what's all this?" I prodded, gesturing at the paraphernalia on the work surface.

"I'm making poison," she said. "It worked before."

"Goddammit," I shouted, "I'm serious."

She shouted back at me with a frightening vehemence. "So am I, Brother Dan! I'm making poison!" She picked up the knife, a hefty carving knife probably used for cutting the branches. She gestured with it as she spoke. The gestures were wild and did nothing to put me at ease. "What else do you think this is? I have the oleander; I have the lantana. I've made herb teas, dried and ground my own seasonings, and read how to make poultices. So, I have the expertise, too. I am making a lethal batch of poison. I don't need the peanut brittle."

"Oh, This is great stuff for the prosecution, Audrey," I shouted back. "Why don't you volunteer it?"

"I have this knife, too, Dan. That doesn't mean I'm going to kill you with it. Poisons don't kill people. People kill people."

197

"Oh, God protect us from bumper-stickers!"

"There are no problems, only solutions." She had no mercy.

"Enough, all right?"

"Lighten up, it's always darkest before the dawn."

"The light at the end of the tunnel is an oncoming freight," I fired back.

"Every cloud has a silver lining."

"Inside every silver lining is a dark cloud."

"All is according to Divine plan."

"You're born. Shit happens. You die."

"If you keep doing the same things, you get the same results."

Not only was she having too much fun, she was winning. "I'm leaving," I snapped, genuinely annoyed. "I need to go to the bathroom. That was plan A in the first place." I turned my back and replaced the walking stick."

"The longest journey begins with a single step."

Still walking away, back to her, I raised my right hand and lowered four of its fingers.

"Dan, you know I did not kill Reilly, right?"

I stopped. "Right."

"And I told you I've tried all kinds of commercial stuff for these gophers, right?"

"Yes," I said, turning around.

"Well is it too late at night for you to add one and one and come up with something approaching two?"

After an awkward and somewhat embarrassing silence, I capitulated. I smiled an apology at her. "I'm the sarcastic one, Audrey. You're infringing on my turf."

"I couldn't sleep," she explained. "I'm worried, really worried. To take my mind off it I started thinking about the stupid gophers and I thought if that stuff is so lethal, maybe it would work in the garden."

"Of course, Sis. I'm sorry. But, damn, what with the cape and the death mask and the chanting . . . what the hell was the chanting?"

"Oh, I guess I got in the mood too, 'double double toil and trouble, fire burn and cauldron bubble; eye of newt and toe of frog, wool of bat and tongue of dog.'"

"I guess I'm not the first one scared off by Shakespeare. Good night, Sis. I'm going to try for another hour of sleep. Don't get carried away, okay?"

"Sure," she said and leaned forward to give me an air kiss, so as not to get her goop on my cheek.

I went back to my room, realizing how tired I was, perhaps how stupidly I had let myself be led astray. I kept wondering if my fear had not been a reaction to something sinister in Audrey that I had sensed but denied. She had always had the capacity to change personas to fit the situation. Had she slid into schizophrenia? Was she having psychotic episodes? The idea that her dark side was a whole other personality haunted me. Was I getting a sense of homicide from her? Each time I got one of these ideas, I put it aside and tried to sleep. That's when the idea would come back. It did not help that a vision of her darkened face with the manic glow in the eyes came at me like a kid's monster. At some point weariness won over worry-ness and I did sleep. I know that when I awoke later, my unshakable faith in my sister had been badly shaken.

CHAPTER FIFTEEN

There was no sign of a witch's cauldron, bats, black cats, evil spells or death dealing paraphernalia in the kitchen at Mission Santa Audrey the next morning. I did see some branches poking out from the lid of the trash container. The mortar and pestle were in the drainer on the counter. An old mayonnaise jar filled with a gravelly looking, earth colored glob of pasty stuff remained too as mute evidence of nighttime mischief.

Audrey, wearing a bright yellow pants-suit kind of thing, suggested we go out for breakfast. She did not feel like cooking anything after spending half the night preparing lethal toxins. I wasn't anxious for her cooking this morning either.

"Is that what killed Assemblyman Reilly?" I asked, pointing to the goop in the mayonnaise jar.

"That's what they say." She stared at it for a second and I would have given a hundred dollars to know what she was thinking. "I'm sure it was more refined, purified into a liquid . . . maybe a tincture."

"Tincture?"

"Alcohol solution."

"Damn, you do know your stuff."

"It's all in books, Dan. Books are everywhere. Anyone can read a book."

"Tincture. Is that what you're going to do with . . . " I gestured at the deadly slop with no taste for it.

"I wouldn't know how. You'd have to know a lot of laboratory stuff. Besides, I don't think the vermin will be as fussy as the assemblyman. I'll put it in their holes with something tasty and aromatic, bacon maybe or cheese, peanut butter should work." She grinned, overdoing it, and raised both eyebrows—"doesn't have to be brittle, you know."

I picked up the jar and held it in my hand. If all reports were right, I was holding death. Death from pretty flowers. There was a kind of bizarro poetry to that. Beauty and the Reaper.

"What time is it?" I asked.

"It's nearly ten. If we hold off, we can have lunch instead. You slept pretty late."

"I didn't get any sleep."

"I'd know if I snored."

"I'll record you next time."

"Aw, stuff it," I observed. "Let me throw on a shirt and some shoes. I'll treat you to brunch."

Once in her car in the garage, I activated the door opener and found the driveway blocked by a sheriff's patrol car. There was no one in it. In a moment, two uniformed deputies appeared from the direction of the front door, guns drawn.

"Sheriff's Department," the closer one called out. "Turn the engine off and dismount the vehicle."

I didn't remembered "mounting" the vehicle in the first place. Who but the law-and-order-ites ever say "vehicle?" Don't any law enforcement people have cars or trucks? I expressed none of these thoughts. Loaded guns trump wisecracks. Close on the heels of the two deputies was Detective Morrison. He strode up to us, one hand in his pocket, the other idly brushing at something on his jacket. He made it clear that he did not consider us a threat. It was insulting.

"Mrs. Davis," he said to Audrey, "I'm afraid I have to ask you to accompany these two deputies, please."

"Why," I said, my big mouth back in gear. "She's not under arrest. She's on bail. I don't think you can do this."

"Mr. Kelly," said the nice detective, "forget about the bail. We've traced that fanny pack to your sister. That involves her in breaking and entering. She's already left the jurisdiction once." He turned his attention to Audrey. "Ma'am, if you'd follow the deputies, please. I apologize for the handcuffs but we have to follow procedure."

"Oh, now wait a minute," I said, stepping forward.

Detective Morrison leveled one of his lethal smiles at me. The man could stop a truck with that smile . . . eyes like spear points: teeth like a row of beachfront condos. "I might not be able to make it stick, Mr. Kelly, but I'd have no trouble with enough probable cause to detain you for more questioning on the break-in at the Homeowners Association office. Would you like to come with us and spend several hours in one of our interview rooms?"

I actually took a step back. "It wouldn't be my first choice, no."

The detective nodded toward the deputies who had holstered their weapons. He observed as they patted Audrey down and escorted her to the patrol car where they cuffed her (loosely, I noticed) and put her in the back seat. She had been taken by surprise and was passive, frightened. I've never known her to give up and give in so quickly. She looked down with a blank expression. She had gone somewhere inside herself. Perhaps it hurt less. It frightened me.

I stared into that patrol car as if I could somehow help her just by wanting to badly enough. I had the feeling she was withdrawing further and further. My misgivings from the night before came back to haunt me. She had seemed to know exactly what she was doing, mixing that poison. Was I watching a tired, eccentric, woman undergoing a psychotic break, perhaps not her first? Nothing funny here. No amount of half-jest, all-earnest teasing was going to help.

"Mr. Kelly?"

"Yeah?"

"We are executing a search warrant of this house. Before they leave, the deputies will assist me."

"Search warrant based on what, for Chris'sake?"

"Evidence linking Mrs. Davis to the breaking and entering. We are looking specifically for copies of association records that may have been made during the course of that criminal trespass."

My heart sank. The mayonnaise jar was in plain sight. If that made them curious, they would see the branches, the mortar and pestle. Shit!

"Did anyone call her attorney, Ladish?"

"Not our job. You can tell him that an assistant district attorney will be seeking an indictment in department thirty-four. He'll argue for remand because of her behavior while on bail. Your guy will argue that it's no big deal. He'll lose. She's going in, Mr. Kelly, put it in the bank."

"What time is all this crap?"

"The appropriate courts sit from eight to ten and from one to four. Just ask."

"And what if we lose?"

"Then Mrs. Davis will be held in jail until her trial, probably a month or two, two or three months. Something like that. In the meanwhile, we will continue to investigate the criminal trespass at the association offices and, of course, the murder with which she is already charged."

As we age and mature we learn more and more to control our behavior. I controlled my behavior by standing there, hands in pockets as one of the deputies drove off with Audrey slumped in the back seat. Another car drew up, an unmarked car. From it emerged two more men in plainclothes. While one of them watched me controlling my behavior, the others went into the house. In about two hours, they came out carrying the poison and paraphernalia, two additional fanny packs, some paperwork and Audrey's computer.

I watched them load the second car and leave. I had to go back in the house. I had to call Ladish. I had to stop my body from shaking.

Ladish's first legal opinion was, "well that sucks." When I continued the tale to include taking her poisonous nighttime paraphernalia and its final product, he expanded his legal analysis to, "Now, that really sucks."

"Yeah, right, no gravity, everything sucks. What are you going to do? You're the goddamned lawyer. Get down there and get her back out."

"No, I don't think so," he said.

"Yeah, lawyers suck too you son-of-a-bitch. What the hell do you think we're paying you for?"

"For being a little smarter about criminal procedure than raving old men who can't take two breaths in a row without putting their foot in their mouth."

"You want maybe I should come down there and we can chat, Spunky?"

"No, I want maybe you should shut up for two minutes so I can tell you how the world works. Think you can do that, Chief?"

"Shoot."

"You said department thirty four. That's judge Greer and it's all over. He's a misogynist and a fanatic go-by-the-book bean counter with a button-down brain. His trial experience is all prosecution. I've got to get it held over till tomorrow, Judge Jameson will have the duty and I used to clerk for him. If there's a reasonable argument, I'll have a slight edge. Are you starting to listen?"

"Yeah, yeah, yeah."

"Now, how was she when she was picked up? She still trying to get them to open a Starbucks down there?"

"No," I said, "that's what's worrying me most. It's like someone blew out her pilot light. She was subdued and passive?"

"She wasn't playing word games with the cops?"

"No. I don't think she will, not this time."

"I'm going down there right now," he said. "I'll see her and I'll move for a twenty-four-hour delay because she's in shock and not competent to enter a plea."

"Oh, she's competent," I complained.

"I thought you were listening. Try again, you might develop a talent for it."

"Gotcha."

"She's in shock and needs some time and rest. I'll call her family doctor."

"Oh, yeah, well. Hey, is there anything I can do? Can I come down there?"

"I know you'll do what you want but I really advise against you going to the jail. When you two get together stupid things get said and bad things happen."

"I've got to do something, dammit."

"Get hold of one of her best lady friends and ask her to pick out an appropriate outfit for Audrey to wear in court tomorrow. No cleavage, no pantsuits, no gay colors. Something a mature, sane, adult woman would wear to court. Got me?"

"Gotcha. I'm not sure about best girlfriends. We've been kind of treating everyone else like suspects."

"God, when this is all over you two should open a charm school!"

"Well, maybe not."

"Find someone to help with appropriate clothing. I don't trust you. I'll keep you posted on our progress. Don't worry, Dan. I'm good and she's innocent, right?"

He hung up without waiting for an answer. I don't think he wanted to hear it.

Perhaps Audrey's only friend was Gloria, but I remembered the pea-green dress with all the giant tropical flowers. Gloria would not make an appropriate wardrobe mistress. The victim's widow was certainly out. I won't forget how she strangled that poor little lacey-doily thing. I had mixed feelings when I made the call to Connie. Connie agreed immediately and told me she'd be over right away. I could only hope that she would have a good sense of appropriate courtroom wear. I was also hoping that whatever she wore to come and help me would be thoroughly inappropriate.

I was not to be disappointed. Shortly before noon, the infernal doorbell philharmonic insisted on inflicting its Lawrence Welkian version of Ode To Joy. It sounded like

Tea For Two. Everything Welk did sounded like Tea For Two. I rushed to the front door out of a passion to stop the music.

In the door frame, hip swung out like Miss October, wearing a tied-up top and thin sweatpants that clung desperately, Connie stood, smiling the kind of come-hither smile that inspires self-abuse in young men. She held a large, insulated shaker and two martini glasses.

"High, neighbor," she said, as though it were an innocent greeting. "Let's play with your sisters clothes."

"Come on in, Connie," I said. "I really appreciate this."

"There's a price," she said sashaying past me. I followed her into the bar of the Mission Santa Audrey. I could not detect a panty line on her sweats and, believe me, I looked for one.

"There's always a price," I said, being cool and sophisticated without having any clear idea where she was going.

She poured two martinis and handed one to me. "It could be a question of age," she said, looking me up and down like she was a judge at a dog show.

"I'm sure I'm old enough," I said.

"I'm wondering if you're young enough," she teased. Her eyes bored into mine. I figured the drink she had poured was not the first one she had had today.

Male pride answered before male-brain engaged, "After all, I'm only in my si. . . fi-ifties."

She stepped up and put her body against mine in a smooth practiced motion. Without even asking male-brain for permission, male arms slid around her body, leaning further towards her to put my glass on the bar top. I discovered quickly that there was a perfectly logical reason I had not seen a panty line.

Her mouth was parted slightly. There was a thing about a woman's mouth and lips that I thought I had forgotten, something about the texture of the lips and the invitation of the slightly open mouth. I brought my head down and kissed her, modestly enough at first, but apparently I had thrown her main power switch and with only the first pitch thrown, we were headed rapidly towards the seventh inning stretch. It's a good thing this had not been rehearsed at all. If I had thought about this possibility, I might have worried about the old machinery being properly tuned. This way, I was delighted to see, the old come se llama had no trouble rising to the occasion.

As unexpected as that was, what happened next confuses me to this day. A part of my brain that I wish to see repressed started reacting. If they ever do a lobotomy on me, I want that part snipped first. I started goddamned thinking. My first effort at communicating was ... "Hey, you're a married woman."

"It's a California license," she almost moaned, "You're from out-of-state."

Maybe I just didn't want her to see my liver spots, I don't know. "No, no, this just ain't right," I heard myself say——and even worse——"We're not going to do this."

Now I felt old and a failure. My lower nature had never before failed in draining most of the blood from my brain and conscience. That had always enabled me to pursue the immediate object. Now, I was pushing away this absolutely world-class body that was practically squirming with enthusiasm and trying to catch my breath. She recovered first.

"Why you miserable old fuck."

I thought, oddly enough, of Taming Of The Shrew; Her voice was ever so soft, gentle, and mild, an excellent thing in woman. "No argument," I whispered sadly.

"You should thank your lucky stars you even got a chance you stupid old loser."

"Again, right you are."

"It would've been great."

"I'd like to think so."

"Goddamn."

"Amen."

She put her hands on my shoulders, most of her exasperation spent. She stared at me for a moment and then said . . . "Why? We were doing fine."

I shrugged. She got her drink and handed mine to me. How the hell do I explain my own insane behavior? "It's just that . . . this is about Audrey," I tried. "I just don't feel right riding the range while she's locked up. I mean there's Clyde to think about too . . . well, maybe not. Maybe I'm a damned fool and this afternoon might not be enough. Then I'd be another of your conquests. If it helps, maybe I'm just not up to it and I don't want you to know."

"Oh, you're up to it, all right," she said. "I had the evidence in hand."

"You're embarrassing me," I complained, swelling with a kind of stupid pride.

"You are an old fool," she said and clinked glasses with me. "And don't start feeling smug either. You get one chance only and you threw yours away you stupid, stupid man." She turned and took a bare two steps closer to her shaker for a refill, but she put enough in those two steps to make me cry for a week. She knew it too.

"Audrey? Wardrobe?" I said, reminding her.

209

"We finish our drinks first," Connie said, back to her casual, mocking self. I knew that we would continue to flirt but a good part of the fun was gone.

"So just how old a fart are you, you old fart?" she asked.

"I'm sixty-four," I said.

She laughed. "Jesus, I've been accused of cradle-robbing, now I'm practically guilty of grave-robbing."

"Oh, thanks a lot." I sensed an unguarded moment in her post coitus-interruptus stupor. "Those vacations the four of you took, houseboats, cabins in the woods, were they wife-swapping parties, then, or what?"

She stopped laughing; suddenly I felt a slightly inebriated advantage. "I mean it seems that everyone in your crowd is boinking everyone else. Was there any guy-guy or gal-gal stuff going on? That would be another level to aspire to I guess. Did y'all go for 'group rates'?"

She was doing well at suppressing her anger. It only showed in the redness of her cheeks and the clenching of her fingers. "No, there was no girl-girl, guy-guy stuff," she said. "As to the rest, there was no wife swapping either. There was no husband swapping. Not overtly at any rate. We were discrete and blind by consensus. It worked out without being discussed."

"The private entrance to Sean's end of the house got me to thinking," I said.

"With Sean living at his end of the house, she pretty much has her own entrance too," Connie said defensively. "That coin has two faces."

To my complete surprise, by the time we were done with that shaker, we were at ease with each other again. We went to Audrey's bedroom and I tried to be of some help but it was clear I was barely qualified to hold things on hangars so Connie could appraise combinations of style and color. Finally, I was dismissed to re-fill the shaker with more martini. I explained that we had no vermouth . . . "Well goddammit then, Gin-tonic, Tom-Collins, Bloody-Mary, Seventy-seven, I don't care. After the first shaker or so it doesn't make a damn. Just don't make anything too sweet. Clyde thought it would be funny to fill my shaker with bourbon and Dr. Pepper one night. I tried to break the damned thing over his head but it was a stainless steel shaker. His head broke. We had to call an ambulance. Stainless steel shaker."

"Jesus, Connie."

"So just make something with what you got but don't get cute or creative on me. This shaker is stainless steel too."

"Good, no pressure. I like that. I know we have gin and tonic water."

"Anything you want," she said, smiling sweetly.

In the end, she picked out two outfits: one a modest tweed business suit with a colorful scarf and half-heel shoes: the other a skirt and sweater combination with flat shoes. She also picked out undergarments, stockings, cosmetics, toiletries, brushes . . . a dozen or more things that I never would have thought of. She found just the right sized overnight bag for it all. Ladish had been right. It required a woman's expertise.

I called Ladish, whose secretary informed me that the hearing would be the next day. Connie, two and a half sheets to the wind as she was, had the presence of mind to call a messenger service she knew to come get the stuff and deliver it to Audrey at the jail. I walked her to the door when her kindly office had been completely satisfied. I thanked her.

211

"Audrey and I are not enemies at all, Dan. Seriously, in the middle of our biggest fight, she would do this for me in a second."

"It was still great of you and I realize what a hopeless failure my effort would have been." I reached out my hand to shake hers.

She drew me in with both hands, body pressed me again and gave me a memory that no senility would ever extinguish. "I want you to remember what you passed up, Danny boy," she whispered, then stood back. "Ta ta," she said with a big friendly smile, then, slowly, maddeningly rotated away.

CHAPTER SIXTEEN

Still feeling the martinis, I started a pot of coffee before going anywhere. I hadn't bothered Brad the Impaler for a while. Maybe we could have a family lunch. I had time for a shower before the coffee would be ready. As soon as I had adjusted for a hot stream of water and lathered down thoroughly, the telephone began rang. In the last week I had forgotten there was any such thing as an unimportant telephone call, so I risked dripping soapy water on Audrey's carpets to catch the bedside unit in time.

"Davis Residence," I said, not at all sounding like a soaped-down, naked old guy in the guest bedroom of his sister's house. I noticed that the window curtains were open and appreciated that I was on the second floor. The angles at least partially preserved the virtue of my nakedidity.

I recognized Jennifer's voice. She was a pleasant, pretty, twenty-year-old who worked for my attorney in Port Angeles. "Ron Downey for Mr. Kelly," she said. "Can you hold?"

"Sure enough, Jenny," I said. Just like a lawyer to call then put me on hold.

Ron greeted me sounding as though he had a chip on his shoulder. "You must be bored down there in LaLa land thinking I have nothing to do but run fool's errands for your amusement," he said. "How's your sister doing?"

"Not well at the moment. What fool's errands? I asked one little favor."

213

"Yes, right, Reinco. That fool's errand. It's a limited partnership. It's an acronym for Real-Estate-Investment-Company. We can all laugh now."

"I don't get it. Who are the partners? What's the joke?"

"The joke is that your goddamned brother-in-law is the senior partner. He and several of his neighbors, same zip code anyway, formed it two years ago. You want the other names?"

"Uh huh," I grunted affirmatively.

"Brad and Audrey Davis, Clyde and Consuelo Miller, Santiago and Marianna Omega, John and Jeannette Bisel and Robert Hornish."

"The dirty, rotten, lying, scheming sons o' bitches!" I mused. "Can you send all that to me, anything else you have? It wasn't a fool's errand. I did ask my family and several of the partners and they all denied any knowledge."

"Even your sister?"

"Even Audrey."

"As far as I can tell, the partnership has not committed significant capital." Ron always sounded like he was making a presentation. I used to imagine him trying to score with a woman, In conclusion, we seek consensus that a physical joining would be in our mutual self-interest. The real Ron Downey continued, "Usually these little friends-and-neighbors companies form for a particular purpose. They may be waiting for their opportunity. They think they have some economic bonanza. They're standing by for their opportunity."

"Is there more you can find out?"

A CASE OF PEANUT BRITTLE

"I can try. This is beyond a favor, though, Dan. Any more investigation means hiring people and billing man-hours . . . you know the drill."

"Oh, the hell with it, then," I barked. "Audrey's too active for her own good anyway. Spending the rest of her life in prison might be just the thing to slow her down. I say let's call it a day."

"Sorry, Dan. Take it easy. I didn't know how important it was."

"Listen, you know my finances better than I do. Everything's on the table, IRAs, savings, home equity . . . let me know once in a while how much I got left. I pretty much know the who now, I need to find out the what and the why."

"This is on the top burner until you say it's not, Dan. Call the cell. If I'm in court it's forwarded to Jennifer and I'll get back to you. I check in with her every hour or so." He gave me his cell number. We had never needed that kind of quick communication before.

Miserable, dirty, rotten, lying sonsobitches! Why would every single one of them lie about Reinco? Even Audrey? I paced the floor, giving Audrey's carpet an unwanted shampoo by foot. I might have started a whole new California trend . . . wiggletoe carpet cleaning: a healthy foot massage, a custom cleaning for the boudoir carpet, an intimate "toes on" approach to a cleaner house. The commercial would show young women in slow motion, wearing flowing negligées and gliding across cloud-pure carpets to their princess beds.

No more martinis for me.

After a very long shower, I considered relaying the news about Reinco to Ladish. I decided against it. He would discuss it with Audrey, no doubt, and I wanted to be there to read her face when I asked her about it. Reinco was all over this mess and she was a partner. I just couldn't top that. The feeling that I was living out some damned conspiracy movie was getting strong again. There'd already been a murder by poison, a car chase, a burglary, bodies discovered in the night, poison making with a witch's chant. What would be next, the big explosion in a downtown warehouse where one package of dynamite blows and we get seven booms seen from seven angles, at least three in slow motion? The one thing I felt sure of is that I didn't kill the son-of-a-bitch assemblyman; I was not in town.

I felt so beat up and confused that I did not see Audrey in jail that day. I waited for the following day, the day of the hearing. Ladish gave me directions and said that he had arranged for a visit in the courthouse for after the hearing, just in case she did not walk free. Because of the lawyer-requested Doctor's visit that morning, the hearing had been scheduled for the afternoon session. "Nominally," Ladish said, "It's scheduled for two-thirty but the times for these things are more ceremonial than real. Be there at two and don't let yourself start getting nervous till after three. I'll be there and I'll find you. Promise."

I was nice and said nothing. Lawyers' promises are mostly ceremonial too.

The next day, I decided to drive in early. Perhaps I could find a parking place near the courthouse where I wouldn't need a second mortgage to pay the fee. I found one several blocks from the architectural felonies that housed the jail and courthouse, and had time for a leisurely lunch. I had a very satisfying ten-dollar steak sandwich for sixteen dollars. Another six-fifty each for two beers, a tip, and I escaped for under fifty bucks. I admired their courage for conducting that kind of business so close to the law enforcement agencies.

Department thirty seven on the second floor was not hard to find. The departments, which are what the natives call the courtrooms, were arranged in a long row along one side of a hallway, or gallery, wide enough for arena football. Along the window wall, you could look out and down to the plaza where countless citizens strode leisurely, confident they would sleep in their own beds come evening. Along this window wall were rows of strait-backed, dark, wood benches. Witnesses and parties waited on these benches. The lawyers strode these corridors, seeking, trolling, hunting, and commiserating with their clients. It was clear by the dress and demeanor of the clients, that very few were there due to subtle contract disputes among major players. There were the faded clothing, emaciated young people who seemed to have left their glasses and right-size clothing elsewhere and had not seen much sun, and the nearly obese in pitifully new bargain-basement clothing who had wet eyes and looked put-upon and angry.

Courtrooms evolved from the days of empire when the state held assizes, head of state or representative being on a central throne and parties arguing before him. The throng stood a short distance from the parties observing wisdom and justice or just enjoying the show.

The court was an arraignment court. The defendant was officially accused and must enter a plea. A steady parade of cases passed. The defendants looked more like the unfortunate unemployed than anything else. There was the occasional thuggy looking jerk whose path I would not want to cross, but, in general, skinny, stupid, shuffling young men with no apparent resources, financial or social. They participated in a ritual dance. The case is called. The defendant and his lawyer appear. The case is read. The plea is entered. Bail is discussed. The judge decides. The next case is called; all this occurred in an almost monotone, excepting only the few righteous "not no way guilty!!" kinds of pleas. The judge, on the other hand, sounded like he was reading Cliff Notes for a chemistry final.

After forty-five minutes, they called our case. Audrey had decided on the tweed suit. She looked small and her hair was combed back, not tight like a schoolmarm, but off her shoulders and face. She looked mostly at the floor but when she was asked a question she answered in a clear voice.

It was Ladish's position that there was insufficient cause to even indict, and that's what he attacked, the indictment. The prosecutor, a baby-faced kid with freckles, talked a lot about fanny packs and exactly how the guilty fanny pack had been lodged in the office door. I couldn't get over it that the might and power of the sovereign state of California was getting so friggin' upset about the location of a fanny pack. Hell, in some parts of that state, fanny packs or ski sweaters are state flags. The prosecutors also talked a lot about the video from the Shop'n'Go, "clearly showing that the defendant was wearing a fanny pack." If that was probable cause for arrest the jails would be flooded and the evidence rooms would have so much vinyl and Velcro they'd be toxic sites.

All the lawyers pronounced "defendant" accenting the "a" like "defend-ant." It's a lawyer thing.

Ladish challenged that there was not enough evidence for a legitimate bill of indictment. Ladish noted that there was no photographic evidence about the all-important fannypack and just how it was stuck near—not in—the door. He also questioned why on earth a member of the association, a member of the board of the association, would risk burglarizing the office when the charter clearly gave her the right to see anything in the office at any time. The state's motivation is a barely concealed tool to revoke bail on another matter, he argued passionately, an attempt to overcome the requirements of probable cause to justify an otherwise unwarrantable search on Mrs. Davis' property. It was not even alleged that anything was taken. There is no clear evidence of a crime, no prima facie case, therefore the indictment should fail and all proceeds of the search should be suppressed in any other legal action against her as fruit of the poisoned tree.

The District Attorney, the Doogie Howser-looking kid with his Dad's briefcase, looked like something unexpected had hit him. He scratched his head. The judge scratched his head. Hell, I scratched my head. I wasn't able to follow all that either. I had no idea what card the pea was under.

When all was said and done, the good judge dismissed the complaint and ordered Audrey returned to her legal status quo ante, which is Latin for a do-over. While our shift was going off and the next one coming on, Ladish caught my eye and indicated I should wait in the hall. At no time had Audrey looked at me. She had not so much as looked around to see if I was there.

I waited in the hall and was gifted with a quick few seconds of Ladish. "We have to sign her out and get her personal things," he said. "Stay here, we'll be back in ten minutes. Promise."

He was nearly true to his word. In less than forty-five minutes he returned with Audrey in hand. She looked

219

distracted, said a neutral hello to me and excused herself to the ladies room. With bird-like suddenness and intensity, Ladish explained: "We were very lucky. I was able to convince the judge that the burglary charge was premature. It might easily have gone the other way. Our bonus is that since the burglary charge had no legs, revoking bail on the murder charge became irrelevant. And, since, the charge was bogus, they had no PC to search the house. Now, it would be a real uphill climb to get any of that poison stuff admissible at the murder trial."

"Uphill?"

"They might try to argue inevitable discovery but they're too late. The argument wouldn't obtain anywhere. What the hell was she mixing poison for?"

"Gophers."

"Christ! God protect me from clients who are non compos mentis."

"I understand completely," I said, hiding a screaming desire to get away from any place where anyone knew any Latin.

"What about the doctor?" I asked. "Why wasn't he there?"

"He was just a delaying tactic to get this judge. There's nothing wrong with your sister aside from the fact that she's unpredictable, crazy as hell and maybe a killer."

The day was getting longer and hotter and the hall seemed smaller and more crowded. "Are you paraphrasing what the doctor said or is this you being cute?"

Ladish looked away with some impatience, then back. I didn't blame him. He was still all gooshy from winning a hard point in court. "The doctor said that Audrey was clearly feeling stress, that her blood pressure was elevated, that she was alert, in control and thoroughly competent to handle her legal affairs."

"I'm glad to hear that," I said.

"The doctor was a delaying technique, Dan. I didn't much care what he said."

"That was for me, Perry Mason," I said. "I needed to hear that."

Ladish excused himself from the fun of chatting any further, pleading the demands of other business. We shook hands and I thanked him. My mind was already on Audrey, never having left that worry about her condition. I was not prepared to look up and see her, the jacket of her suit unbuttoned, hair down about her shoulders and walking her jaunty walk. A big smile lit up her newly made-up face and she ran to me and hugged me hello.

We family-talked back and forth for a few moments while we walked to the elevators. Congratulations. Missed you. Love you. Where'd the lawyer go? We were lucky. I was worried . . . blah, blah, blah.

Outside the building, she paused at the top of the steps and took a deep breath of air. It seemed to include the great blue sky, the sunshine, the warmth, and the bright-clean cityscape. When she exhaled again it was as though she was blessing all she could see. She sighed, a long, luxurious sigh, the kind a cat would do if it knew how after one of those exuberantly elegant cat-stretches. "It was only one night, Dan, but oh, my God, how sweet is freedom."

I took her elbow and directed her towards Fourth. "This way," I said, "It's about three blocks to the parking garage. You want to go straight home?"

"God, no," she complained. "I turned down most of the food in that horrible place. I want a quiet restaurant, something by the sea, something with an ocean view; I want the sun's warmth on my face and the hypnotic sound of surf giving me peace. I think I could eat an entire animal just now if I weren't mostly vegetarian. Oh, I know, there's a place in Coronado where they have a wonderful seafood bisque."

"And a view of the ocean? Sounds great. I already ate but I could sip some wine and watch the surf."

"What surf?"

". . . Sound of surf giving you peace?"

"Not at Café Flaubert. What gave you that idea?"

"'Nice restaurant by the ocean with an ocean view', that's what you said."

"We'll go over the bridge to Coronado. Honestly, Dan, I don't know what gets into your head sometimes."

"You . . . I . . . I don't know. Just give me directions."

"At least if they did have a Starbucks at the jail I could have had a latté and biscotti for breakfast instead of some overly-salted mush stored on, cooked on, served on, and tasting like—aluminum."

Back to the Starbucks routine. Good. That freed me to worry less about little sister and release the anger and suspicion about Reinco. "Your mood seems to have bounced back. I was worried about you, dammit."

We were in the parking garage and at the car now. The light wasn't that good, I couldn't read her face as she got in the passenger's seat. I guess the semi-darkness was good for confession.

"I couldn't tell you, Dan. I had no time to think. When those deputies took me and I heard them talk about searching the house, I wanted everyone to see me as a good, vulnerable, innocent person in trouble, not a perky, joke-making fool. I wanted you to worry about me. I wanted people to see you worried about me. I don't have a lot of defenses, having some control over how others see me is one of them. Even that crude matron with the ugly shoes and food-stained uniform treated me a little better."

I had never appreciated how much of her role-playing was deliberate. Admiration and pride swelled in me. "You manipulative bitch."

We drove up the graceful arc of the Coronado Bridge connecting San Diego and Coronado. Coronado was the broad terminus of a long narrow peninsula that defined the western limits of San Diego bay. The North Island Naval Air station occupied half the landmass, the rest being a civilian community that was as close to officers' country as a civilian community can get. Rumor was that a stern cadre of admiral's wives and those captain's wives who wished to become admiral's wives ruled it. There was an 'enlisted' neighborhood of low-rent housing. The main street that also bisected the 'island' (so called because once it was an island) contained many upscale shops and souvenir dens. Just past the foot of the bridge, in all its regal splendor, sits the world famous Hotel Del Coronado, a wonderful turn-of-the-century white building with its famous red-tiled roof and numerous dormers and cupolas. Just past that, we turned right one block off the main street to a pink, stuccoed, cottage. It looked like it had always been a bistro or boutique, large windows on three sides of an end room and an ornate carved door. In another clime its small size and high-peaked roof would have made a great Christmas card. There was table service in a small, walled in patio. Huge

223

red and white Cinzano umbrellas jutting from the centers of the cedar tables shaded the clientele.

Perfect. We ordered a bottle of Pinot Gris. I think Audrey just liked saying that; and a bowl of the bisque for her, a shrimp torte for me. I poured and let her enjoy her first sip of the wine, then gently eased into the subject.

"Why have you been lying through your goddammed teeth about Reinco?"

Her face was a study in expressions but I discounted all of them but the first: shock. That was probably genuine.

"I haven't lied to you, Dan. I haven't told you anything about Reinco. How could that be a lie?"

She didn't seem terribly upset. I had to be very careful. She was thoroughly capable of fooling me. "You're evading, Audrey. You know all about Reinco and you pretended that you didn't."

She lifted the glass to sip but lowered it again. She leaned forward slightly. Aha! I was about to get the "sincere" gambit.

"I don't know anything about Reinco. Are you on drugs? Seriously."

"No, I'm not on drugs. What's your story? It's now or never, Audrey, I'm fed-up."

"Why don't you tell me what it is that I'm supposed to know that I'm lying to you about?"

I leaned forward too. Sincere is good. I was sincerely pissed. Our faces were close and our lowered voices almost hissed through our teeth. "What you're supposed to know, Miss Innocent, is that you, your beloved impaler husband, the Millers, the Omegas, and several others of your neighborhood glee club are full partners in Real Estate Investment Company. Reinco.

224

Now, as Granddad used to say, 'put that in your pipe and smoke it'."

I leaned back in victory and treated myself to the Pinot Gris. Shortly, I felt cheated. I was reading her face for meaningful reactions but it was completely blank. She stared at me for several seconds, slowly leaned back in her chair and studied the sleeve of her suit.

"Well, I can certainly see why you're mad at me," she said in a calm voice with no emotional clues. "I'm sorry."

"Are you sorry enough to tell me for the sake of all that's holy what the damned truth is? For once?"

A smile crossed her face, but there was neither joy nor humor in it. "I don't know what the truth is," she said. "You have to believe me. If you tell me that I was made a partner in Reinco, I believe you. That doesn't mean I knew anything about it. For years at one time or another, Brad has given me papers to sign. I've always signed them. Taxes, property stuff, wills. For all I know I own another house, a movie theatre, a water park. I don't know."

"Jesus, Audrey."

"I know how stupid and naïve that makes me sound, but there you are. I trusted Brad to do all those business and paperwork things that bore and confuse me. It worked out fine, at least I thought it did. Now, I've lost my home and everyone, including you, thinks I am crazy enough to have killed someone over a stupid skateboard park."

She looked about to cry and reached down for her purse. I produced a handkerchief but she waved it away. "No, Dan. You don't get to see me cry today. You don't get the satisfaction. You think I'm a killer. You think I manipulate everyone." She grabbed her purse and strode

225

off, strait back, proud, righteous. "I'll be back when I've tended to the wound you have inflicted this day," she said. I think she meant it, at the same time, I knew that she had phrased it as an exit line.

I wondered how the hell I had become the bad guy for finding out the truth. Her explanation was credible. I knew from past conversations that at least a good deal of the business end of that marriage was conducted by Brad. If he wanted her signature but not her knowledge it would have been easy to pick his moment, some time when she was distracted by other, more entertaining things, then give her two or three documents to sign. She would have done it without even looking. For someone like Brad, neither witnesses nor notaries would have been a problem. I realized that it was more probable that Audrey was duped in a business matter, than that she had maintained such a lie to me for so long, or, certainly, that she had planned and executed a murder. How quickly I had assumed she was lying. The primary characteristic of faith is that logic is irrelevant to it. I had to examine the degree of faith I still had in my mercurial sister.

CHAPTER SEVENTEEN

Audrey perched on an ersatz Spanish colonial chair in the main room of Mission Santa Audrey.

"Okay," I said, pacing the room, "All your pals at Reinco have claimed ignorance of its existence or their relationship with it. It's a real-estate investment company . . . seems elementary that Brad and his buddies had some real estate investments in mind, and that they want to hide something about it."

"Gee, Dan," Audrey sarcasmed at me, "this'd be so much better if you had a Meerschaum pipe and a deerstalker hat. I guess I'm Dr. Watson, huh? Good. It's about time the doctor was a woman."

"I'm trying to put this together, Audrey. I'm not the one accused of murder here."

Through the great picture windows, the setting sun bathed the large room with a wash of crepuscular color. Two Tiffany bridge lamps scattered some of the light turning the eastern wall into stained-glass-like glory.

"Tea or Sherry," Audrey offered in a British accent.

"Tea, I guess," I answered, still thinking of investment conspiracies, cabals of mortgagees, evildoers twirling their moustaches at the Savings & Loan.

"With or without your seven per-cent solution of opium?" The accent lingered.

"Jesus, Audrey, can we just get some coffee or tea in here?"

"I'd ring my little silver bell for a domestic, but I've given the staff leave for the day." She rose, pretending to arrange the 'folds' of her voluminous skirts, and left. "I shall be back presently, Holmes," she declared. "I'm confident you'll have it properly sorted out bye and bye."

I didn't need Sherlock. I could have used Sam Spade or Philip Marlowe . . . Mike Hammer would have been refreshing. Give 'em hell, kick ass, and punish the bad guys. Break noses. Shoot people. That's the ticket. "Make my day, Punk," there you go - the American way.

No wonder we love the fantasy. I felt impotent in a hundred ways, trying to pluck truth from thin air with nothing but the precision of an intellect I just didn't possess. How depressing that my sister, truehearted wonder that she was, might go down in flames because of my incompetence.

I called Ron Downey's office and got the recorded message giving office hours. Rather than call his cell, I left a message asking him to hire a private investigator to come help us out. Trying to do this on our own was madness. I wondered if Monk was available.

Audrey returned with a tray holding cups, saucers and a teapot. She carried the tray and presented it in my direction, ritual like, as if for approval, before she placed it down on a split-cedar table that pretended to be primitive woodcraft and had probably set her back two thousand dollars at a trendy boutique.

"Thank you, Dr. Watson," I said, wanting to be nice.

"Skateboard Park," she said.
"Huh?"

"Maybe they wanted to buy that useless bit of land the kids were using as a skateboard park. That's real estate, right?"

I gave it some thought while she poured tea. The tea, it turned out, was some of that good-for-you, organic, herb tea whose strongest taste was hot water. I longed for some cheap, caffeine-laden, crappy tea-bag stuff that would satisfy. I guess they're all out of coffee-flavored herb tea.

"Skateboard Park Real estate. Right," I said to humor her. "Yeah, it's a link."

"Well what've you got?"

"We've got Connie and the assemblyman shtuping each other, giving two jealous spouses their motive. We've got Clyde and the widow doing the nasty, two more jealous spouses. We've got weird Eric slithering throughout the neighborhood, sniffing panties and stealing bric-a-brac. Crazy people don't usually grow steadily saner, you know. They usually get suddenly crazier. We've got Brad the Impaler trying to get you, and any financial claims you have, out of his life. What lawyerly thinking it is to kill a neighbor, frame your ex for it, use the defense expenses to bleed her dry, then throw her to the wolves. That kind of circumferential thinking would give Machiavelli a woody."

"'Circumferential?'" eyebrows raised in theatrical shock.

"Okay, I might've made that up . . . approaching the center of something by going around in a big circle first." I checked my teacup. There wasn't enough stuff in it to color the water much past a dish watery tint.

"Well, have you got any circumferential ideas of your own?" she asked. She took a proper, ladylike sip of the hot water and seemed pleased. Hers must have been

229

made from the dried leaves of the genus Smugiferous blatant. "What do you want to do next?"

"I've called for Ron, my lawyer in Washington, to send us an investigator. We should've done it first thing. Look, these guys know what to do, how to research things . . . y'know?"

"When will she get here?"

"She?"

"You wouldn't have noticed if I said 'he'. What's the matter with 'she?'"

"Nothing. Nothing. Nothing. Look, I want to see Biddy again."

"Why?"

"Something she said. She said that Sean was angry at 'them.'"

"Them?"

"Reinco. She said Sean was angry at Reinco and promised to 'get them all.' Those were her words and now we know who 'they' are."

Audrey shifted in her seat, "yes, and 'they' includes me."

"Suppose he threatened one or more of them to 'get them.' Maybe he had the tools to do it."

"Now the suspect list gets a little bigger. How does that help?"

"It's a more specific motive. We've got to find out more about them. The only one who knows anything so far is Biddy. Maybe she knows more. At least, she's not part of Reinco."

"We should call her."

"I should call her. She doesn't want to see you, Audrey."

A CASE OF PEANUT BRITTLE

"Oh, I know. I can't say I blame her. Let me know later how your tete-a-tete turns out."

#

"You can go to hell for lying just as quick as for stealing, you know," I said when we parked in the marina parking lot late the next morning and Audrey got out. "You were supposed to just drop me off here."

"Oh, don't be ridiculous," she barked, slamming the driver's door. "Biddy's all grown up. It's time she buried her dead and faced forward."

"Insightful and sensitive grief counseling from Audrayfa, wicked witch of the Southwest," I accused.

Biddy had been reluctant at first to grant a second interview with me, claiming she was simply too busy. She had work to do on her sailboat. I had pressed gently, then she had said that if I came to the Bonita Mar Marina, dressed informally and with soft-soled shoes and a willingness to work as we talked, she would see me. Now, Audrey and I, dressed in jeans and sweats, walked out to the dock looking for slip number forty-four. Audrey wore a pair of her own boat-skips, I struggled with a pair of old tennies that formerly belonged to Brad the Impaler and were too big.

Marinas always impress me. I can jaw all day about politics and economics and the national debt, etc. etc. However, walking through a marina and passing, every few feet, by another forty, fifty, two-hundred thousand dollar toy . . . literally acres of that . . . is too much for me. There are thousands of marinas throughout the country. That's money that, even while you're looking right at it, you can't conceive. Who are all these people? The toys have to be periodically hauled, scraped, painted, dingle-dorfed; it all costs money. Moorage fees run from ten or twenty a month per foot to hundreds

What're you doing this weekend?

Oh, I'm rimalizing the fripper fittings on my boat.

All weekend?

It's slow work. Got to get it done before the cold weather. Rimalizing compound has to set properly.

Aaaauuuurrrgghh!!

I had a small boat once. An emotionally crippled, substance abusing, materialistic, self-absorbed mistress would have been a lot cheaper and probably a lot more fun.

I felt the heat of Biddy's hostile stare before I saw her in the cockpit of a sloop no more than twenty-six feet at the water line. I saw no scrapers, brushes, or other tools in the cockpit. I saw that the sail cover had been removed from the mains'l and the ties that normally secured it to the boom had been loosed. Perhaps her "boat work" was going to be raising the sails and rinsing and scrubbing them. Not a terrible job, but we'd all end up wet no matter how careful we were.

Biddy wore a pair of white canvas jeans, loose enough to get some work done comfortably; working pants, not a fashion statement. Standing in the cockpit with the sun shining down at her, her long, graceful body was achingly pretty. If only that long, patrician face would smile revealing the charming person that was locked up in grief. We approached and she glared at us. Within voice range she called, "I thought I had been quite clear, Dan."

I waved a jaunty hello at her and, like an encyclopedia salesman, kept coming. When we were by the boat I said, " . . . Permission to come aboard?"

232

"I have things to do. I don't know why I should. I have no particular reason to help the two of you."

"I've called you a lot of things, Biddy," Audrey called back, not even slowing her approach. "I've accused you of being a snob, a politician, a hypocrite, and a phony. Never before this have I thought you were stupid. You should help us because you should allow for the possibility that I am not lying. You are helping the real killer. Is helping the real killer is somehow in your interest?"

It had probably saved Audrey a lot of time and passion, and perhaps prevented tragedy amongst the nations, that she had never considered a career in the diplomatic corps.

Biddy was undaunted. "And I have called you a scheming bitch and I still do. There is perfection in the world after all. You're perfect." It awed me that while some women can say "sir" and make it sound like "asshole", Biddy could say "bitch" and make it sound like a precise observation.

Under different circumstances this initial confrontation might have been prelude to an entertaining girl-on-girl fight, but that wouldn't do us any good. "Ladies, ladies," I said. "Sheath your weapons. Let's declare the boat neutral ground for a few minutes. Biddy, I have not deceived you. Audrey coming is a surprise to me too."

Audrey spoke up before I could muzzle her. ""Biddy, we don't have to be friends. I understand your anger. I don't blame you for it. But, you're wrong. Dead wrong. Just allow for that possibility. You're better than this. You should be mad at someone else. We're trying to find out who."

I let some air out of my lungs in relief that Audrey had played civilized and rational. Biddy hesitated a moment and I filled that moment, repeating . . . "Permission to come aboard?"

Biddy took a step back and waved her arm absently, indicating that we might board. She positioned herself aft, sitting so she could access the inboard engine controls built into the seat by the tiller. She looked at some gauges on the starboard side of the entrance to the tiny, mostly below-deck cabin. She reached down and started the quiet little inboard engine and looked at me, "Cast off forward," she said, "then come back and cast off aft when I tell you."

Audrey, realizing that she had not been granted crew status, sat in the middle of a built-in bench along the port side. A similar bench ran the length of the cockpit on the starboard side. As the boat eased forward allowing even more slack on the bowline, I lifted the eye end of the line from the pier cleat, then walked aft and, at Biddy's signal, released the stern line. Biddy, manipulating the throttle lever with fingertip gentility, eased us through the marina and into San Diego Bay. She increased power then stood and the tiller swung up so she could maneuver the craft while standing.

"A little work on the boat?" I said, quoting her.

"Just had engine work done. Test drive, and I want to air out the sails. Meanwhile, I want you to raise the mains'l. Here," she said, pointing to a line affixed to the mast. "That's it."

"I can see where the halyard is," I said. I felt little-boy pride at not having to ask her about her nautical terminology. I thought of her as "Little Miss Yacht Club," showing off. I would not cooperate by being an ignorant landlubber. The boom holding the mains'l stretched across the cockpit at head level if you were seated. It extended aft past the transom. As I raised the sail against the gentle breeze, the boom strained against the belaying sheets, the lines holding it 'amidships'. Biddy made a course correction, heading directly into the wind and the boom settled down. She cut the engine and the sudden silence was magical, just water slaps against the hull and the distant white noise of the city. She sat down and held the tiller with one arm.

"I'm releasing the sheets now," she said. "Always be careful of the swinging boom. Whenever I jibe or come about, I'll shout fair warning. If you're not paying attention, you're going to get your head split and spend some time in the water." Audrey and I exchanged glances. Biddy, enjoying the moment, allowed a brief smile. "You invited yourselves."

She released the sheets from their friction locks and allowed the boom to swing nearly twenty degrees to port. We beat against the wind for several moments, heading approximately south, toward the Coronado Bridge.

"That bridge," Biddy said. "is what got Sean into politics. The powers-that-be wanted a bridge. They wanted to finance it with a bond issue. The public voted it down. Then, they decided on a port-wide initiative. Once again, it was rejected. They established a special commission that recommended against it. Then they built it."

"I remember" Audrey said ". . . not exactly that way, but, I remember that."

"Sean's sense of democracy was so offended that he sold his business and went into politics full time. He was criticized for being a neat freak . . . well, he was and it was difficult. But his dedication to right and wrong was his raison d'etre. He didn't march in and make those ridiculously idealistic speeches to win the crowd . . . he was the crowd. He was the idealistic young guy going to Washington, like in that movie."

"Mr. Smith goes to Washington," Audrey volunteered. "Jimmy Stuart."

"A Frank Capra film," I added.

"Whoever killed him took more than an assemblyman away from us, more than a possible senator and more than a decent husband. They took an honorable, moral man away; he was the best of us." Biddy gazed toward the long strip of flatland called the strand that defined the western line of San Diego Bay, but her eyes did not seem focused.

Audrey and I were silenced for once by a tangible sense of loss.

Biddy averted her face in a show of scanning the waters. She returned her attention forward and yelled, "heads down!" as if it were a curse.

Suddenly, as she pulled on the tiller, the boom crossed the cockpit like a bat swinging, barely missing our heads.

"Low. Ball one," I called when I realized it had missed.

Biddy curled one corner of her lips into a near smile.

"Set the jib," she ordered. "There's a sailbag within reach of that forward hatch."

I crabbed forward, found the sailbag and brought it up. I passed the port and starboard sheets aft, with some help from Audrey, connected the halyard to the jib, then, attaching jib clips to the forestay, hauled it up and secured it. From the cockpit, Biddy adjusted the port and starboard sheets so that the wind filled the jib at a shallow angle.

"Not bad," Biddy said when I returned to the cockpit. "You passed the test."

I smiled and acknowledged the compliment with a nod. One does not overdo with this lady. Audrey shifted back and forth. Biddy looked down at her, "Audrey, you are either desperate to ask a question or you need the ladies room. There's a marine toilet in the cabin. There is no privacy so please close the cabin hatch. Do you know how to use a marine toilet?"

"In fact, Biddy, I do know how but I do not need it. I want to know about Reinco."

Biddy dismissed Audrey by looking at me. "I believe we already covered that. Sean wanted to stop them or harm them in some way. They were doing something or planning to do something that he felt was morally or legally wrong. I know nothing more."

"We were hoping there might be something else. Nothing, eh?"

Audrey spoke up. "How about Clyde," she said. "Did you know he was part of Reinco?"

Biddy pulled hard on the tiller and managed to manipulate the jib sheets as well. "Heads down!" she called. I thought her warning was a bit delayed. Once again, I nearly felt a breeze as the boom came whizzing by my.

"Batter up! Swung on and missed."

In Audrey's case, I think the swinging boom actually touched her red hair. She looked mildly shaken, death grip on the gunnels, wide eyes shifting right and left as if looking for escape routes.

"Really," Biddy said in a non-committal tone of voice.

"Yes, Biddy," I said. "Reinco is, essentially, the same people who are the homeowners association at Bonita Bluffs. Any bells?"

"No," she said. She was avoiding more answers. I wondered if we'd learn more if, somehow, we shook her up a bit.

Audrey was way ahead of me. "Not even any pillow talk from Clyde? Come on, Biddy, lovers always gossip."

After several seconds of silence during which the the anger was nearly palpable, Biddy apparently won an internal battle. Her muscles relaxed and her vice-like grip on the tiller eased to normal. "You are wrong, Audrey," she said, a soft and quiet voice. "You have either listened to or started rumors that appeal to the crudest and most prurient of minds. You set the bar very low. Neither speaks well for your character."

While I took valuable time formulating something appropriate for that, Audrey, feeling herself under no such restraints, replied immediately. "Well what do you expect, Missy, when we see how the two of you are, we hear about the luncheons and other assignations and we never hear anything from you but denials?"

"Gossips," Biddy pronounced.

"Gossips," Audrey answered, "and I don't want to hear your better-than-thou lessons on ethics. The most vicious rumors come right out of your country club crowd: poor taste and backbiting are not limited to one class, your 'mine doesn't stink' attitude is bullshit."

I was sure Audrey could not have said that. There must be something else to do. I could go down to the cabin and sit on the marine toilet for a while. I doubted there'd be a cooler down there with beer in it. Damn.

"I'm going to come about and make a run back to the marina," Biddy said. Again she swung the tiller, this time holding it until we had come about to a nearly reciprocal course. The boom took its third great swing, this time, terminating so that it pointed almost directly abeam. She had also adjusted the jib so that now, with a following wind, it billowed great and graceful against the sky. With a great white sail on either side we were a bird flying over the water. The increase in speed was dramatic, as dramatic as the apparent decrease in fresh, cool breeze.

"I am not a snob," Biddy said to Audrey. "I have never been a snob."

Audrey shrugged her shoulders. "You probably can't help it, Biddy, but you are. Maybe some of us are jealous of you and don't give you the benefit of the doubt."

"I don't think that way. Some of you have simply not, have never, accepted me."

Audrey studied Biddy with what looked like a measure of compassion. Her lips, not preparing an acid remark, seemed softer. "Biddy, next time the neighborhood association has a potluck meeting, bring a dish you make yourself."

Biddy allowed herself a short, self-deprecating laugh. "I'm not a good cook. A dish I prepared would be mediocre at best. Why embarrass myself?"

"Because most of us don't have cooks or caterers, that's why. Because it would make you a little more accessible, because if it really stinks, we'll enjoy making fun of you and laughing at you. You have to let us have that. Laugh with us, then we'll help you make a better one next time. How the hell can you be part of a potluck when you bring a gourmet dish that 'Cook' has prepared?"

The boat skimmed along beautifully. Blue sky. Blue waters of the bay. White puffy clouds and these two making nice. It was like a telephone commercial.

"I brought things like that because I thought you'd all like something . . ."

" . . . Better?"

"Oh," Biddy said, beginning to understand. I hoped she was not the killer; she was starting to seem nice. It occurred to me that she was also 'available' now, 'on the market.' With no sense of quilt nor shame I re-assessed this attractive woman, arguably too young for me. Yeah, an age gap, but it was not science-fiction size . . . she could be within range.

After several moments of gliding along in silence, it was Biddy who started talking. "Clyde Miller and I," she started, "met each other as parts of a foursome, the Bradshaws and the Reillys. I see now that it was just about the time that Connie was tiring of Clyde. He is a dreamer, really. He fantasizes about greatness and power but is too impatient to do the work of a truly ambitious man. Connie set her sights on Sean. He resisted at first but Connie was quite seductive and, yes, they did start an affair."

Audrey, overcome by the tribal bond of the sisterhood, actually reached a hand out to Biddy, just nodding her head in sympathy and allowing Biddy to continue. "Sean was going places and Connie wanted to go along. She did not care that she was ruining my marriage and her own. She schemed for ways to get rid of Clyde and take as much of a settlement as she could get away with. Poor Sean, by then, was sexually obsessed with her. Clyde and I started to depend upon one another for support. We became the most intimate of friends and still are. Not intimate, Audrey, intimate friends. The poor man has a

240

drinking problem and I would never abide that, besides, I was committed to my marriage."

Biddy and Audrey started getting downright friendly, exchanging some things by speaking too low for me to overhear. The sisterhood had raised its secretive flag. I lost interest. The way back to the marina, of course, was a lot quicker than the way out. In no time we were lowering sails, returning the jib to its bag, furling the mains'l against the boom and securing it. Biddy took us back into the marina under power and we were properly dockside as gracefully as we had left. The mains'l sail cover had been secured, the cabin locked and the cockpit devoid of human clues. Seconds before we stepped onto the pier, Biddie, while looking about in a last casual check of the boat, said casually, "I don't know if it has any importance, but, Sean's outrage against Reinco had something to do with that ridiculous skateboard park."

We hung on her words, exchanging stares with each other. A blissful smugness at having been right swept over Audrey's countenance like a west wind. She blessed me with one of her sweetest "I told you so" smiles.

"How so, Biddie?" I asked.

Her final look-around finished, she walked with us to the parking area. "As you said, there was a time when we and the Millers were closer, for pragmatic reasons. At the beginning of the skateboard park fiasco about which Audrey became so fanatic, we were siding with the Millers and the association. At some point, shortly before the end, Sean was ready to change his position. He was as angry as I have ever seen him. 'I'll get them,' he insisted, "I'll get all of them.'"

Yeah, a politician and two bounty hunters murdered, an almost secret investment company, conspiracy, my sister, whose neck is on the line, probably framed: all over a neighborhood skateboard park? The fact that Sean Reilly changed his position after the park became controversial did not mean that he did so because of the park. A big error in logic, post hoc ergo propter hoc: after the fact, therefore, because of the fact.

Skateboard park my ass.

CHAPTER EIGHTEEN

The shadows were getting noticeably longer as we approached Mission Santa Audrey. She drove and I maintained the paranoid watch from the passenger seat. I couldn't help looking for maroon SUVs as we neared home. There were none, of course, just a silver four-door thing of recent vintage. I can't tell what the cars are any more. For all I know they're all made in the same factory. Some come out the Chevy door, some come out the Ford door, some come out the Toyota door. They're all silver gray. Foreign, domestic: tomāto—tomato.

The foreign cars were either enormous, black lacquer and chrome sculptures of luxury or odd-looking little things that did not look like 'real' cars at all, some of them with names like kitchen appliances, "Crosley" and "Morris" come to mind.

It nearly worked the other way with the names. "What's that?"

"It's the new Amana Turbo Drive."

"Is it as fast as the Admiral, or the RCA speedster?"

"Don't know but its lines are a lot like the DuPont, Sylvania model."

I pointed to the gray thing parked near her house. "What is that," I asked. "Is it a Buick or a Ford?"

"I think it's the new Honda," she said. "I think Harriet Harrison has one. She likes it. I wonder if she's visiting with Connie. It's just like those two to be cooking something up."

"Speaking of cooking up . . . "

"Way ahead of you," she brightened. "There's a roast and veggies in the crock-pot. I started them this morning. I think I'll put the car up for the night."

I was too tired to ask her how one goes about putting a car up. I was also a little surprised that the automatic garage door was open. I thought I had closed it when we left. Still, having explained the car out front, I was not concerned as we slid into the garage and stopped, putting the car "up," I suppose. But, while Audrey was at the door to the house interior, fussing with the keys, I heard a crashing sound from inside, then running footsteps approaching.

I shoved Audrey to the side just in time. The door to the house blasted open right in my face. I lost my balance. Whoever it was finished the job the swinging door had started by stiff-arming me and I went down hard. I had spread my hands out trying to cushion the fall. One of the assailant's feet smashed down and pushed off from my forearm. As I struggled to all fours, a second running man charged at me. This one used my upper back like it was second base and disappeared around the corner of the garage.

I looked to Audrey who had stumbled when I pushed her. She had had the foresight to land against two laundry baskets. She looked all right, albeit a bit shaken and confused. I took inventory of my own body and felt several places, knees, hips, right arm and lower back that were not going to feel good for a while. Nothing seemed broken.

"You okay, Audrey?"

"Considering that you knocked me down then I watched two guerillas stomp you like a welcome mat . . . fine, thank you. And you?"

I did the old-guy-getting-up ballet, accompanying myself with a bit more than the usual grunt-and-groan concerto. I heard an unfamiliar voice nearby, shouting at someone. "Settle down or I'll hurt you more."

What in the name of god's green earth was going on?

Around the corner of the garage and at about the same time I heard his whining, I recognized Eric Miller, Connie's adorable little perv son. He was stretched out, belly down partially on grass and partially on decorative flowerbed gravel. He did not look happy.

Astride him, still slapping the sides of Eric's face in a casual manner, was a man somewhat shorter than Eric and easily twice his age, a man who also had a good thirty pounds on the kid. He adjusted his position so that he had one knee on the small of Eric's back and could adjust the pain without putting himself out too much. Eric learned quickly that not moving was the least painful alternative.

I nearly felt sorry for Eric. Almost. Sort of.

"What's going on here," Audrey said, arriving on the scene in full rant. She turned an angry face to the stranger. "What are you doing to this boy?"

"I'm controlling him at the moment," the man said. "You are Audrey Davis?"

"I suppose so," Audrey said, "although I won't be for long. I'm getting a divorce and I will take my maiden name back. Kelly. Then I will be Ms Kelly, thank you. So you might just as well get used to it. That's the reality. I am Ms Kelly, not Mrs. Kelly and certainly not Mrs. Davis."

245

Her quick, defensive wall of words took some attention away from the stranger. I read on the man's face, a scowl that he hid with a quick smile. He was adjusting to Audrey. "I'm Barney Cross," he said. "Ron Downey hired me to work for you; for your brother. I'm a private investigator."

"Dan Kelly," I threw in, feeling irrelevant.

"And are you going to let this young man go Mr. Barney Cross?" She asked.

"No. That's not my plan," he said. "I'd like to hurt him a little more, then have a chat with him." He delivered this cold-blooded threat in a casual voice that oozed credibility.

"We can call the police, you know," Audrey said.

"Yes Ma'am, you can, and I'd certainly hold that option open. My way is faster, simpler and more efficient."

Audrey would not be cowed. "Eric Miller, your victim, has permission to enter our house to do some chores. You, who do not work for me——do not."

Eric felt supported enough to enter his opinion. "Audrey, can't you get this thug of me? I wasn't doing anything wrong. Just my job an' shit"

"Not your turn yet, creep," Barney said and hit him again on the side of the head.

"That's it," Audrey snapped, recovering her cell phone from an otherwise invisible pocket. "I'm calling the police now."

"You telling me ma'am that this fella's duties include messing around in your bedroom, going through your under ware things. What kind of job has he got, anyway? Maybe I got this all wrong, huh?"

"No, uh uh, Barney," I said, really warming up to him. "You've got this kid pegged."

246

"Don't be ridiculous," she said, scowling at Barney and me. She paused dialing however, " . . . my bedroom?"

"He pulled something from a drawer. It was black and shiny and looked like it had little red things, roses maybe, embroidered on it."

"Aw, Audrey. It's all messed up," Eric begged. "It's lies. I know they all tell lies about me."

"Yeah, right," Barney said. He released Eric long enough for Eric to stand, then he grabbed his belt with one hand and put his other in Eric's right front pocket. From it he withdrew a pair of black silk panties with red embroidery on it, red roses and an "AD" for Audrey Davis. The impressively strong detective then yanked down hard on the belt and pervo Eric hit the ground sitting. Barney rolled the kid over again and replaced his knee in the sweet spot.

"Nice work," I said, beaming with appreciation. "Looks like your timing is great too."

"No big deal," he said, revealing a pleasant smile. "I got a message third hand from Ron but it sounded like you guys needed help quick. I came to the house but no one was home and I decided to wait. I saw this dufus kid gain entry and couldn't resist seeing what he was up to."

"I don't think we need all the physical details," I said, thinking of pervo's possible activities and innocent Audrey.

"No, it's not just that. It took me a while to get into the house sight unseen. He was still doing things downstairs. At first I thought he was looking for jewelry, I-pods, video cams, you know. But he was hanging around the home office, y'know the desk downstairs. He didn't go up to the bedroom till several minutes before the sound of

247

your car spooked him. I can see that he's a creep . . . but he had other business here first."

"Eric?" Audrey cajoled.

Eric had apparently selected a strategy and was determined to stick to it. He gritted his teeth and studied the ground.

I watch some cop shows and, like I said, I know a couple of cops, so, I thought it was time to invent a plan. "Audrey," I said, "how about going inside and checking on that roast in the crock-pot. You can also maybe make a couple of drinks for us. Okay?"

She looked at me like I was Darth Vader.

"Come on," I urged. "Trust me, and, don't call the cops yet."

With some reluctance, Audrey returned to the house via the garage. A quick look at Barney and I felt we had a tacit agreement.

I approached close to Eric and put a big smile across my face. "Eric, old boy," I said to him. "This fella doesn't know you as well as I think I do. That's one of the reasons he's being so nice to you. Also, he doesn't want to offend me, his new employer. You understand that, right?"

Eric said nothing till Barney gave him a gentle nudge in that painful spot in the small of his back. He nodded his head.

"But I want you to hear me reassure Mr. Cross that I think you are a real piece of crap. If I were a violent man, like, say, a detective or something, I wouldn't think twice about abusing you. Do you understand me? I want to hear you say it."

"Yeah, Dan. I get you an' shit."

"I'm sorry, who are you talking to and who is this man standing next to me? Who are the two adults you're going to talk to."

"All right, all right. Mr. Kelly and Mr. Cross."

"I knew he could do it," Barney said. "He's smarter than you were saying."

I felt I was on a roll. My dark side was having fun being a bully. "Tell us what you're doing here, Eric. If you don't explain to me, I'm going to ask Barney to talk to you. I don't really have to be here for that part. I'll go in the house with Audrey. If you pick plan A, I'm going to ask Audrey to re-think that whole police business. If you pick plan B neither me nor Audrey is going to be responsible for how it goes and the telephone call goes through anyway."

"No cops and I'll tell you stuff," Eric said, far more courageous than I might have predicted. Barney and I looked at each other and shrugged.

"Deal," Barney said. "Speak."

"First you let me sit in a better position an' maybe have a cigarette an' shit. This sucks."

"Yeah," Barney said without moving. "We could send out for pizza and beer. Or, right now you can think of how much fun it's going to be to be able to walk home without needing some kind of help. Up to you big guy but I'm getting kinda restless too. Speak."

"Okay, okay," Eric said. "First off, In spite of all the shit an' shit, I don't think Audrey killed anybody. Somethin' else happened. I don't know what, but it wasn't . . . Miz Kelly. Okay?"

"We're looking for stuff we don't already know," I urged.

249

"Like what the hell were you doing here before you got the urge to sniff her panties," added Barney.

"Lookin'. . . anything. I was looking for anything like real-estate stuff an' shit."

"Why?"

"There's something going on. I think it's got something to do with real estate. My Mom and Dad are part of it. I know they are. I just don't know what it is, but they're up to something, and some other people too. I was looking for real estate shit."

"What would you do with it?"

"I dunno! Depends on what it is, don't it? My Mom and Dad are right in the middle of whatever this shit is and I think Audrey . . . ow! . . . Miz Kelly getting' bagged for murder is part of it."

I was floored. He was saying the kinds of things I'd been thinking, but to hear them said aloud in the real world was daunting. Barney Cross released the pressure at the small of Eric's back but his knee was still there and reminded Eric every so often that he could inflict pain at any moment.

"What would you do with information you got," Barney asked.

Eric looked up and smiled, a tight, desperate smile. "I was lookin' for something I could use to mess with 'em," he said. "I like Audrey. My parents are assholes. I'd mess 'em up. Big-time! I'm on your side."

It was clear to me from Barney's blank expression that he was as impressed with that as I was. "So you found nothing," he said. "What about the bedroom tour. Looking for grant deeds in her panty drawer?"

"I told you," Eric said, showing the shame of a little boy caught, "I like her."

"Oh, Jeeze," I said, exasperated. I turned away. Some stuff is just past what I can understand.

"What do you know about Reinco?" I asked over my shoulder.

"I heard about it. It's a company or something," Eric said. "I think Brad is a bigwig. I don't know. Seems like he's a bigwig with everything."

Barney put his face within two feet of Eric's and asked in a conversational way, "Do you think you can run faster than me?"

Eric showed some growth by thinking about the question for a moment. "Yes, sir," he answered; some instinct informing him that truth might be a good idea. "I think I'm faster than you."

"Good," Barney said. He smiled and stepped away. "Would you bet life and limb on it? Right now?"

Eric looked around quickly for the right answer then said "no." He was not ready to bet life or limb on it.

"I want a quick word with Mr. Kelly, here," Barney said. "After that, I'll probably let you go. Meanwhile, I want you to lie there." He turned his back to Eric and approached me. "He won't go anywhere," he said. "He doesn't really know anything."

"I agree, except that he knows the people involved and I guarantee that he's right."

"Oh, yeah. But we need stuff for court. Okay if I turn 'im loose?"

"Don't let him keep the panties. Audrey will want to burn them."

He looked back to Eric and made a motion with his head. Eric jumped to his feet and was out of sight in seconds.

Audrey appeared from the house. I assumed from her timing that she had been watching from inside. "Are you two barbarians finished with your testosterone festival?" she asked. She had brought not drinks but a small paper bag that she held at arms length motioning for us to retrieve the panties from the flowerbed they had been dropped in, and put them in the bag.

"Mr. Ross, you intimidate teenagers very well. Apparently you can illegally enter a house without disturbing other burglars, and you dress conservatively. Do you have other talents?"

Audrey, still upset, was trying to bait Barney Cross, but he seemed amused by it. "Well, Ma'am," he said, "I play a little piano, show tunes mostly, some rock; I'm pretty lucky with cards, poker and blackjack, and I shoot a good game of pool, nine-ball's my game. Does any of that help?"

"I was thinking of professional skills, Mr. Ross, although I suppose in your profession, almost anything can be called professional."

"That would include intimidating teen-agers, Ma'am," Barney said with an affected humility that he clearly did not feel.

"Your Honor," I interrupted, raising my voice. "Can we at least go in the house and examine those drinks we were talking about earlier? Do you think we can do that? Can we? You think?"

"Well don't get all grouchy, Dan," she responded, back on more familiar grounds. "I was just trying to find out if Mr. Ross is adept at reading legal documents." She ushered us into the house. "Is that all right with you? Is it all right with you, Mr. Ross?"

"Yes, Ma'am."

Audrey stopped dead in her tracks and turned to Barney Cross. "Okay, first deal," she said. "No more 'Ma'am'."

"Only if you call me Barney," he said, and the first quid-pro-quo between these two was set.

"Legal documents?"

"Most legal documents, yes," he said. "I've taken several law classes. I am weak in tax documents, international law makes me cry and I don't understand the jargon of entertainment and maritime law. Your garden variety articles of incorporation, contracts for services, uniform commercial code disputes . . . been there."

She led us into the heart of Mission Santa Audrey where she had prepared a pitcher of Martinis. "I know I shouldn't assume," she said, leading us the large pitcher and three glasses, but I already had two votes of three. I can certainly make you a root-beer float if that's your preference."

"Martinis are fine," he said. Pretty soon these two were not going to need me around.

"Real estate," she said.

"Not a problem. I have some experience."

"We certainly need to find out as much as we can about Reinco," I agreed.

"We need to find out about the skateboard park," Audrey said, smiling at her new friend who would not take her crap any more than her brother would.

"Audrey," I said, "No one is committing three murders over a stupid skateboard park."

"Ron sketched in that part of the story," Barney said. He sipped his drink, then raised the glass to complement Audrey on the drink. "This does seem to start with the skateboards."

"You might as well say it starts with the peanut brittle, Barney! Maybe we should investigate homemade peanut brittle . . . or poisonous domestic flower gardens. There's a biggy."

"Skateboard Park," Audrey said.

"I can certainly look into it," Barney said, hearing the determination in Audrey's voice.

"Ah, come on," I argued, the lone voice of sanity getting lost in Audrey's wind. "The property's too small to build on in this neighborhood. Too small for anything."

"Skateboard Park." Audrey said again.

Barney turned to me. He was starting to enjoy himself. "Have you anything else you want me to do tomorrow?" he asked, innocently.

"No," I admitted. "I suppose not."

Audrey turned to me, eyes flashing with humor and determination. I felt I could see the words actually forming on her lips. "Okay," I shouted at the ceiling. "Barney, tomorrow, why don't you go wherever you have to go and do whatever you have to do to find out all you can about the god-blessed, stinking, pain-in-my-butt, waste-of-time skateboard park, and, in your spare time, what, if any, connection it has with Reinco, Audrey's murder charge, peanut brittle or the energizer bunny."

Audrey twice started speaking and I held up my hands, begging silence. Finally, after giving silent assurances that she would not provoke me, she blessed us with one of her nearly haiku profundities.

"I'm just saying."

I could not close the topic on that. "You win, but I'm telling you both, and you can put this in the bank . . . it's not going to be the skateboard park."

CHAPTER NINETEEN

It was the skateboard park.

We, meaning Audrey and Barney, agreed that Barney and I would work together. Stepping into Sean Reilly's shoes so to speak, we would look into the things he was most likely to have investigated. We assumed that, being an assemblyman and an attorney, his approach would have included a search of the public records. Barney said that most professionals use the appointment calendar almost as a diary, a journal, for later reference. We asked Biddie's permission to see Sean's appointment schedule. She allowed it with the air of a tired caregiver being asked to change the bed sheets again.

We were interested in the last three days of the calendar, covering the time during which, according to Biddie, the assemblyman's attitude had changed. If we could find out why, we might discover what changed him from ally to target.

We learned nothing that did not confirm Biddie's portrait of a hard-working public servant. With Barney's talent for interpreting mere telephone numbers and times into concrete activities by cajoling this person, conning that one, flirting with another . . . we traced the activities of his last few days and dismissed most as irrelevant.

On a hunch, I asked Barny if we could find out if Sean Reilly had checked into Reinco. We were lucky. His administrative assistant remembered that Sean had asked about Reinco and had gone to the hall of records to confirm the names of the partners.

By late afternoon we were at the County Administration building. Some of the areas, like the hall of records, had sign-in/sign-out sheets that helped. We merely took the notes from the calendar, matched the times and looked for his name. That led us to the county planning department in the late afternoon where we located the records and stats for Bonita Bluffs. I am so glad that Barney was with me because I would have missed the biggy.

He almost jumped looking at one map. He harassed the busy county employee until he got the master-planning document he wanted. This he analyzed then drew back from it, clearly impressed. He had not said a word to me and, seeing the sudden passion of his pursuit, I had remained silent. Now he summarized his expert findings.

"Holy shit!" he whispered.

"What holy?" I asked. "Holy what? What have you found? What is it?"

"It's a zoning screwup," Barney whispered, not wanting anyone else to hear. "The whole of what you call Bonita Bluffs is zoned the same. The assumption is that it is strictly residential. But, look here, this wording means that commercial development is allowed."

"So, how does the Skateboard Park, have anything to do with it? They weren't going to be commercial."

Barney hushed me with a hand gesture and we returned the documents and maps we had asked for, requesting photocopies. He led me into a small receiving area of the county building, and, surrounded by polished marble walls, he explained. "When Sean checked on the skateboard park land, probably researching the restraining order, he discovered what I just did. He discovered that the land, the whole of Bonita Bluffs, could, under some very achievable circumstances, be developed commercially."

Fine, I was thinking. I wouldn't be offended if a Dunkin' Donuts opened near my house. "So what? And what does Reinco have to do with it?"

"He knew about Reinco, who they were. They are all Bonita Bluffs homeowners. It's not a great leap of logic to figure out that the homeowners were getting together to put the entire acreage on the block. I'm only guessing, but I think that explains the 'I'll get them all' statement

"Yeah, right, so?"

"I'll bet the farm that Brad Davis and most of the other owners formed Reinco with the idea that when they had accounted for all of the Bonita Bluffs properties, they would market them as a commercial property block. A sixty-two acre block of undeveloped, premier commercial property on the California coast. There would be no price competition. The Skateboard Park and one or two remaining owners were details, obstacles to be overcome. Sean Reilly became one of those obstacles. Someone removed him."

"What am I missing? These upper middle class pseudo estates occupy the whole of Bonita Bluffs. It's already developed."

Barney, eyes glowing with excitement, fought to keep his voice low, still, in the marble hallway it reverberated seeming to add gravitas to his words. "What you're missing is the money involved, Dan," he nearly hissed. "This is the only undeveloped, Cliffside, coastal real estate between Los Angeles and Mexico. Sixty-two acres suddenly available for a luxury vacation resort or a theme park or a sunset condominium complex with facilities . . .

257

use your imagination. Take the value of all the homes now on the site, double it, multiply that by ten, then you're approaching the value of the property as a managed, upscale, commercial property."

"You're talking millions of dollars, aren't you?" I said, awed by the figures. "Ten, fifteen million dollars. Twenty million dollars."

"We're way past a few million dollars, Dan," he said, even impressing himself. "What do you think Hyatt or Disney or Hilton might bid for several dozen acres of Cliffside California coast with beach access?"

"Wow!" I said. "But, wait . . . is what they're doing illegal?"

"No," he said. "They're taking advantage of a clerical error, but they're not doing anything illegal."

"Then what could Assemblyman Reilly or anyone else do to them?"

"He could get the mistake corrected before any sale contract was complete."

"Couldn't Reinco argue that they had just made a property investment, now they were cashing in?"

"Probably not. Every damned one of them built their primary residences on that property. They're raising their kids, sending them to school . . . everything that a residential community does. No—someone found the zoning error after the fact and wanted to get all the ducks in a row before the county realized its error and corrected it. At stake could be millions for all the partners."

Brad's 'deal' to have Audrey give up her rights to the property now took on a whole new dimension of malice. For that kind of money some people were capable of sacrificing an assemblyman and a pair of bounty hunters.

It certainly explained Reinco and the conspiracy. It was important enough to motivate murder. It justified my instinctive suspicion of Brad Davis and anyone who shared his pit of darkness. My immediate exultation over a discovery was muted.

"How does this help Audrey?"

Barney and I were awaiting the photocopies we had requested. His whispering was hoarse and intense. "Right now, the best we can do with this is give it all to Paul Ladish so he can develop alternative theories for the jury to consider. We're not helping Audrey directly, just opening to other possibilities."

I was reluctant to get on a roller coaster ride of Audrey's emotions. "Let's not tell her. It'll only raise false hopes."

"It helps."

"The state has the same case against Audrey as it had before. Nothing has changed. We sit on this."

"It suggests an alternative. That could lead to reasonable doubt."

"Mum's the word, just for now."

I saw in Barney's clear, gray eyes that he disagreed with me. "You're the boss," he said, yielding. "But I still think we should give the information to Paul Ladish. Maybe he can think of ways to use it that we haven't thought about. He is the lawyer."

Now I was being asked to entrust explosive information to a lawyer and hope that he would only use it when and if it would further my interests. A voice teased my brain with a sardonic tone. I'm your lawyer. I can help. Trust me.

This was not comfortable. For Audrey's sake, I agreed to Barney's suggestion. We took the photocopies to

Ladish' office. He was not in so we left it for him with a note ordering him to keep it confidential for the moment.

#

Audrey thinks that I drink too much. She does not understand. Our very straight-laced grandfather used to say; "there are times in a man's life when nothing is as satisfying as a good old fashioned damn!" I agree. There are times in a man's life when nothing is as satisfying as a good 'old fashioned.' I'm a scotch drinker so I replace the old fashioned with scotch-rocks, water back.

After the revelation at the county planning department, and our agreement to keep the discovery confidential, there was nothing to talk about. Still some anonymous someone had offed the good assemblyman with organic poison and the biggest motive seemed to be greed. Greed . . . seduction by the multi-million dollar jackpot waiting for the Reinco partners when they sold their homes en-block to a developer. The kind of greed that even with all the money involved, would drive Brad the impaler, to cut his ex-wife off. Just how many millions of dollars must one have before it's enough?

For some it's not the amount of money at all. It's having: having more, and never having enough. For people like Clyde, it's buying power over people. For others, millions meant mistresses, yachts, penthouse living, servants, and shiny cars. What would it be for Connie Miller? Enough to buy high social status for herself and her husband? A pool-boy on the side? Maybe one of the Reinco partners had a drug habit or some other irresistible vice.

A CASE OF PEANUT BRITTLE

What price the death of an annoying, neat-freak boy-scout politician? Then, in for a dime in for a dollar, a couple of street thugs in the bounty hunter racket. Small price to live a life that satisfies all your fantasies.

I had invited Barney for drinks and dinner with Audrey and me, but, with a mischievous glint in his eye, he said that he had other plans. I knew he wasn't married and I knew that no man has that kind of look unless he's anticipating some adventurous sex.

"Okay," I said as we parted, "I'll drink your share."

When I got back to Casa Santa Audrey I made myself a healthy dose of scotch in a bucket glass over some of the natural, mountain spring, tree-hugging, water that Audrey kept around the house. I felt her critical eyes on me.

"You're not going to drink yourself stupid tonight, are you?"

"Yes, that is my plan. Care to join me?"

"What did you and Barney find out today?"

"Oh, just some business stuff. We're pretty sure it was Reinco, the partners, that Sean Reilly was going after. Apparently one of them took it seriously."

"Nothing else?"

I could hear the suspicion in her voice, a tentative quality. She knew I was holding back. The woman was a witch. "We found some legal stuff we didn't completely understand and forwarded it to Ladish. He wasn't there. Have you got any decent jazz CDs?"

She ignored the question, opting for a school-marm sneer. "I've seen that mood before. You want to slurp your scotch and go into some foggy dreamland with a jazz soundtrack."

261

She was right, of course. I was looking forward to it, only I called it relaxation. "Almost anything that's not like your doorbell music or the electronic suppository music you use for ringtones on your cell."

"And what am I supposed to do while you're easing into a stupor."

"Well, you can stop exaggerating. Let's compromise. Light classical and you join me. We can talk about old times, granddad, that summer the whole family spent at the rented cottage on the beach, the year you were in the high-school musical. Come on, Audrey. You never did tell me just how you got the lead," I said, raising and lowering my eyebrows like Groucho Marx.

The suggestion that we talk about her was clearly having its affect. "Maybe we could have a family night, Bro. It would be a welcome change from . . . all this," she said gesturing with her arms to pretty much include the world.

"That's the ticket," I said. Now my challenge would be to start off talking about her, then change the subject to something that actually interested me.

"We should eat something first," she offered. "I'll see what I have. I know there's lots of salad makings."

The last thing I wanted to do was have something all green and California healthy. These people ate like range animals when they should be eating range animals. "Tell you what," I offered. "We'll switch to wine, sharing a bottle. Let's call out for pizza. We'll drink wine, eat pizza and rap about our childhood—but no photo albums."

It started to sound so good that I was sold on it too. She smiled one of those rare but beautiful Audrey smiles, like the sun rising warm and fresh. "You make the call," she said, "number's on the fridge. One-third

262

vegetarian and two-thirds whatever dead animals you want. I'll pick out a bottle or two from our wine cellar."

Wine cellar, a wood frame thingus along the wall in the pantry. "Don't you trust me to pick a bottle?"

"Not even a little bit," she said, the lilt in her voice putting indictments and violence aside. I had lit a candle in her. She was committed to a night of remembrances with her dear brother; she was happy. We'd end up feeling all warm and gushy.

I felt guilty, having suggested it in the first place, merely to get her off my back about spending some time drinking. How the in the name of the universal Earth Goddess does she do that? Hell, I wasn't averse to a mellow, pajama party kind of family night. It's just that, I start off planning on one thing–getting all woozy in a darkened living room and listening to some Miles Davis, Coltrane, or the Duke, scotch in my hand and nothing on my mind, and–BOOM–a few words with Sis and we're on a family outing of her design, with–I don't know–Spike Jones on an old victrola.

By most objective measures I am smarter than this woman. Why is it, then, that I am so handily manipulated into committing to her plans? If she were a romantic object, I could understand it and I wouldn't mind. But here, there's nothing for me. I'm all ready for plan 'A' and I find myself smack-dab in the middle of plan 'B', and it's not even my plan 'B'.

The pizza came, with the garlic bread I ordered, and without the garden salad she asked me to order. It was half vegetarian and half sausage and pepperoni. I was happy to pay for it. She contributed a bottle of genuine Italian Chianti. God bless my sister. I had been worried that she'd bring some politically correct wine made from

263

free-range grapes. I took one look at the Chianti and asked her if there were more than one. She grinned and nodded her head.

The pizza was excellent. The sausage was special, not overcooked and seasoned nicely. Two pieces in, Audrey got me to try one of the vegetarian slices and, just to show her what a hell of a guy I am, I went for it. Imagine my surprise when, in nothing flat I had downed it and started wondering just how much of her half she was going to eat.

We satisfied ourselves with the pizza, going through at least three-quarters of it. The same was true of the Chianti. Audrey got up for another bottle and on the way turned her music system on to a soft jazz station that she had been hiding from me. Jerry Mulligan was practicing his scales. Audrey came back with a fresh bottle and corkscrew, indicating that we should retire to the family room. "I want you to tell me about that horrible sunburn you got the summer we were at Lake Powell. There was always a big secret about it and now I want to know."

"Oh, that was a long time ago," I said. I poured the final glass from the first bottle and motioned for the corkscrew for the second.

"No way. There's a story and I've never heard all of it. You didn't wear sunscreen, right, I get that. You fell asleep, big deal. But you were laid up for the rest of the week, for the rest of our stay at the lake . . . and Dad kept laughing."

"Okay," I said, wanting that corkscrew and realizing that we were both old enough for this stupid memory. "Remember Elsa Von Kokeritz? Do you?"

"Yes. She was a classmate. Of course I remember Elsa."

"Well, I stole a bottle of wine and she and I went on a secret picnic to that little sandy island. Remember?"

"Ya, ya, wc callcd it Pirates Island or something."

"Well, we drank the wine and we went skinny dipping and a little bit more, then fell asleep on the sand for the rest of the afternoon."

"And you got sunburned. There's got to be more to it than that."

"We both got sunburned all over. Get it? Her family took her home."

"You got . . ." she started, then stopped, getting the whole picture. She started laughing that 'real' Audrey laugh. "All over? Oh my god, that must've hurt." Apparently that was hilarious. "No wonder you haven't told the whole story. Did Mom know?"

"No, but Dad did. That's why he kept laughing when I couldn't walk or ride the bike or sit."

It was wonderful to see Audrey relaxed and laughing, even though it was at my expense. To share in kind, Audrey told me stories about embarrassing moments of her adolescence, stories involving the onset of menses and the first time she got felt-up. I pretended to sympathize but she was almost too candid. Too much information. Things I just did not want to know about.

"Remember the nuns at Our Lady of Graces School?" she said, also into the second bottle now.

"Oh, yeah," I answered. It was not a pleasant memory.

"And their three-cornered rulers that they'd rap our knuckles with?"

"At least the girls got the flat end," I complained. "The boys got the sharp end."

265

"Well," she giggled, "I did that to Eric a while back."

"You mean Eric the knicker-sniffing perv? The Miller kid?" I pictured a stern Audrey in a black and white Dominican habit, chasing Eric with an immense three-cornered ruler and smiled. This was good.

"Yup," she said, looking proud.

"A three-cornered ruler?"

"No," she admitted, clearly wishing that it had been. "It was the flat side of a bread knife."

"Tell me more." I demanded. "Tell me why you didn't use the edge?"

"It was while I was preparing the peanut-brittle for Sean," she said. "I caught Eric snitching some and I hit his hand with the flat of the knife. I was only sort-of teasing about it."

I sat straight up. Why had she never mentioned Eric connected to the peanut brittle? "Eric was in the kitchen when you were preparing the brittle for Sean Reilly?" I asked.

"Well, I guess so," she answered.

"Tell me exactly what you said to him, Audrey," I demanded. "It's important."

"I said something like . . . 'leave that alone. That's for Mr. Reilly.'"

"Jesus H. Christ, Audrey!" I nearly snapped. I felt joy at the discovery, but frustrated that it took pizza and Chianti to loosen her up. "You've just connected Eric Miller with the peanut brittle and the knowledge that it was going to Reilly."

"I suppose," she said, connecting the dots. "But isn't that a bit far-fetched?"

"I don't think so," I said. "At any time, even for a few seconds or so, did you leave him alone with the brittle?"

"No, Dan. Of course not. He was there for his pay. I paid him and sent him home. Then I took my shower."

"And the candy wasn't in the box yet."

"No, but he'd gone home."

If life was like a cartoon my cheeks would have been cherry red: my mouth would have bellowed like a great siren: all kinds of punctuation marks would have exploded from my head. I could hardly stammer. "And little Eric would never enter a house unless someone specifically invited him in, right?"

Her look was interesting, like someone who's just found out that the payments were twice what she thought they were.

"You're sure that you didn't box the candy until after your shower."

"But you told us that you boxed and wrapped it then took your shower. "

"No, silly. Boxed it. The box and ribbon were upstairs, so I thought I'd take my shower then get the stuff and go downstairs to finish the job."

"So Eric was aware that the candy was there, unattended for at least ten or fifteen minutes and he knew that it was going directly to assemblyman Reilly."

I could barely contain myself. This was the kind of thing we'd been looking for all along.

"Oh, my God," she said.

I got up and headed for the door.

"But why would he do anything like that?" she called after me.

267

"Because he knew that Sean Reilly was banging his mother. Maybe he didn't like that. For all I know he wanted to bang her himself. The kid's nuts."

I was at the door thinking in some primitive, almost pre-lingual way. It ends now. I get the perv in my hands and slap the truth out of him. Crazy bastard; crazy son of crazy parents.

"Where are you going?" I heard from behind me. She had gotten up and was following me to the door, but she was too far behind to stop me.

"I'm going to have a chat with that piece-of-shit kid," I said. "I don't care how young he is or how old I am. We're having it out."

I half-ran, half-jogged over to the Miller house. I had no idea what I would say. I was following a Chianti lubricated primal urge. If I didn't kill him right away, maybe a confession, maybe a trial as an adult. Maybe they wouldn't hold it against me if I broke his goddamned face a few times. Audrey was a few steps behind me. I wouldn't let her catch up. I wanted my hands around his neck an' shit.

I tried the front door of the Miller house but it wouldn't budge. I banged on it with my fists. Just as Audrey caught up with me an older woman I recognized as a Connie's housekeeper opened the door.

"I'm looking for Eric," barked. I pushed past her into the foyer. I saw Eric across the entryway. His eyes grew large as they locked with mine. He paled and escaped into Clyde's office. In a second I was at the door of Clyde's precious den. All the polished wood, shiny brass and cigar smoke would not save Eric now. Neither would his daddy. I jerked the heavy, carved door open. I stared for a moment, hardly believing my eyes. It was as though I had

268

opened a door to hell and caught the devil in a meeting. A breathless Audrey fell in beside me and saw what I saw.

CHAPTER TWENTY

Distributed comfortably about the room were, Brad, at Clyde's desk, Clyde and Connie, and two couples whom I did not know. Eric stood behind the protection of his mother's chair. They stared at us, startled to silence.

"What is this?" Audrey demanded from behind me, catching her breath.

"This," I said, inspired by the sudden truth of it, "is a meeting of the Reinco partners."

The housekeeper pushed into the room. "I'm sorry, Mrs. Miller. I tried to stop them. Honestly, I—"

"—It's all right, Mrs. Farris." Connie, first to regain composure, stood. "I'll deal with this."

Mrs. Farris withdrew.

"I'm here for Eric," I said. I looked past Connie to her cowering teenager. "I'm going to wring his neck." His face was a study in the struggle between arrogance and animal fear.

Clyde found his voice. "This is an invasion," he whined.

Brad, at Clyde's desk, was closest to the phone. "I'll call the police," he said, looking directly at me."

"Good idea," I shouted. "Call the police. Meanwhile, Clyde, I'm here for your perv son. Finding you vipers cowering in the snake-pit with guilty looks on your faces is just a bonus."

Clyde appealed once more. "Brad, are you going to make the call?"

270

Brad, my favorite puppy-kicking, Impaler paused. "In a moment, Clyde," he baritoned. "We can always call them."

"You ridiculous old man," Connie said. "You are not going to attack my son. We will call the police."

"That shivering bag of trash hiding behind you is the one who poisoned the peanut brittle," I snapped. "He killed Sean Reilly and framed Audrey."

Connie put a protective arm out as if to hold her son back, but Eric didn't look like he wanted to go anywhere. "Ridiculous," she declared. "He is completely innocent."

"Like we're going to take your word for it," Audrey said. She stepped forward to stand beside me, like when we were kids facing neighborhood bullies. I felt proud. Don't mess with the Kelly kids.

Brad began to dial. "I've had enough."

"You complete that call and I'll I blow the whistle on Reinco, like Sean was about to do. I'll do it before the night is out."

His finger hesitated over the phone pad. "What is it that you think you know?"

"I know that if the county has time to correct an obvious oversight, your scheme collapses. You had to be through escrow before the law changed."

I cast a sidelong glance at Audrey. She did not know the details about Reinco. I hoped she would play along.

Connie's eyes were dark and flashing anger. "What makes you think Eric is involved with this?" She kept one eye on Audrey and approached me with something close to menace. "Jesus!" she said when she got close. She waved a hand in front of her face as if to clear the air. "You're drunk as a skunk. They both are," she said to the rest. "I can smell the cheap wine a yard away."

"There's nothing cheap about that wine," Audrey corrected.

I continued. "Eric was alone with the peanut brittle and he knew where it was going. He was the only one who could have laced it with poison. Audrey was in the shower. Eric knows all kinds of things about plants, like which ones are poisonous. He's the guy and I'm going to get it out of him."

"Why the hell would Eric want to kill Sean?" Clyde demanded.

"Because he knew that Sean was putting it to Connie," I responded cordially. "She wants to trade up. They've been at it for months. After Eric got kicked out of prep school he spent a lot of time in the neighborhood. When he wasn't stealing things from all of you and fondling ladies' underwear, he was learning the neighborhood secrets."

Connie reached her arm back to slam my face but an incensed Audrey was suddenly between us clenching Connie's wrist. "You try that again," Audrey said, in an even voice, "and it will be the last thing you try tonight." Connie backed off.

Audrey is my favorite sister.

The others in the room, whom I took to be Reinco partners, had been spectators, but one of the men had had enough. "Dammit, Brad, the police. Call them."

Brad looked directly at me. I saw a difference in his expression. He was taking me seriously. That could be good, or, extremely dangerous. "Tell me something, Dan," he said. "Tell me two things."

"Yeah?"

A CASE OF PEANUT BRITTLE

"Tell me what whistle it is that you think you can blow . . . and tell me what kind of future you would like to have for you and your sister."

"The whistle is simple," I said. "The whistle is about a surprise sale of commercial property on a particularly scenic part of the California coast. Over sixty acres. Bidding starts at two hundred million dollars. Do you like my whistle?"

Brad smiled a smile whose memory I will take to my grave. I looked into his eyes and knew that killing would not be outside his envelope. "That's a good whistle," he said. "Now, how about dreams for the future."

"The usual stuff, appropriate to the market." I said, trying to hide my naïveté about whatever market there was. "The big dream is all charges against Audrey being dismissed; all legal threats against Audrey being lifted and a generous settlement of her interests. And, Eric, the homicidal, peeping-Tom, knicker-sniffing pervert brought to justice."

Brad turned to Connie. "The man does have a point."

Connie spat at me. "You dried up old creep, bastard. My son had nothing to do with killing anyone." She turned to Brad, "and you, what an arrogant son-of-a-bitch, what gives you the right to tell me what to do and bargain with my son's life like it's some kind of game?"

"Connie," Brad said, cool as an icepick, "You admitted to me that you and Clyde have considered counseling for Eric. Could be long-term. What difference does it make what the institution is called. There's a way out of this for all of us."

273

Eric looked from one to the other with wet-eyed concentration. He saw his own doom being calculated by selfish adults.

That reminded me of something from an old movie, but this time I remembered what movie it was. Toward the end of The Maltese Falcon, Humphrey Bogart bargains with Sidney Greenstreet to make a deal and provide a fall guy.

Time stopped.

Yeah, something about that old movie had itched at me several times. I couldn't put my finger on it. Sidney Greenstreet, villain without a conscience (Brad the Impaler): Humphrey Bogart tries to get Greenstreet to give up Peter Lorre (Eric) as a scapegoat. They bargain right in front of Peter Lorre, like Brad was doing now in front of Eric, appealing to Connie. Give up Eric and we can buy our way out of this. They're ready to deal.

There was more. Humphrey Bogart's partner Archer had been shot at close range in an alley. The Bounty Hunters were shot at close range on a dark street. Archer was street smart; so were the bounty hunters. Archer would not allow a stranger to get that close to him; neither would the bounty hunters. But, Archer would let beautiful Mary Astor approach him. She had hired him. And the bounty hunters? Who would they let get close?

And, what would Eric have against the Bounty Hunters? They were about to give someone up . . . the person who hired them. The murders were linked.

"Yeah," I said aloud. "She hired Archer. She was beautiful. He didn't know how dangerous she was. It had to be Mary Astor."

I might as well have announced that Martians were dancing in the tennis court. "Maltese Falcon," I explained. Every eye was on me but I focused on just one person.

"You," I said, facing Connie and knowing in my heart that it was true, "and I know how."

"You're drunk and crazy," she backed away from me. Her voice had shown outrage but I was sure I saw fear in the way her eyes darted about for support and how she seemed short of breath.

"You knew that Audrey left for Washington to see me. You wanted to paint her as a fugitive. That's when you hired the bounty hunters. Tighten the frame, point the light at Audrey. It didn't work. Brad got Audrey out of it. The bounty hunters demanded more money or they'd come to us. They had become a liability. You followed them to National City. You walked up to the van, smiling, maybe waving a checkbook. You got close enough. They rolled down the window. You shot them. The first one never knew the danger. He was distracted by his sexy client, Connie Miller."

"You're full of it," Connie responded. Clyde did not seem that surprised at my accusation. Brad was intrigued to the point of a cynical grin on his face.

Connie smiled a bitter smile. "You got all this from an ancient movie? You're amazing! Bounty hunters, eh? How exiting and romantic." She looked for support or encouragement from her allies but found none.

"It's pretty much what happened," I said. I glanced at Brad, a statue, but he was paying attention. Audrey's eyes were wide, mouth half-open like a popcorn-popping adolescent at the scary parts of a horror movie.

"What has any of this got to do with Audrey killing Sean Reilly?" Connie challenged. "I hate to say this, but I think they've got a pretty strong case against her."

"Maybe," I admitted, "But it's based on an assumption we've all been making, an assumption that is wrong."

Clyde, who had been standing as if to support Connie, without making any movement to do so, sat down. "I can't wait to hear this part."

"The assumption we've all been making is that Audrey presented assemblyman Reilly with poisoned peanut brittle."

"That's not too far fetched," Brad said. "He ate it and died from it."

"I don't think so," I said. "There wasn't a damned thing wrong with that peanut brittle. Connie added the poison after the fact."

Audrey had sat down on the arms of one of the chairs. Her expression was one of intense disbelief. "Dan," she said, "Why don't you tell us what you think happened?" I could tell by her tone that she was beginning to patronize me. She was losing faith in my handle on the truth.

"You've lost it," Brad said, clearly agreeing. He pushed the phone aside. I think he wanted to get back to negotiating.

"Just listen, " I started. "Sean had given Connie warning that he would ruin the Reinco plan. Connie was far too invested to allow that. There was no time. That night, she arranged to meet Sean after the party. She used Sean's private entrance. That's when she poisoned him. I'll bet the poison was in the mouthwash she knew he'd use. The open candy box was there with a little brittle left. She

276

poisoned the remaining candy. She not only silenced him but left a clue pointing to someone else."

Connie clapped her hands, a grin on her face that looked manic to me. "Bravo," she said. "That's a grand story. It even fits most of the facts. It's just not true. None of it."

"I didn't expect you to admit it right away."

"You pathetic fool," she said. "Your whole cockamamie story is that I went to the Reilly house about ten thirty, after the dinner. I framed poor, innocent Audrey, who had already insulted, threatened, and assaulted Sean several times before she poisoned him."

Audrey looked about to fight back but I cut her off.

"I think that's what happened." It felt like I had gone out on a long, high limb and turning back toward the tree, saw Connie holding a chain saw and smiling.

"Well, think what you like, you crazy old coot. I have absolute proof of where I was when you say I was poisoning poor Sean. I'll get it now and put and end to this nonsense."

"Proof?" I said, nonplussed.

"Wait here," she said and left the room with a quick march that projected confidence.

"Eric has some problems," Clyde said, filling an awkward silence. "Some things may not have been entirely under his control, in terms of competence that is," he concluded.

"Competence to stand trial?" I jabbed. "I can't believe you."

Eric, frightened to silence, looked for help from one face to another. He had sat in the chair his mother had occupied. He slumped and looked at the floor. Clearly Dad was aboard to sell out his troublesome son. Well, Father knows best.

Brad picked up the banner and drove forward with it. "It's hard to tell what a troubled young person with problems might do. They cannot always be held responsible, morally or legally." He looked directly at me, cocked his head slightly to the side and smiled a negotiator's smile. "You and I should discuss a settlement of this whole affair," he said, and then added quickly, "including, of course, complete satisfaction of Audrey's interests."

"And Eric?" Connie asked, returning. She had a DVD in hand. "What about Eric?"

Brad displayed his most sincere voice and smile. "Does anyone, including you, Connie, not realize that the boy needs help? Why not solve two problems at once? Audrey gets relieved of her legal problems. The best lawyers we can find defend Eric and settle for commitment to an institution that can help him. We then continue with our plans. We've worked so hard."

It was a reasonable and logical solution. Eric, the knicker-sniffer, gets three squares, a bed, some good drugs, and counseling. Connie had not immediately and with motherly outrage roared "Not with my son you don't." She, instead, was weighing the deal, glancing at Clyde, perhaps for signs of fight or resignation.

She made the "timeout" gesture and placed the DVD in the player installed on one of the bookshelves then lowered the large screen for viewing. "Before I show this," she said, "I have to say it is very difficult for me," she paused, looking down at the floor and giving people ample time to feel sorry for her and to pique their curiosity. "It was meant for a small audience of lawyers," her voice was small and tragic. "I have been concealing, some very personal problems." She looked to Clyde in an almost kind way, like a pet owner blowing a kiss to a dog she's about to put down.

"I made this video on the night Sean was killed, right after the last guest had left. There's a TV going in the background that should establish the time. This is embarrassing and it was meant for negotiations before a divorce. I apologize for it."

She backed away from screen with a remote in her hand. "I was at the end of my rope."

The screen came alive. It showed an unconscious Clyde in bed, the sliding glass door opening to a balcony overlooking the ocean, a portable TV set on the right, and Connie in a baby-doll outfit. On the video Connie narrated . . . "Another frustrating night at the Miller household." She stepped to the bed. She grabbed the front of his Clyde's T-shirt and pulled him up, "Wake up, damn you, wake up," she shouted. She looked at the camera. "I endure this night after night. We had friends for dinner. He drinks himself to a stupor and passes out. This is my marriage." Video Connie turned again to Clyde and slapped him in the face several times. "Every night," she complained. "Every night is the same. He won't get help. He won't stay away from the scotch. I'm making this because I don't think people will believe me otherwise."

Constant in the background late night TV forges ahead. The talk show host/comedian babbles and introduces guests. Through the window, indifferent to the marital tragedy, a full moon sits on the horizon and reflects shimmering light off the Pacific. She looks so vulnerable, so sexy. Any man would want to show her what a loving mate could be.

Connie touched the remote and the blank TV seemed to hiss at the silent room. Brad hid his reaction with a bland expression. Clyde stared at Connie with his mouth ajar, his cheeks blushing. While Eric studied his own knees, Audrey was literally at the edge of her seat.

"That's embarrassing," Connie said, but her expression seemed more like victory to me. "I had to show you where I was at that moment. Dan gave you a fantasy." She turned to me, completely victorious. "Dan, you're an outrageous joke. I want you and your murdering sister out of my home."

"The TV show could have been recorded," I said.

"Oh, screw you, Kelly," she turned her back. "Get out of my house."

"A recording," I argued. "A disc and you did the video later."

"Oh, hell," she sighed, speaking to the ceiling. "Prove it."

I moved toward the door. Audrey did not.

"Brad!" Audrey called out. "We have business to complete."

Brad nodded his head. "Go ahead then. I would like to resolve this."

"I would too and right now," Audrey said, then, pixie-like, turned, putting her face inches from mine. "Danny, Danny, Danny," she scolded as she might say 'tsk tsk tsk.' "What am I going to do? You even forget things that you taught me. That should make you feel pretty bad."

"I don't know what you're talking about," I said.

"Run the video again," she demanded. "As soon as we get a picture, freeze it."

Brad shrugged and nodded to Connie. She resisted briefly then complied and we were treated to the first few frames. Connie in her baby-doll, the double bed, the window, the TV.

"Yeah," I said, "So?"

"Window," Audrey said.

"Yeah," I responded, "full moon on the horizon, reflecting . . ." and I stopped. God, sometimes Audrey is brilliant! Did I teach her that?

"Ah," Audrey said. "Tell the rest of the class what you see, Dan. What time is it when the full moon is on the western horizon?"

"It's just before sunrise," I said. "The only way a moon is full is when it's at the opposite side of the sky as the sun. A full moon rises at sunset and sets at sunrise. This video with the eleven o'clock late show on TV was made just before dawn."

"So what?" Clyde asked.

"So Connie went to all the trouble to fake an alibi for the time that Sean was poisoned." The mystery continued to unfold in my head. "Clyde," I said. "You weren't that drunk that night. She drugged you. She wanted to fake an alibi."

Connie paced. "I couldn't begin to do all that technical stuff."

Eric's face was pale and it seemed that he had to push himself off the chair to stand. "Mom?" There was doubt and pain in his voice. She looked at him and something in her look must have convinced him. "You bitch!" he yelled. He looked directly at me. "Two days before, she made me show her how to record an' shit." He faced Connie, tears in his eyes. "If I knew you'd frame Audrey I would have told you to go to hell."

Connie could have gone on denying, perhaps to some effect. She silently appealed to her husband and to her son and saw no help. Her shoulders slumped and she collapsed in a chair. She looked up at the ceiling and, surprising us, smiled.

"Hell," she said, looking at Clyde with clear disdain, "the only reason I had that much poison ready was that I was planning it for you, Sweetheart."

Clyde looked as though he had just taken a dose of it.

Connie seemed relieved at being unmasked. "Once I pruned Clyde out of the picture I was on my way," she said. "I already had Sean in my pocket, then he had to go all righteous on me.

"Yes, Dan," she said. I could hear the defeat in her voice. "I went there that night. I had the poison with me. I convinced him to sample the brittle. I knew he couldn't stand to eat it without rinsing his mouth and I knew that he couldn't spit. I put the poison directly in his rinse glass. I sprinkled some on the brittle. Sorry, Audrey."

Audrey looked disappointed, then recovered. "You cold-hearted bitch."

"No," Connie said. "I really liked Sean a lot. I'm sorry that he's gone."

"You had prepared the poison for me?" Clyde was still absorbing it.

"You fantasize about politics and power, intellectual masturbation. I wanted the real thing."

"This is emotional," Brad said. "Let's not lose focus. There's more at stake than an unbalanced woman who went too far. There is an answer we can all live with. Let's not throw away years of effort and planning. It's in your hands . . . Dan? . . . Audrey?"

I hung back. Audrey was the one who had lost her home and had a murder indictment hanging over her head.

She stepped forward to her hero, Brad. Brad the varsity star, the lover, the dream. "You were . . . it for me," she said. "Through it all, I still dreamed about you, thought something would change and we'd   . . .. I'm not mad at you any more."

"A good beginning," he beamed. "Now, let's bargain."

Audrey showed him a one-finger sample of her new nail polish. "Brad, you've taken most of what I have. Now you offer to return it. You'd still be defining my life. Make that call. It's over."

"Audrey," he almost begged and did not look as big as he had. "No, you have no idea what you're spurning. There's always room to make a deal."

"I'm dealing with myself now," she said. She turned to me and seemed at peace, smiling. "I knew that you'd help me out of this."

"Sis, you're the one who solved it at the end with that moon thing. That was smart when we needed something smart."

"Great! Tell everyone how smart I am."

"Not likely, kiddo."

"Okay then, go back to your drab rain forest and I'll even send some malt scotch up to you."

"I don't know," I said, realizing that we had just tuned out the others. "You might have had a point about me rusting up there. I've been thinking about maybe taking a trip or something. There's a lot of this world I haven't seen. Wanna come?"

"Good for you. Sure, how about Paris?"

I been almost joking, but it started seeming like a good idea. Perhaps I was getting stale and, perish the

283

thought, old. I had to admit that this San Diego adventure had energized me more than I would have thought.

"You're on, Sis," I said. "Let's make our next adventure a little less tense, okay. Can you stay out of trouble for a few weeks in Paris?"

"I think I can avoid murder indictments if you can climb out of your rain-forest cave."

"Sure," I said. "Meet the new, adventurous me."

"Maybe the new you will become a vegetarian and quit drinking."

"Yeah," I laughed. "That'll happen."